Adam Lloyd Baker

NEW YORK GRAPHIC

Adam Lloyd Baker, a former grave digger, embalmer, theology student, and movie projectionist, lives in London. *New York Graphic* is his first novel.

NEW YORK GRAPHIC

Adam Lloyd Baker

ANCHOR BOOKS

A Division of Random House, Inc.

New York

Library of Congress Cataloging-in-Publication Data

Baker, Adam Lloyd.
New York graphic / Adam Lloyd Baker.
p. cm.
ISBN 978-0-385-49843-2
1. City and town life—New York (State)—New York—Fiction.
2. News photographers—Fiction.
3. New York (N.Y.)—Fiction. I. Title.
PR6052.A3246 N49 2000
823'.914—dc21
99-088713

www.anchorbooks.com

Printed in the United States of America

146866421

For M+D

'It was a texture. I felt like I could reach out and touch it, it was so intense. The blackness was so intense.'
– Charles Duke, Apollo 16

'As I looked out into space I was overwhelmed by the darkness. I felt the flesh crawl on my back and the hair rise on my neck.'
– William Pogue, Skylab 4

Chapter One

Father Ryan Lubick was standing in a parking lot near the UN building when a manhole cover fell out of the night sky and cut his head off. It happened like this:

The weather was in turmoil. October 1 and New York was locked in the worst blizzard on record. Total whiteout. On the Weather Watch Network Big Mickey's storm desk was predicting indefinite freeze and the city was coming apart. One hundred and fifty frozen to death. Fourteen shot dead in arguments over bread and milk. People looking to use their cars were digging them out of drifts starting at the roof and working down. The cops patrolled on skis.

A state of emergency had been declared and a decree came down from Gracie Mansion that the Highways Department should keep the major avenues navigable. They upturned barrels of salt in the streets and saline slush trickled into drains and sewers. Negligent utility companies used some sewers as conduits for power lines thick as a man's arm. Drop by drop salt water ate away at the cable insulation and laid the wires bare.

That night, as Father Lubick locked St Sophia's church and made his fateful walk to the parking lot, a subterranean power line two streets away was on the verge of shorting out. Coincidentally, that section of sewer tunnel had become obstructed by refuse and was now clogged with bubbling, fermenting turds that expelled thick methane vapour.

The spark occurred at midnight fifty-nine. The resulting detonation rattled windows in a half-mile radius and a great geyser of shit propelled the manhole cover skywards like a champagne cork from a bottle. The metal lid charted an elegant parabola above the rooftops, flipping over and over, waiting for someone to call heads or tails, and fell to earth at the exact spot where Father Lubick was bending over to pick up his car keys. It came down edge first. The side of the manhole cover was blunt but its terminal velocity was such that it sheered the priest's head from his shoulders.

He lay there for an hour, the snow turning red, until a lady taking her Dalmatian for a nocturnal walk saw him and dialled 911.

Virgil Strauss heard about the incident as he drank coffee in Levy's Café. Warm light inside, darkness outside. He imagined himself to be a figure in an Edward Hopper painting and liked it. A silent TV and a busboy wiping tables; a study in isolation. The nighthawk gestured for a refill.

Virgil had a radio the size of a cigarette pack in the inside pocket of his raincoat. Emergency traffic coming through on earphones. A head full of static and incident codes. The distress of the city numerically encrypted by police dispatch.

So there is a body in a parking lot. Usual Friday night shit. But moments later details crackle through the waveband and dispatch is scrambling black and whites because they have a priest with no head. Virgil snatched up his grey fedora. The incident was three blocks away. He was out the door and trying to unzip his camera bag as he ran through the snow.

He reached the parking lot before anyone else. The Dalmatian lady was gone. He skidded to a stop next to the priest. Estimate cop response time at one minute forty-five. Maybe thirty seconds to take pictures.

A body, a head, a yellow oxidized manhole lid. He made a snap judgement he wasn't fucking up a crime scene and composed the shot. The priest's head was face down in the snow. No good. Virgil rolled it over with his foot and fired ten shots, superfast monochrome, no flash. The Leica was back in its case by the time he heard sirens.

First on the scene were two mortuary vans, each with snow chains and a plough. The drivers argued jurisdiction until a cop showed up and settled the matter by flipping a coin.

The attendants dumped the body in a body bag and emergency strobes turned the scene red and blue. A big, black guy briefly span the priest's head on his forefinger like a basketball before dropping it in the bag and zipping it shut.

'Least the man didn't know anything about it,' he said to no one in particular, and heaved the gurney into the back of the recovery vehicle.

Virgil knew this wasn't true. He'd read books about it. A severed head is not instant death. The heads of French aristocrats guillotined during the Revolution sometimes showed signs of life for a minute after they were cut from the body. The executioner would hold up the head by the hair, the eyes would swivel around to look at the crowd and the mouth move as if to form words.

When a human is cleanly decapitated the brain has enough oxygen stored for seven seconds of metabolism with additional juice from the substrate of the scalp, face and neck muscles. Death, as the textbooks say, is from anoxia consequent upon haemorrhage.

Maybe that's what happened to the priest. All of a sudden his head plopped down in the snow and the man couldn't understand why he couldn't feel his body any more and why nothing happened when he tried to call for help. And the last thing he saw was muddy snow, then nothing but the light and euphoria of a dying brain stem. Did the priest think he was ascending to paradise? Or did he realize a life of prayer had precipitated nothing from heaven except a manhole cover and a fine drizzle of shit?

Virgil thought about it as he walked back to Levy's Café. If three years of street photography had taught him anything it was that people take a long time to die. Lots of mess, lots of screaming, lots of crying. These incidents didn't disturb him. He took pride in his professionalism, his detachment.

'I am a camera with its shutter open, quite passive, recording, not thinking.'

He hoped his coffee wasn't cold.

*   *   *

11

The girl was where she said she would be. At the back of Levy's in a Leatherette booth beneath a Rocky Marciano fight poster. A petite blonde, leather pants, nose ring. Late twenties, maybe early thirties. She had hard eyes and a tattooed dragon coiling up her neck. She was very thin, smoked Salems, and her hands trembled.

'Pleasure,' she said, taking Virgil's hand as he slid into a seat opposite her. A stud in her tongue and a voice made husky by cigarettes. 'You look out of breath.'

'Yeah. There was some stuff happening in a parking lot a couple of blocks from here. Had to check it out.' She ordered bagels and lox twice.

'Let me get these,' she said. Virgil didn't protest. He had only twenty-five dollars to his name. He lived rent free, but his clothes were threadbare. He needed money fast. The pictures of the priest were good but there was no point calling supermarket tabloids like the *Globe*, the *Enquirer* or the *Weekly World News*. He carried the number of their Boca Raton offices in his wallet but the papers had pictures of a presidential aide sucking dick at a Romanian Embassy party and wouldn't interrupt their feeding frenzy for a dead priest.

Virgil knocked back corticosteroids with his coffee. He was fighting contact dermatitis triggered by the film developing chemicals he used. The eczema was clearing up. He no longer had to wear gloves all the time.

'You're English,' said the girl.

'Sort of,' said Virgil.

'You were taking photographs, right?'

'Right.'

'What happened?'

'An explosion in a sewer. A guy got his head cut off by a manhole cover. A priest. Type of thing happens most winters.'

'So you took pictures.' She didn't seem to judge him. She didn't seem to care. Too involved in herself to be touched by anything he said, but he liked that. He didn't get to talk about his job much and when he did people got squeamish.

'It's what I do.'

'Crashes and dead people all day?'

'Not ordinary stuff like crashes and murders. It's got to be strange, like a cosmic joke. I'm a connoisseur of weird shit. Like the dead priest. There is a guy who has spent his whole life telling people there is order to the world and a guy with a white beard working it all out. And then by dumb chance he gets his head knocked off.'

'Depressing.'

'It's what it is.'

'You want to prove life's a bitch.'

'I just want to remind people how lucky they are for each day, you follow me? That priest got up this morning and didn't have the first idea he would end the day in a mortuary freezer wearing a toe tag. You have to live for the now. What's your name?'

'Marcy.'

'How did you hear about me?'

'I asked at Hunter College and a couple of kids remembered you from a photography course. Got your number.'

'You were at Hunter?'

'I was a nude model in the art class.'

'No shit. Don't you get embarrassed?'

'It's my body. Not me.'

'Why do you want a photographer?' He rubbed his eyes.

'The kids said you used to work with a private detective called Johnny Ray. Spied on people. Took pictures.'

'Might have.'

'Would you do it again?'

'Depends on the money. Depends what you want me to do.'

'Some people made a fool of me in the past, and a little payback is due. I was thinking in terms of compromising pictures.'

Virgil thought about his empty wallet.

'No violence?'

'No violence.'

'Yeah. What the fuck.'

'All right. I've got to think on it. Decide exactly what I want to do. Can I call you?'

'Any time.'

'Nice to meet you, Virgil.'

She left, and Virgil tried to work out who she was and what the fuck their conversation was all about. She was pretty but street tough. She probably wouldn't call and he probably wouldn't see her again. That was okay. New York was a city of transients. The bagel had been nice.

The phone behind the counter rang and the busboy said: 'It's for you, Virgil,' and passed the receiver.

'Hello?'

'It's Lee.'

'What have you got for me, Lee?'

'Old lady. Been dead in her apartment for a week.'

'Can't use it.'

'Pet dog ate her eyes.'

'I'll be right down.'

'East 12th Street.'

There didn't seem much reason to hurry.

Even with the taste of smoked salmon in his mouth Virgil felt hungry. He hadn't eaten much these past days, as money from his last sale dwindled away. He had a part-time job as a security guard but wasn't due a pay cheque for two weeks. No matter how bad it got he wouldn't swap his camera for a straight job. He worked in a photocopier shop once, but bullying management and customer bullshit sent him home feeling tired and emasculated. It made him lie in bed at night yearning for a post-apocalyptic world in which there was just him and empty streets. Never live like that again. But Christmas would be his thirtieth birthday, and he didn't have an apartment, a car or a vocation other than photographing dead people. He was blowing it day by day. He had a month to make serious changes in his life.

'Good to see you, Lee,' said Virgil, as they both waited for the dead lady to be brought down from her apartment.

'Nothing for me today?' asked Lee.

'I'm broke. I'll remember you double next time.'

'Don't fuckin' forget.'

Lee was a scalpel for hire. He was an ex-coroner's investi-

14

gator offering freelance autopsies. He drove through the city at night in a white van with his radio tuned to the emergency frequency and his bone saw and rib cutters ready on the passenger seat. He was competent at biopsies, toxicology and serology. A sign on the side of his van advised anyone wishing to utilize his skills to dial 1-800 STIFF.

Virgil tipped Lee and regular ambulance guys when he could, so he got to scenes while they were fresh. The ambulance guys felt okay about taking his money because he wasn't one of those guerrilla TV vultures trying to break into the networks via road carnage on public access. Virgil was an old-style newspaper lensman. He was a street archivist in the tradition of WeeGee; wiseguys drilled full of holes in a barbershop chair or face down in a plate of spaghetti. Virgil worked hardcore hours: ten till six, holes in his shoes and pockets bulging with film. An artist.

They carried the lady down the apartment steps and let Virgil pull back the blanket. Her lips had been eaten away giving her a happy smile. No eyes. The body was frozen hard and would have to be thawed like a Christmas turkey before a pathologist could get to work.

The dog ate the eyes. Eyes are liquid and a trapped dog gets thirsty a long time before he gets hungry. But the missing lips were down to rats. Soft tissue, easy to tear. Burial parties collecting the dead of Ypres and the Somme noticed the same phenomenon. Fat rats in every trench and lipless corpses grinning in the mud.

New York was infested with rats. Black sewer rats, Norwegian grays and cross breeds. Indefatigable, yellow-fanged vermin. A seething, swarming pestilence rising up from the subways and sewers. They were everywhere. They fed off garbage piled in the streets.

The city's trash cans were sealed because an elusive psychopath called Vishnu Jones had deposited three bombs inside garbage cans in the past month. Home-brewed napalm from gasoline and polythene nuggets triggered by a mercury tilt switch. No statements, no demands. So the bins were sealed and garbage trucks couldn't collect the growing piles of black sacks because

15

they didn't have chains or ploughs to get through the snow yet. Rats fed and thrived.

Private pest control firms tripled their charges and only took calls from rich bitches on Madison and Fifth. City Hall broke out emergency funds and turned the public killing service from a squad to an army, and now red exterminator vans were common as yellow cabs. At the New York Bureau of Pest Control, a sub office of the Sanitation Department, people were queuing out the door and down the street, shivering in the snow, each wanting their apartments cleared of vermin. Best thing to do was put a steak on the kitchen floor and wait in ambush with a hammer.

The intense cold slowed the spread of disease, but with vermin and garbage worse than Calcutta slums no one knew what plagues would be unleashed when the thaw came.

Rumours of contagion and pandemics circulated town, mutating like Chinese whispers. Virgil heard of an apartment block in the Bronx where the residents had vomited blood until they died. Three hours after the bodies were found the area was quarantined and a team of plague specialists from the Center for Disease Control were scrambled out of Hartsfield airport, Atlanta. A news blackout was imposed. Dark whispers suggested the apartment residents were wiped out by an adaptive viral haemorrhagic never seen before. Relatives of the deceased wanted to bury their dead but the bodies were dissected by men in biosafety level-four spacesuits at the Special Pathogens Lab in Atlanta. Slivers of their loved ones were dispersed to university departments around the world on microscope slides. Rumours of spreading sickness persisted and people trekked through the snow and out of the city on foot rather than stay for the thaw.

Virgil imagined medieval scenes of plague. Cartloads of dead wheeled down Fifth to mass graves in the park. Brokers staggering from their offices clawing at pustulating buboes. He wouldn't want to miss it. But in the meantime there was a corpse on a stretcher, so he took pictures.

'Thanks, boys,' he said when he was done. He shouldered his camera bag and checked his watch. Two hours till deadline.

He was so anxious to reach his darkroom he got clipped by a limousine as he stepped into the road.

Virgil's darkroom was in the basement of the Majestic, the last porn cinema on 42nd Street. During the twenties it was a burlesque theatre leeching off trade drawn to see Louise Brookes shake her stuff in Ziegfield's Follies at the New Amsterdam. During the seventies, the glory days of the pornography business, it had been a mob money machine. These days Times Square was a Business Improvement District. Disney imagineers were converting the Amsterdam to a venue for live extravaganzas, and six peepshows had been levelled to build a site for Madame Tussaud's. There was a Virgin Megastore where the Pussy Parlour used to be, and Samson's Titty Parade was now the O_2 Café, where hipsters could stick a rubber tube up their nose and snort pineapple-flavoured oxygen.

The Majestic was a derelict hulk, a neo-gothic ruin, incongruous like the Bates mansion rebuilt on mainstreet. The mob were getting last use of it showing skin flicks before it succumbed to the zoning laws and a wrecker's ball. The place was run by Larry Onions and nobody bothered him as long as the theatre turned a profit. He let Virgil use one of the old dressing rooms in the basement as a darkroom and another as a place to sleep.

Virgil strode into the crummy atrium, waved at the girl on the pay booth and unlocked a door marked Private. A passage led down to a warren of dressing rooms. Each room had a table, a chair and a big mirror, all covered in dust that rose in drifts when a subway train thundered beneath the floor. It was a ghostly place but Virgil was in too much of a hurry to feel spooked. Once in the darkroom he unpacked his camera, hit the safelight and blinked until he adjusted to the murk.

He ran the film through hydroquinone and had the roll out of the developing drum and into the fixer in moments. He halved the processing time by using a hot water solution but the negatives would still take twenty minutes to fix. There was nothing to do but set his watch and say hello to Larry.

Out and up through doorways and stairs to the old theatre stage. He was behind the screen, bathed in phantasmic light.

17

A swing door took him into the auditorium. A searchlight cone of brilliant colour lit a broiling cigarette nimbus in sick dream light. Reflected movie radiance illuminated the faces of a few skulking, masturbating viewers. On the screen genitals, close-up to the point of abstraction, deflected attention to vacant eyes and cheap fashions of a decade ago.

The cinema was a dead thing. The fittings were decrepit and the film emulsion was bleached white through over-use. A century of celluloid dreams sunk to lecherous senility. Nothing left now but the reflex desires of the lowest, reptilian cortex of the brain.

Larry Onions was sixty-three. A lifetime of Marlboros had turned him to a yellow, desiccated husk. He had a cough like a cold ignition and his laughter died away to a deep, emphysemic gurgle. He looked like Harry Dean Stanton. Virgil once asked Larry why he didn't quit smoking. Larry said: 'Kid, the damage is done.' He was probably right. Virgil never mentioned it again.

Crude partition walls had been erected in the theatre auditorium to make three little cinemas. They were served by a single projection room in the middle of the building. Larry serviced and operated the three machines and also slept on a camp bed in the projection box. He had made it his home. He cooked meals in a microwave, watched TV, drew pictures.

'How's life on planet Onions?' asked Virgil, entering the projection booth and throwing himself down in an armchair.

'Good.' Steady eye contact, upbeat voice. Noticeably different from Larry's usual torpor. Virgil was intrigued to discover the reason for Larry's good mood.

Virgil sat with his back to the projectors. He didn't like to look at them. They were disgustingly insectoid: the lamphouse seemed like a sting-loaded abdomen, the anamorphic lens seemed like a bulbous, compound eye, and the spindly struts holding the mechanism upright looked ready to creep and crawl.

'What's new, Pops?' asked Virgil.

'Not a great deal.' Larry lit a fresh Marlboro with the embers of the last. 'I watched the fight last night.' His voice slipped to a minor key, which told Virgil the man had lost a big bet.

'The New Jersey kid?'

'Simmons. That's right. He fought the Mexican.'

'Good?'

'Spic hammered him into the floor.'

'How much did you lose?'

'Nickels and dimes. And the Cardinals beat the Jets so it was a bad day to the bone.' Larry said it with a dyspeptic wince, so he must have taken a heavy hit.

'Should spread your bets a little.' Virgil took a video tape from his raincoat pocket. 'Casablanca. Taped it last night.' Virgil was going through a Bogart phase and was taping Bogey's movies as they appeared on TV. He lent the cassettes to Larry after he finished watching them.

'Is it as good as I remember?' asked Larry.

'Better. Bogie is the type of guy you don't meet any more. Stoic. Does his crying alone. There's this terrific scene where a young married couple are at the roulette tables in the back-room of Rick's Café Americain. They're trying to win enough money to buy black market exit visas, but they keep losing. Bogie rigs the wheel so the guy keeps winning if he bets on twenty-two. "Cash it," he says, pointing at the chips. "And don't come back." Isn't that great? Not to need approval. It must be like losing your sex drive when you get old. What a relief not to have that monkey on your back.'

'I'll watch it later,' said Larry. He dropped the cassette on to a pile of paperbacks next to his chair. He often sought refuge from a fucked-up life in fantasy books, sub-Tolkien quests with a map and an elf-lore glossary. Whenever a big science fiction movie opened at the legit theatres across the square Larry would be in the queue. A haggard old man in a line of children, with all the usherettes frowning at him thinking he was some kind of pervert. 'Real life is something to be risen above' was his motto.

They talked about the parallels between Star Wars and *Lord of the Rings*. It was a comfortable conversation because it was one they had enjoyed many times before.

'I've got a score,' said Larry, leaning forward and adopting a confessional tone. The admission came out of nowhere. A

19

moment earlier they had been discussing similarities between Obi Wan and Gandalf.

'What?' said Virgil.

'There's a buzz. Some mystery man is buying up quality jewellery and antiques. Stuff under normal circumstances would be too distinctive to fence. Particularly artefacts with a strong religious connection. They call him the Tooth Fairy. Now I happen to know that there is an angel at Metropolitan Plaza, where you work as a security guard. You know the House of Usher? The store that sells antique fireplaces from Europe and shit like that?'

'Yeah.' Usher architectural salvage offered 'Antiques and Relics of Olde London'. The window displayed an ornate marble bas-relief depicting Athenian javelin throwers, three iron steps from the Eiffel Tower and a U-boat periscope.

'The shop has just bought a wooden angel from France. It's from an altar screen that got burned in a fire at Chartres cathedral. They broke off the angel and auctioned it in Paris.'

'How do you know?'

'Friends of friends. Anyway, this angel is in the shop, but the day after tomorrow it gets driven to the new owner in Connecticut. I want to jack it but I can hardly walk into the mall and take it from the shop. Too many cameras. But you could tell me when it's leaving the building. Watch it drive out of the car park, on your closed circuit TV. I would intercept and fence it at a place I know in the Village. You would get thirty-three per cent. What do you say?'

'No is what I say.'

'Why?'

'You're not exactly a criminal mastermind. You're associated with disasters. Titanic. Hindenburg. Larry Onions.'

'Think about it. Please.'

'I'm thinking about it,' said Virgil, leaving to check on his pictures. 'And trying not to laugh.'

Back in the crimson twilight of the darkroom Virgil powered up the enlarger and put on gloves and a mask to filter the fumes of ammonium thiosulphate he was using for print fixer. The water in the developing trays was steaming. He could see the picture he wanted on the contact sheet and found it on the strip of negatives. The negative close-up of the priest's eyes, black with white pin-prick pupils, was an image dredged from the darkest, nauseating dreams, and therefore perfect. He pegged the prints to an overhead string to dry. As soon as they could slide in an envelope without smearing, Virgil was out of the Majestic and running down Broadway to Greenwich Village.

Slick software disguised the fact the *Village Advertiser* was produced by one man working in a cupboard above a delicatessen. The man was Walter Queeg, who mixed sensational gossip with ads for bullshit art shows. He put the free-sheet together at night and had copies on store counters across town by nine. Nobody knew when he slept.

Virgil's pictures were voyeuristic and detached, and Walter loved them because prurient art got his paper snatched up like free money. But tonight he wasn't in a generous mood.

'I can't use the woman with the fucked-up face. It's not a story. It's just squalid. The priest is good. The priest I can use. But it's got to be fifty bucks.'

'I was banking on a hundred.'

'I know. But I lost a couple of big advertisers and things are tight. It's not just you, Everyone is taking a pay dip, including me. It's all I can offer you, Virgil. I wish it was more.'

Virgil slid the print across the table and pocketed fifty.

'I guess it will have to do. You know I have to look for a better market, Walter. I can't get by on fifty a picture.'

'The *Post* and the *Times* won't go for decapitated clergy. I hope you find a better market, I really do, but I'm always here if you've got a picture to sell. Fifty bucks is better than nothing.'

Virgil trudged back to the street of dreams and the Majestic with a big bag of groceries cradled in his arms like a baby. He lived in a basement room with bare brick walls. There was a chair, and table and a camp bed. He had put up some shelves for books and ornaments. He didn't mind the austerity. It was like a monk's cell, and he liked it that way. The lack of clutter kept his mind clear. It was a Bushido thing.

He unpacked the groceries but was too tired to climb the stairs to use the microwave in Larry's projection box. There were cock-roaches on the floor so he took off a shoe and whacked them with the heel. He leant back on the camp bed and fell asleep in his clothes, one shoe on his foot, the other in his hand.

It was then voices of all the corpses he had photographed came to him. The lung's final, whispered exhalation piped through mummified throats, rustling like feathers, like wings, like leaves, and Virgil strained to hear, but the voices spoke together and he couldn't decipher the urgent message of the dead.

WANTED

Death Globe Motorcycle Riders wanted to perform at the Deuce Hotel/Casino in Las Vegas, Nevada. Duties will be to ride simultaneously with two other motorcycle riders inside a steel globe at speeds of up to 50 m.p.h. Must have minimum of 3 years' experience and able to work 6 days per week – two shows nightly. Rider is responsible for upkeep of the motorcycle he is designated to ride. Rider must have a clean bill of health including 20/20 eyesight. Alcohol and drug abusers need not apply. Salary $100 per day, paid weekly. Rush resumes and recent photograph to:

SHOWTIME ENTERTAINMENT
Attn: Bill Burry
1366 West Flamingo Road
Suite #635
Las Vegas, Nevada 84726

Chapter Two

Two hundred dollars bought a swipe card; a key to the Shimomura Arcade, the pay-to-shop mall on Third Avenue. The mall occupied floors two to seven of Metropolitan Plaza, a hundred-and-ten-storey skyscraper based on Kansai Airport, Osaka. The sleek Philip Johnson rose above the city squalor as if a giant shard of ice had erupted through the sidewalk. A quarter of a million square feet of performance architecture: a fibre-glass simulacrum of a Moroccan bazaar with bioclimatic control and a Vegas lighting rig that kept the scene at perpetual twilight.

At the end of the day the glass and aluminium tower cladding ticked and creaked as it contracted around the chevron girders of the superframe.

Virgil watched the last shoppers knock back dregs of cappuccino and pick up their purchases. He had an aerial view from a roof gantry and looked down on the little people as if he were observing a colony of ants. The shoppers dawdled, reluctant to leave the sterile perfection of the mall and face the arctic Gotham streets. But they could take a little of the magic home with them on the subway in laminated bags. Anna Sui. Isaac Mizrahi. Shue Umura. Totemic names.

Virgil didn't like being a security guard. His uniform was too tight and his secret-service earpiece relayed nothing but the crackling dissonance of an empty waveband. His Kevlar body armour made him feel like a cockroach, a sensation enhanced by his exile to passages and crawl-spaces recessed in the arcade walls.

Virgil had studied theology at Hunter College before switching to photography; a combination which qualified him for nothing at all. So he got the security job and took photographs while he decided what to do with his life.

He wanted a real job. He wanted to be a staff photographer for the *New York Graphic.* The *Graphic* worked from floor eighteen of Metropolitan Plaza. It was Manhattan's own supermarket tabloid: a mix of Broadway gossip, political scandal and prurient photojournalism. A real freak show. Virgil's kind of place. But they wouldn't give him a job. In fact he couldn't get further than the reception desk. He would hand over his pictures at the desk and read *National Geographic* while he waited. The photos came back with the night editor's ritual rejection: 'Good picture. No freelancers.'

This night was no different. The headless priest and mutilated lady. Good pictures. No story. Nothing for Virgil to do but pace shadows.

Virgil enjoyed the pleasant melancholia of the evening shift: four till midnight. From his crow's nest in the mall roof he watched the last customers leave and the sudden infestation of drone workers clear up after the day's traffic. Waxers polished the travertine floor. Florists, sweepers, a couple of shopfitters. Contract crews all gone by eight, and he was left alone with shadows. Pre-set timers shut down the sea breeze and switched off the sky.

He descended to the basement down stairways and tunnels which twisted like a great intestinal tract before expelling him into the light and heat of mission control.

It was hard working nights. Bright lights messed with his body clock, deranged his hypothalamus, gave him headaches, fevers and sweats. The speed of nervous conduction raised three milliseconds for every degree centigrade his body temperature increased. Virgil fought dizzy spells by basking under the breeze of an air-duct grille.

From a swivel chair on castors he had a panoptican view of the mall; a monochrome, time-lapse montage relayed by twenty CCTV cameras. Shop fronts and stairwells, viewed in ellipsis. Nothing moving but the steady increment of a date/time display.

The only action he ever saw was from a camera ranged on the exterior of the loading bay, the only closed-circuit position to impinge on the real world. On Fridays and Saturdays he could watch fights and frenzied fucking. He always had a blank tape ready in the back-up VCR in the hope he could sell some footage to a reality TV show.

Closed-circuit cameras gave Virgil the creeps. Every major building had them, inside and out, and the Highways Department had erected video surveillance in the street to monitor traffic. The FBI put the images together. Using a Computerized Facial Recognition and Neurometric System they could set a computer to track a person as they walked around town, sat in the park, went to the bank, rode the subway home. Twenty-four-hour surveillance. Unblinking cameras watching, recording.

Metropolitan Plaza had its own mainframe, nick-named HAL 9000, which supplied a constantly updated floor-by-floor read-out of electricity consumption and air quality in the business suites, corridors and bathrooms. Virgil could change the climate in any area of the building at the click of a mouse. He could search for blockages and leaks in a wire-frame simulation of the twenty-five thousand feet of plumbing that snaked through partition walls and ceiling voids. But mostly he just read magazines.

There was a post-it note stuck to the console. 'Will you please pick up your garbage. I am not the cleaner.' The note was from Craig Timpson, a prissy man who pulled the shift before Virgil. The offending candy wrapper was scotch taped to the console. Reece's Peanut Butter Cups. Virgil didn't eat peanut butter. So who did? This was not the first time traces of intrusion had been noticed in the private recesses of the building, and Virgil couldn't shake the feeling he was not alone. Someone, or something, shared the passages with him. It avoided the camera and alarms. But it was out there, in the corridors and tunnels. That was why Virgil never sat with his back to the door.

The silence and solitude were oppressive. Being trapped with his own thoughts made Virgil claustrophobic, so he switched on the radio for comfort and scanned the papers. Atrocities rendered abstract in headlines. MINDLESS KILLERS WITH A BANKRUPT IDEOLOGY, SUICIDE BOMB KILLS 17 AT EMBASSY, CHILD DIES IN OVEN and local news like Vishnu Jones, Manhattan's own mad bomber, threatening to switch from little incendiary charges to a thousand-pound nitrate fertilizer device if City Hall didn't pay his fifty million in five days.

The headlines seemed fragments of a bigger message, but the meaning twisted and eluded him like an Escher diagram. He cut out the texts and pasted them into his notebook. The book contained two hundred pages and each was a collage of sex organs, lonely hearts ads, strange newspaper stories, pictures of car wrecks, and over them all headline buzzwords: GUNSHIPS, SEXUAL OBSESSION, PEEPSHOW MURDER. There was such an accretion of scraps each page was stiff as board and the book couldn't be closed properly. It was the thirty-seventh notebook Virgil had filled and he felt compelled to continue. These pictures and stories were the background noise of life, like the rushing of blood in the inner ear. News of misery and disaster infused the airwaves, a constant assault upon the senses, roaring white noise like a TV tuned to a dead channel.

Nothing happening on the monitors. Silence. Stillness. No distraction to suppress the anxiety working at him like a toothache. Money.

He didn't want the castration of straight work. Maybe his salvation lay in the surveillance job Marcy offered last night. But there was no immediate cash to be earned. No certainty she would get in touch. So by this circuitous chain of thought he returned to Larry's offer. Use the cameras to rip off the House of Usher, the antiquarian fixtures store.

He didn't like the idea. He'd spent time in a juvenile correction facility as a kid and institution life had put him in fear of jail.

Virgil decided to do the job and he didn't need Larry to talk him around, tell him he made the right choice. He had known the old man for several years and their relationship had inevitably taken on father/son overtones Virgil rebelled against. The decision to get involved in Larry's pocket change criminality was his alone.

As he dialled Larry's number on the office phone Virgil hesitated between each digit until his finger rested on the last nine and he watched the button slowly depress. When the digit registered and the dialling tone began he felt a subtle sense of having crossed some Rubicon.

'Who is it?' Larry sounded half asleep. Phoney orgasmic shrieks in the background.

'Virgil. The proposition you had for me.'

'You're calling on a land line?'

'Yeah.'

'So you changed your mind.'

'Yeah.'

'What time do you finish tonight?'

'Midnight, but I can make a call. Extend my hours until morning.'

'Okay. The package is set for noon delivery, so it's got to leave early. Watch the underground car park from six. When you see movement make the call. I'll be at a payphone. I'll give you the number later.'

'All right.'

'And give me a description of the van.'

'Right.'

Larry hung up and the disconnect tone had the finality of an ECG flatline.

UNWANTED GIRL PUT OUT WITH RUBBISH

A recently born baby girl was thrown down a garbage chute by her mother and left to die because she was not a boy, a Brooklyn court was told today. Martha Kopoto, an illegal immigrant from Nigeria, was apparently under cultural pressures to produce a son. Social workers were unable to track the mother and child after they left hospital and the baby was later found jammed in the chute covered in garbage at Kopoto's apartment block in Flushing, Queens.

Chapter Three

The Briony Secure Care Unit for violent and emotionally disturbed teenagers was Alcatraz with Disney stickers. White cells, barred windows and teddy bears. Virgil spent a year there. He was sixteen.

Briony was a four-storey brick building in Little Odessa. The slavic locals protested when they heard a half-way house for delinquents was to open in their district, but from the shitty state of the neighbourhood Virgil couldn't see it made a difference. Every building was crudely fortified and spattered in graffiti.

At breakfast a nurse with a clipboard made her rounds distributing medication. Some children had to be tranquillized because they were gleefully homicidal when straight. They made weekly visits to an observation room where they were filmed ripping dolls limb from limb.

At least half the population of the secure unit were perpetually stoned on sedatives. Thorazine for the psychos, sodium amytal for the manics and dilaudid for anyone considered subversive. Chemical intervention was the main therapy the centre had to offer. Quick, cheap; a short lifetime's torment erased by flooding receptors in the brain with slow, dissolving rapture. Feral children doped to submission and economical productivity.

When the nurse gave a boy medication she would check his mouth with a pen-torch to make sure he hadn't retained the capsule ready to spit it out. The kids on medication were thin because they never finished breakfast. When the tranquillizers

33

hit they would slump in their chairs and remain immobile for the rest of the meal.

Virgil spent the day dosed on Ritalin; a speed-based psycho-stimulant that gave him an obsessive attention span. He enjoyed the buzz, never tried to skip his daily dose and became so trusted the nurse let him help with her rounds. Virgil loved to speak the names on the pill bottles. The -dones, -dates and -drines. Hard consonants like German.

Virgil was sent to Briony because the head of the Roman Catholic orphanage in which he stayed liked to dose the boys on alcohol and diazepam and invite them to share a shower. One day the good reverend invited Virgil to his study, unbuttoned his cassock and ordered Virgil to 'suck for Jesus'. Virgil stabbed the priest's dick with a propelling pencil. The guy was self-evidently a paedophile, but none of the inspecting bodies chose to notice. Virgil was convicted of grievous assault.

When he first arrived at Briony he was on twenty-four-hour lock-down, but after a couple of months they let him out during the day to visit the boardwalk. It took him a while to adjust to the outside world. When he went to Wendy's for coffee he found himself opposite a sign which said: NO LOITERING. THIRTY-MINUTE TIME LIMIT TO CONSUME FOOD. It was the kind of stuff that made him want to pull a gun and demand some fucking respect.

His room wasn't bad. It was sunny and freshly painted. This confused him because in his orphan status he was supposed to feel deprived and victimized, but materially he was better off than a lot of kids with parents.

He never knew why he wasn't adopted. White babies are a seller's market, so he should have been an easy trade. But things never worked out. He was fostered by an English couple who couldn't have children, but the wife started IVF treatment and found she was carrying triplets, so Virgil was dumped back at the orphanage. All he got out of that was a cool accent.

Briony was run by a thin man called Mr Whipple. He welcomed Virgil in his office when he arrived and told him about the community programme.

'Nice to have you,' said Whipple, laying a hand on Virgil's shoulder. 'We have opportunities for kids who can be trusted. Plenty of companies on our books want to give you a second chance, so tell me what line of work interests you. You don't have to answer now. You can think about it.'

Virgil didn't know what job he wanted to do. Whipple said he had an opening for a night porter at a big hotel on Second. Virgil took the job because the alternatives were sweating in a restaurant kitchen or zapping bar codes at a supermarket till. The anti-social rota suited him because he didn't like people. The job wasn't stimulating. He worked at the Mayflower Hotel for four months, and afterwards couldn't account for the hours. He had a vague recollection of the sights and smells of the hotel but otherwise it was more wasted time. He was counting down the days until he was out of the paternal hands of the New York State Division of Youth.

He enjoyed himself on two occasions. Firstly, when he found three hundred dollars a guest had hidden in a Gideon's Bible and forgotten. Secondly, when a lady caught fire in the bar. She had a surgical dressing on her nose following plastic surgery and lit her bandages while putting a match to a cigarette. Virgil extinguished her face with beer.

Larry was the barman. That's how they met.

Walking to and from the subway was his first chance to savour the downtown lights of Manhattan. Sometimes Virgil would walk all the way down Broadway and catch the train at Union Square, just so he could enjoy the street lights. He never had any hassle on the streets and came to believe the nocturnal city was his true home.

He expected the city at night to be a violent place but the first serious incident Virgil saw occurred at the hotel.

Pitkin was an armed robber out on parole. He was a big black guy and they had him waxing cars all day and evening. There would be a row of Jaguars, Ferraris and Rolls-Royces parked down a side street next to the hotel, and Pitkin had to polish each car with an aerosol of cleaning foam. He would lean over the hood of each car, write 'CUNT' in foam, and then vigorously rub the word in with a cloth. After a while they

35

promoted him to night porter and he shared a staff room with Virgil. His hobby was stealing hotel stationery.

'Son,' he said to Virgil, 'there are two things you should never pay for in this life. Sex and office supplies.'

Pitkin had two main gripes. The first was his feud with Schneider, the security man who guarded the foyer at night. Schneider was a cop who got invalided out of the force. He resented a crook like Pitkin working for the hotel and gave him shit at every opportunity. His petty taunts had Pitkin spluttering curses through each shift like a Tourette's case.

Pitkin's second gripe was that he had to kick back half his take home to his immediate boss in order to keep his job. The moment the money stopped his boss would phone his parole officer and say Pitkin had been caught stealing. Blackmail. The man had him by the balls. Or so Pitkin said. The story may or may not have been true. Pitkin always said he preferred an entertaining lie to a boring truth.

One night Pitkin was on duty but wouldn't talk to Virgil. He helped Virgil push a trolley of snacks up to a suite rented by Sting and his entourage, but didn't say a word. Sting's minder gave Virgil a big tip but Pitkin wasn't interested in splitting it. He didn't seem interested in anything. He stood in the middle of the corridor staring into space for a while, then said: 'I'm sorry, man. I've tried. Lord knows I've tried.' Then he hit the fire alarm. 'Could you leave your rooms, please,' he said, banging on each door. 'This is a genuine alarm. Could you please leave your rooms and make your way to the foyer.'

The bewildered and bleary guests crowded the corridor and stairways as they made their way down to the ground floor. They cleared out and Pitkin checked each room for valuables and filled a pillow case with jewellery and cash. When he was done he made his way to the elevator, sack of stolen goodies over his shoulder like Santa, and pressed Ground. As the elevator doors slid shut he tossed Virgil a camera. Not a shitty snap-shot like he already owned but an expensive, fully manual Leica. Virgil hid it under his jacket and made his way down the stairs to the foyer.

Virgil could have alerted management to Pitkin's theft but

he didn't. This wasn't due to any great affection for Pitkin. It was simply that minimum wage plus tips wasn't enough to get him involved in police shit.

Pitkin was already dead when Virgil reached the check-in desk. He was lying face down on the carpet, a blood stain creeping from under his chest. Diamonds and dollars scattered around him. Pyjama-clad tourists kept a distance. The only guy who came close was Schneider. The guard had a smoking automatic in his hand. He kicked over the corpse and spat on Pitkin's face. The dead man's eyes were closed.

Virgil never forgot the way Schneider sweated and swayed with a look of post-coital bliss on his face. He hadn't believed people could be truly evil, just fucked from the get-go like the kids at Briony. But there was evil in that man. Something black and clear and cold. After that night Virgil avoided Schneider as much as he could.

It was the first dead body Virgil had seen. When he went home he kicked himself for not having the presence of mind to take a photograph of Pitkin's corpse. He heard about a guy who videoed a Mig crashing at an air show in Nebraska and earned a fortune. A wing clipped the ground on a low level fly-past and the plane cartwheeled into a hanger where a Lockheed P38 Lightening was being fuelled and prepped. The explosion was so cataclysmic it registered on seismographs in the next state. A network paid the guy fifty thousand dollars for twenty-four-hour use of the footage. After that he sold it for newspaper stills and to every station who wanted it. It was like the day the Challenger shuttle blew up. A slow-mo fireball on every channel. The guy made a mountain of cash.

Pitkin wouldn't have objected if Virgil took pictures. His favourite song was the Steve Miller tune Take the Money and Run. He sang it all the time.

The next day Virgil saw a roller-blade courier get knocked down at Madison Square. The courier was clipped by a taxi, tumbled across the sidewalk and broke his leg when he hit a light pole. A snapped femur protruded from the skin of his thigh. Virgil had his new camera with him and so took a picture.

Having got the shot he then had to arrange processing. Kodak outlets wouldn't develop anything involving blood or nudity, so he had to find an independent camera store with a liberal-minded owner. He got the pictures developed, but it cost him fifteen dollars. He vowed to shoot monochrome from then on and process his own pictures at a fraction of the cost. He bought a book on developing from Barnes and Noble.

The photograph of the injured roller-blader wasn't great. It was blurred and there was insufficient detail of the leg. You couldn't see the femur properly. Something yellow protruding from blood. The blood was very red. He would later learn this was because it was well-oxygenated arterial blood. He would also learn how messy it was when people get cut up. Lots of shit and half-digested food. Globules of subcutaneous fat oozing from the skin like margarine. But all that was for the future.

Of the friends he had at Briony four got killed in gang scenarios, one got busted for stealing cars and one died with a needle in his arm. Virgil swore he would get out, he would make good and do it by thirty. He wouldn't die in the street and he wouldn't live behind bars. An easy resolution to make, but he had a stolen camera to remind him he walked a narrow line.

PASSENGER HORROR

Philip Brome, 43, a businessman from Baton Rouge whose wife had recently left him, cut out his eyes with a knife and fork on a United Airlines flight to Sydney. He had been undergoing treatment for depression since his marriage break-up.

Chapter Four

D awn. Larry stamped his feet to get warm. He was standing by a payphone near the service entrance to Metropolitan Plaza. He was waiting for the call from Virgil to tell him the House of Usher van was on its way up the ramp and into the street. His partner in crime was Vinny Palermo. Palermo was a spotty kid with a gangster fixation. His real name was O'Dowd, but he changed it to sound Italian and started hanging around pizza parlours in the hope of making his bones. The plan was to use Vinny's pizza-delivery scooter as the getaway vehicle.

Vinny was all for whacking the driver and his mate. He wanted to pull an Uzi and spray the windscreen with bullets. Larry insisted there be no guns except the paintball gun he would use as a threat. The paintball gun looked like a chromed automatic from a distance.

Larry didn't want to use a real gun because his best friend died in the gas chamber after a warehouse job went bad. His friend was Carson Welch. They had met in jail. Carson was doing time for cheque fraud; Larry was sent down for gluing tin foil to zlotys and krónur to get them accepted by vending machines.

Larry and Carson was paroled in nineteen eighty and both got jobs at a fish-packing plant in New Jersey. It was a shitty job. They started work in the shellfish boiling room at two in the morning. Their job was to lower great baskets of shellfish into vats of boiling water then skim away the brown scum that formed on the surface. It was exhausting, disgusting work, and there was nothing to do after clocking off but drink to oblivion, but the sights and sounds of the packing plant pursued Larry even in his dreams: a quayside auctioneer barking prices, crates of crushed ice, writhing lobsters, crabs and eels.

Carson tried to make a little extra money as a presidential impersonator. His face, mannerisms and voice were exactly those of Jimmy Carter, and he joined the books of a company called Meet The Prez that arranged for lookalikes to appear at parties and be photographed shaking hands with the birthday boy. It was a cumbersome business, as each appearance had to be accompanied by a blue curtain and a podium with the presidential seal. Carson didn't get many bookings because he stank of fish, and people only wanted Jimmy Carter if Nixon wasn't available.

One night Carson told Larry of a warehouse full of cigarettes in New York state he was planning to jack. Security was lax so it would be smooth, in and out. It was a two-man job and Larry was the only guy Carson could trust. Larry thought about the offer for several days, and eventually let greed conquer fear. He bought black clothes and gloves but then, the night before the raid, slipped over in the shower and broke his wrist. Carson went ahead with the job. He used a casual drinking buddy for help.

What happened that night was never fully established. Carson and his buddy got into the warehouse and things turned bad. Shots were exchanged and a security guard was hit in the head. Carson's buddy escaped and was never seen again. Carson fled the scene but was picked up hours later. Before the security guard slid into a coma he told police one of his assailants looked and sounded exactly like Jimmy Carter. It didn't take the cops long to come up with a name.

Nobody could prove Carson had his finger on the trigger but the security guard died and Carson was shipped to Sing Sing and death row. From that day forward Larry felt he was living on borrowed time. He should be dead or behind bars, but by a quirk of fate, an accident with the soap, he had been spared the gas chamber. He had the same kind of guilt Viet vets felt at making it home.

Larry didn't visit Carson as much as he should during the

appeals process. He bought newspapers every day and read the occasional reports of Carson's attempts to gain clemency.

The next few years were spent in the usual routine of rejected appeals. Carson spent twenty-one hours out of every day in a six-by-nine cell. He received only twice-weekly visits to the exercise yard, and was not allowed to do prison work. His mother visited him when she could and they talked through a perspex screen. Carson spent his days writing glum and misspelled poetry to a nun in Wyoming. In his letters he mentioned he could see a pond from his cell window and enjoyed the way the evening light fell upon the water. He often wrote he would rather die than continue his life in prison.

Larry was on the outside thinking about his friend and all the things Carson was missing. Live Aid. The end of Communism. The Gulf war. Every pleasure Larry enjoyed was tainted with guilt, like the freedom to walk down the street and the freedom to drink a cool beer when he chose.

Carson's final Supreme Court appeal was rejected and he was scheduled to die on Tuesday 27 March 1983 at one in the morning.

Crowds and film crews began to arrive mid-afternoon. The lawns surrounding the hospital wing had been cut, flowers planted, and the hospital building had been freshly painted in anticipation of the media coverage. Members of the public set up barbecues behind the police cordon surrounding the entrance to the hospital.

For his final meal Carson requested steak and fries followed by pecan ice cream. He was allowed to see his mother for the last time. She said he seemed withdrawn and agitated.

At half-past nine a hearse from a local undertaker arrived ready to receive Carson's remains. Prison security moved to a state of institutional emergency and was closed to all but essential traffic.

At half-past ten he was driven the short distance to the execution block by minibus. At midnight forty-five he was taken from the holding cell and strapped into the gas chamber.

At ten to one most national and local news networks were broadcasting live from the prison grounds. A crowd of fifteen hundred people had gathered, many of them waving Final Justice placards. Local radio stations were playing: Don't Fear the Reaper and Jumpin' Jack Flash ('It's a gas, gas, gas . . .').

Carson was given the chance to make a last statement but he just shook his head and they sealed him inside the chamber.

While all this was happening Larry was nearby watching TV coverage in Gino's bar next to the prison walls. He was surrounded by off-duty prison officers with beers lined up to toast Carson's demise the moment word came through he was dead.

Images of Carson's last minutes haunted Larry's dreams ever after, and he started injecting dope just to smother the nightmares. He thought how it was to sit in the steel pod with no sound but your own breathing. Straps cutting into your wrists and ankles. Hostile faces watching you though the porthole. Then the rattle and plop of sodium cyanide crystals rolling down the tube and dissolving in a pail of sulphuric acid between your feet. Did Carson hold his breath as long as he could, hanging on to his last few seconds of life? Or perhaps he bent forward and breathed deep just to be rid of the world. People can only guess what death by cyanide must be like. Burning, choking, asphyxia. Nobody comes back to tell the tale. The horror of those dreams leaked into Larry's every waking moment.

Carson was buried in Indiana. Larry couldn't go to the funeral. Instead he paid a hundred and fifty dollars to have an asteroid named after his friend.

So Larry stood outside Metropolitan Plaza all but shitting his pants. He had done a little forgery, a little insurance fraud in his time, but never anything like this. Smash and grab in a rush-hour city street. He had never been so exposed. All his life he had pissed away money that came into his hands, so here he was at sixty-three, bronchial, arthritic, waiting to hold up a van. Time to admit he was never going to make the big score, never get the house on the beach. He should be led away and shot like a lame horse.

Larry and Vinny Palermo were at the back of Metropolitan Plaza flanking the ramp down to the docking bay. Vinny cut a bella figura in suit and shades; bad acne, but cool as ice. He was carrying a satchel. The route of Larry's worried pacing through the slush was mapped out in butts and ash, like the chalk silhouette at a murder scene.

More and more trucks were starting to arrive at the ramp head: couriers delivering mail, garbage trucks picking up cubes of refuse from the basement compactor, produce vans unloading perishable foods for the cold room. If the traffic got much heavier Larry would have to call off the job.

The payphone rang.

'Yeah.'

'Virgil. They're coming. White van. Two guys up front. Angel in the back.'

Larry dropped his cigarette, put on his shades and gave Vinny the get ready signal. He worried about being shot and worried about having a heart attack.

The payphone rang twice to alert them the van was approaching the exit ramp. Increasing engine noise, and there it was emerging into daylight: a white Toyota with House of Usher stencilled on the side.

Larry pulled the paintball gun from the back of his pants, stood in the middle of the ramp and shouted: 'Get the fuck out the van.' He was so breathless it came out a Mickey Mouse squeak.

The driver hit the brake and he and his passenger stared at Larry in astonishment.

'Get out, Right now.'

Vinny pulled a small, carbon-dioxide fire extinguisher from the satchel and threw the empty bag away. He punched out the side window and directed a jet of carbon-dioxide into the vehicle. He pulled the passenger from the van. The guy fell in the road in a mess of carbon fog and glass granules. He gasped for clean air and the driver followed his example and bailed out.

Vinny opened the back of the van, pulled the angel from under blankets and spiked himself in the leg with the angel's raised sword. The angel was three-foot high and made of scorched wood. There were splinters at the statue's feet where it had been snapped from the reredos. Vinny limped to the pizza-delivery scooter parked yards away. Larry moved to follow but the van driver wrapped his arms around Larry's leg like a dog on heat and said: 'No, you don't, fucker.' The guy crawled up Larry's body until he was standing and wrapped his fingers around Larry's throat. Up close Larry could see the guy was about thirty and a body builder. He popped the man in the stomach with the paintball gun and the guy fell to the ground, red paint on his hands and staining the snow, screaming, 'I've been shot. Jesus, I've been shot.'

Vinny gunned the little scooter engine. Larry struggled to get his leg over the saddle and hold on to the angel, and when he was finally on board they wobbled away down the road weaving through gridlocked traffic. Vinny was hunched over the handlebars and Larry was sitting on the back of the accelerating scooter holding the angel, wings spread for take off. It was the most exhilarating moment of Larry's life.

'What a rush,' he said when they parked next to the river and alighted.

'Man,' said Vinny with distaste, 'you ought to change your shirt more often.'

When no one was around Vinny tipped the bike into the river and it sank leaving bubbles and a rainbow sheen of oil.

IMPOTENCE

Millions suffer every year.
NOW YOU CAN HELP YOURSELF TO
OVERCOME IT!
Simple. Safe. Satisfying.
THE PNEUMATIC DEVELOPER.
Comes complete with suction pump,
energizer rings, lubricating sachet
and full instructions.
Try it for three months and if it doesn't
work we will refund your money!
Send just $19.99 to:

Dept NYG
Lazarus House
Persk Street
Glendale
Queens NY 18374

Chapter Five

Larry didn't want his life to end in defeat. He didn't want to be a lonely old man walking the streets with nothing to do. He was a specialist when it came to nurturing hope. He had swept floors, served fries, dug ditches, and always with a flickering faith things would go right for him some day.

Disappointment set in during his late twenties. He became aware he was running out of time. It was already too late to become a doctor or a lawyer. He realized flipping burgers on a griddle might be his entire life. He grew to hate his apron, the spitting fat, the spatula in his hand. He took the easy way out and ran off with the weekly takings. He got caught. He went to prison. He shot up morphine while in prison to smother the disappointment of his life. When he got out he did petty criminal shit to feed his habit and ended up back in a cell. The cycle of his life was set.

He didn't have a bad junk habit. He didn't shoot dope cut with detergent. He didn't snort coke cut with battery acid crystals and Lignocaine. He stuck to soft shit like Mandrax crushed in a joint, or prescription candy like Xanox chased with vodka.

The only wife he had was a mail order Philippino bride who ran away after two weeks. He didn't even get laid.

Larry had an older brother called Caspar. Caspar liked to take toys apart to see how they worked. As a teenager he graduated to repairing radios. He started a repair shop but turned to retail. When he died of heart failure in 1985 he had four Brooklyn shops selling Walkmans and beat boxes. Caspar bequeathed Larry a gold watch and Larry pawned it for dope money.

Caspar was buried in a mahogany casket with gold plate handles and The Last Supper carved on the side. Larry stood at the graveside sweating in his court-appearance suit. He would be lucky to get a pine box when he died. But he realized how absurd it was to envy a man his coffin and turned his eyes away. His gaze fell upon Caspar's widow: a willowy blonde, a magazine chick; the personification of elegance and beauty and all the things he would never have.

Larry held down a couple of straight jobs. The best was trainee barman at Joanna's, the bar in the lobby of the Mayflower Hotel before the place turned to shitty apartments. He had a lab coat and manicured fingers. He had to memorize a hundred cocktails and make two a minute. He was taught to serve ladies first and make small talk without mentioning hot subjects like the primaries or Grenada. One time James Spader and Susan Sarandon came in the bar and he was happy to mix perfect Russian Quaaludes, swilled in a gleaming Boston shaker. It was the best job he ever had, and he fucked up by stealing from the till. Sometimes, if he was in a maudlin mood, he'd walk into a bar, order a Martini, and toast missed opportunities.

Larry finally quit dope Christmas Day 1989. He woke up alone in the room, shivering and hungry, and badly in need of a hit. There were carols on the radio and he had the DTs. It made him face how much he needed morphine bliss to get through the day.

He hit the streets looking to score but the streets were empty, not even cop cars about, and he walked miles through driving sleet looking for a connection. He trudged round the parks, the squares, the waste ground where sellers usually hung out, but it seemed everyone but him was pulling crackers and kissing under mistletoe. When he passed through residential blocks he could see fairy lights through net curtains. Occasionally he heard laughter. His coat was soaked through and the sole was flapping off his left shoe.

Eventually he found a dealer called Bradley sitting on a bench near the river, sucking a cigarette even though the butt was sodden and rain was dripping from his fringe. Christmas time was a seller's market. No question of being picky. Bradley didn't have morphine ampoules or any of the usual shit Larry needed. Bradley had a pinch of smack in a twist of foil and took all the cash Larry had in exchange.

Larry cooked up when he got back to his room. He assembled the full paraphernalia of heroin use: the candle, the spoon, the cotton wad. He filled a dropper, one of a batch he got pretending to be diabetic, tied off his arm and sat for a long while looking at the needle. He hadn't shot heroin before, never touched unclean shit.

After much thought he squirted the dirty liquid down the sink and threw away his hypodermic. Then he threw away all his hypodermics. Tossed them down the garbage chute and never shot up again. In his experience junkies quit, when they quit for good, with little fuss. If you live long enough a day dawns when the need for dope simply evaporates, and that phase of life is over. It happened to Larry. He simply stopped.

NEW BREED OF KILLER PARASITE WORM FOUND IN BODY OF AIDS VICTIM

Pathologists have uncovered an entirely new species of parasitic worm infesting the body of a 37-year-old Aids patient from the San Francisco Bay area. The man was initially thought to be suffering from abdominal cancer, but it was only after his death that tissue congesting his intestines and liver was analysed and found to be non-human. Gene amplification techniques revealed the tissue to come from a close relative of the tapeworm. However, scientists say the new parasite is larger and much more aggressive than the common tapeworm.

The origin of the new parasitic killer is unknown.

The creature has yet to be given a name.

Chapter Six

T ravel through the city and see nothing but a wind-blasted
landscape. Each avenue, each park, reveals a fresh vista
of icy desolation. This is it. This is the deluge. The wind has
driven the beggars away and the hawkers and the hookers and
the crazies. Abandoned cars. Deserted buildings. Just snow and
whiteness. Six more hypothermia deaths since yesterday.

The Weather Watch Network describes the collision of a
warm Mexico breeze and an arctic storm front as an unantici-
pated high-level disturbance. It is the term they used two weeks
earlier when 'overcast with the possibility of rain' turned out
to be a second ice age. The global weather system gone haywire.
Cut to footage of Caribbean palms thrashing in typhoon winds, a
4×4 upturned in floodwaters and lava bleeding between cracked
tectonic plates.

It is a bad time for the Manhattan branch of the Service
Employees Union to be on strike. Picketing janitors retreat
indoors and nurse their frostbite.

Virgil hated the weather. He was used to the controlled and
artificial environment of office buildings and malls. A world in
which he could predict everything except what fell out of the
sky.

The come down from the raid had him looking over his shoulder for cops.

He bought the *Graphic* and stood in a doorway to thumb
through it.

The *Graphic* had picked up some pictures he took a couple
of days ago. A window cleaner got his left foot tangled in a

rope and fell off his gantry. The body in the street. The leg two hundred feet up and swinging in the breeze. The pictures were due to run today, but a malicious computer nerd hacked the *Graphic* mainframe and infected the software with an encryption virus. The text turned to gibberish. Because the paper was manufactured by machines, and people who behaved like machines, the *Graphic* hit the streets with the headline #:R"QS'£N $PG @ [¾:$0I. The digitized copy of Virgil's picture was so corrupted it was nothing more than a kaleidoscopic swirl of pixels.

He screwed up the paper and tossed it amongst garbage sacks.

Larry Onions had saved a booth in Levy's Café. He was sitting with a man Virgil hadn't seen before. Virgil slid into a seat and towelled his face and hair with napkins. Larry passed an envelope of money beneath the table. Virgil put the money in his pocket. The thickness of the wad dispelled any qualms at profiting from a robbery.

'Who's your friend?' asked Virgil.

'Benny Fordice. Benny has a proposition for us. You might be interested. Tell him the story, Benny.'

Benny was in his late forties. His suit was cheap and he had a gold crucifix lapel badge. He looked tired and pissed off and the scowl lines on his face suggested it had been that way for a long time. He smelled like a juicer. He told his tale.

'I work at St Sophia's church near the UN building,' he said.

'I know the place,' said Virgil. 'The headless priest, yeah?'

'Father Lubick. That's right. I'm a verger. You know what that is?'

'Vaguely.'

'It's like a caretaker with ceremonial duties. Now St Sophia's is a big church, and in the bell tower there is, or was, a two-ton bell called Great Peter. Last week the bell fell through the roof and damn near killed me. You see the bell swung on a couple of rusted iron pins, and when I pulled the rope to ring it the damn thing fell through the choir ceiling and buried itself in the crypt.'

'No shit. Why didn't I read about this in the papers?'

'The snow kept people away from evensong. There was nobody except myself and a couple of clergy in the building. We managed to put a lid on it.'

'Go on.'

'Like I said, the bell buried itself in the crypt. The point is we didn't know we had a crypt. We thought there was solid bedrock under the floor. Instead, we find a warren of passages with old caskets in them. Now the treasury room is in the east transept of the church. A bunch of display cabinets with gold and silver relics and chalices and stuff. The room has heavy walls and iron bars on the door. But nobody anticipated someone coming up through the floor. Didn't think it was possible. So for the next week, until the builders have shored up the floor, the stuff in the treasury is vulnerable to theft. The clergy haven't emptied the cases because they are just plain dumb. All you have to do is get in the building, jump in the hole, dig upwards under the treasury room and bag the stuff. Simple.'

'I don't mean to get personal, Mr Fordice, but I'm wondering why you, with a cross in your lapel and all, would want to rip off your own church.'

The guy sat back.

'I work a sixty-hour week for nine thousand dollars a year. I keep the pews clean, hoover the floor, polish the brass, take care of hymn books, order candles, arrange the right vestments and altar cloths. All the shitty jobs. In the winter I don't get to see daylight. If there is an evening choir concert, or something, I have to stay late whether I like it or not. To cap it all my wife left me. Said I'm a loser, and I can't disagree. So I'm paid jack shit and splitting it fifty-fifty. I get half of nothing at all.'

'You're fucked up the ass.'

'Tell me about it. I can't even quit. I mean what kind of CV do I have? Fifteen years of pushing a vacuum cleaner. And the worst of it is, I don't believe a word of this Bible shit. I'm spending my life helping these guys worship thin air.'

'A good answer.'

'This isn't theft. This is my fucking due.'

'So what do you think?' asked Larry.

'What do I think? I want to go home and get into dry clothes and eat.'

'You can eat here. Let me get you something.'

'No. I want to eat in my room, sit in my own chair and watch TV.'

'But the crypt.'

'Fuck the crypt. No disrespect, Mr Fordice, but I can tell this is a disaster in the making.'

'It's the chance of a lifetime. It's the house on the beach. Whatever you want,' said Larry.

'No, Larry. Chances to wind up in jail come along every day. Take my advice. Don't get involved in any movie heist bullshit now that you're too old to bend your fucking knees.'

Virgil knocked back his coffee and left. Even as he stepped out of Levy's into the cold he was composing his apology to Larry. If he didn't keep the guy sweet he wouldn't have anywhere to sleep tonight.

Virgil visited the Sanitation Department to arrange the extermination of the roaches that infested the Majestic basement. Once in the echoing halls of the building he joined a queue and resigned himself to a long wait. There were so many wet people with scarves and raincoats and tubercular coughs it was like a boat-load of refugees being processed at Ellis Island. The smell of damp garments was noxious, and the shuffling impatience was unsettling. The clerks stamped and collated a series of blue forms and dockets for each applicant and then there was nothing for the petitioners to do but join a long crocodile of New Yorkers that spiralled up a marble staircase and out of sight. Virgil got in line and was given a pink raffle ticket.

'Keep the ticket safe and remember your number,' intoned the guy handing out the tickets. 'No ticket: no interview.' He said it to every person who passed. Virgil's ticket was 943.

The roach problem was worse than the rats. There were roaches everywhere and nobody knew where they came from. They were sluggish in the cold but when the thaw came they would come swarming out of the city walls. The Sanitation

Department sent out vermin control operatives to deal with the problem before it got out of hand. Demand for asthma inhalers had already increased by twenty per cent. Hospital trauma departments were reporting infestations of Pharaoh ants gorging themselves on blood-soaked bandages and dressings. The only guy celebrating the arrival of the insects was a gourmet entomologist who went on TV stir-frying cicadas in a wok.

There was nothing for Virgil to do as he waited but read a letter that arrived that morning. He opened the envelope and read it slowly to kill time.

Dear Virgil,

It was very nice to meet you the other night at Levy's Cafe. I really appreciated you taking the time out from your photography to talk to me. I am sorry if I was not at all clear about my intentions when we spoke. I wanted to meet you and see if you were the kind of person I could feel relaxed with. I need a trust-worthy person for what I have in mind. You seemed a nice guy so if you are still interested in my proposition then give me a call at the number listed at the top of this letter. Early afternoon is best.

*I hope you are well and I
look forward to hearing from you.*

Best wishes,

Marcy.

The girl in the leather pants. He could half remember her face and knew it was pretty. He would call her that afternoon and arrange a meet. Maybe he should buy some smart clothes with the money he got from Larry. A new shirt or something.

Virgil closed his eyes and put himself in a place far from the miserable people around him. Minutes turned to hours.

'Nine forty-three.'

'That's me,' said Virgil, stepping across the threshold into a large room. The room smelled musty, and motes of dust drifted in the lattice beams of light shafting through the blinds.

A thin man in round spectacles sat behind a desk. A laminated security pass clipped to his jacket identified him as Mr Reynard. He took Virgil's ticket and threw it away without looking at it.

'Name,' he said. 'Address.' Virgil told him. 'The nature of your problem?'

'Roaches, mainly. And a few woodlice. Some ants now and again. And I can hear things in the wall, but I'm not sure if it's rats or mice.'

'You are in luck, Mr Strauss. Someone just phoned to cancel an appointment. Three o'clock on the afternoon of the twenty-fifth of October.'

'Great.'

'Next October.'

'What?'

'We're booked solid for the next two years. If I were in your position I would accept a twelve-month wait and be grateful. I need your blue forms.'

Virgil handed Mr Reynard his paperwork with two fifty-dollar bills between the paperwork.

'I'll see what I can do,' said Reynard. He pocketed the money.

Through a half-opened door he could see a room full of boxes stacked one on top of another, until each pile began to crumple under its own weight. Each box was filled with blue extermination papers and was nibbled at the corners by mice.

Virgil called Marcy and she arranged a meeting on her own turf. The place was the kind of Village café Virgil often passed but never went inside. Cafés like this were excluding. They were filled with dreadlocked, body-pierced artists in huddled cliques talking up fleeting bullshit art movements like post-post-modernism, neo-pop surrealism and Dada revivalism. You couldn't go inside one of these places and just read a paper. Luckily, the snows confined the weirdo population to their garrets.

Marcy had a table by the window and was watching pedestrians through rivulets of condensation. She had a moustache of cappuccino froth on her lip. They shook hands and Virgil took a seat. The girl wore a lycra top and Virgil couldn't help noticing the size of her breasts and remembered he hadn't got laid in a while.

He ordered a protein shake and a nut cutlet, and while his order was being prepared the girl slid an envelope of photographs across the table to Virgil. The photographs were professional quality porn spreads of Marcy in wet-look S & M rubber, in a nurse's uniform, in a frilly French maid's outfit. Each spread started off as a striptease and ended with her straddling elephantine vibrators. From the pictures he could see she had large breasts with well-defined, brown nipples. The breasts did not sag, nor did they seem to have the rigidity of prosthetics. Her vagina was neat, dark skinned and surrounded by thick, black pubic hair. Her stomach was taut like she did a lot of sit-ups. Marcy looked healthier in the pictures than she did in the flesh.

Virgil crossed his legs to hide his erection and put away the photographs. He hoped he didn't look flushed.

'Why do you want to show me this stuff?' he asked, making

a big effort to look at her face rather than her chest or lap. He couldn't meet her eyes but focused on the bridge of her nose in the hope she wouldn't notice the difference.

'This is who I am. This is what I do. I'm recognized more for my cunt than my face.' She said it with a smile and Virgil found himself smiling back. He felt easy in her company despite her beautiful figure, which made him feel shabby and unattractive. 'I want you to know all about me. Ask anything you want.'

'Do you do hardcore stuff? Movies and shit?'

'I don't do pictures with other people any more. Just on my own. It limits my opportunities.'

'Why's that?'

'I got Aids.'

'Jesus. How?'

'Nobody in the skin flick business thought they'd catch it. The guys always pulled out for the pop shot, so that was okay, right? People like to see a guy ejaculate in the open. Proof that he isn't faking. So I thought I would be all right. But there was this one guy. Producers loved him because he had a thirteen-inch dick, thick as a wine bottle. Over a couple of years he screwed every girl in the business, then they all started getting sick. I took a test and heard news I didn't want to hear.'

Virgil couldn't think what to say. He had never been face to face with a person who knew with absolute clarity they were at the end of their life.

'Don't they use condoms in hardcore flicks?' he asked.

'They do in gay stuff. Sort of turned it into a fetish item. But it never caught on in straight skin flicks and magazines. Some of the guys can't get it up with a rubber. I can only do softcore, and it keeps me poor. None of the models in the softcore market make much money, except maybe *Playboy* bunnies. They get a quarter of a million and a Mercedes, but they're the exceptions. The big wages are in the hardcore industry.'

'I don't understand why you're telling me all this straight off.'

'I'm on a mission of revenge. I don't have time for gradual introductions. I don't have much time left for anything. I got two people I need to see shafted before I check out.'

62

'What's your beef with these people?'

'When I was at college a guy took me to his apartment, got me drunk and fucked me. The guy's name was Mathias Haas. He's a big-ass lawyer now. His girlfriend took pictures of me sucking dick and taking it up the ass. He used the pictures as blackmail to make me keep fucking him. Said he would mail the photos to my classmates, my tutors and my family if I didn't do what he wanted. He made me do degrading things. Then, when he got bored and decided he didn't want to see me any more, he mailed the pictures just for the hell of it. I had to leave college. I couldn't stay there after that. That's how I ended up in this line of work. My life could have been different.'

'You want retribution.'

'Payback in kind. Humiliate those two in front of their family and friends.'

'Who's first?'

'I want to save Haas till last. First up is Mary Gollecky. She was his girlfriend. She's manager of a big department store now.'

'What do I get out of this?'

'A thousand for each of them. An extra thousand if they are both done right.'

'You could buy a hitman for that kind of money.'

'Don't think I didn't consider the possibility.'

That night Virgil prowled the streets listening to the emergency waveband and watched rats play with garbage. He hadn't eaten or slept for a long while and was trembling and dizzy. But that was okay. He liked to feel his body operating at the limits of endurance. It was the same when he quit smoking. Everyone told him how hellish it would be but he enjoyed the cold sweat and the strung-out sensation. It made the world more intense, made it sparkle.

He got food in Chinatown, stood in a mini-Kowloon and ate curried prawns from a styrofoam cup. Eighteen inches of snow but the place wouldn't shut down for anyone or anything. There were guys selling bootlegged CDs and fake Rolexes off trestle stalls. Virgil nursed his camera. He could have bought a better one with his cut from the robbery but he realized, with an exquisite pang of self-pity, that the battered Leica was his only true friend.

The first call of the evening was a suspected serial killer case and, although it wasn't true art, Virgil hoped he was on to big money. The location was a lock-up garage on the East Side, the interior looked like an abattoir. The walls were dripping with blood and organs and half-digested food. It was as if someone had redecorated the place by slitting a man open and dipping a paintbrush in his guts.

He got the story from one of the cops. There wasn't a maniac on the loose. It was some weird sex thing gone wrong. Two Wall Street brokers got their kicks blowing air up each other's ass. They got drunk early in the evening and broke into an engine shop to try out a big air compressor for filling tyres. One guy fed the hose up his backside while the other worked the controls. The guy operating the pressure dial confused maximum with minimum. When the guy with a tube in his asshole signalled okay for the switch to be thrown he instantly burst.

It was a bad photo opportunity. Just red walls. No object around which he could compose a shot.

The second incident was better. Two executives working on the top floor of an office building got into a fight and one guy threw a bronze figurine of Muhammad Ali at his colleague. The guy ducked and the statuette smashed through the window and fell ten storeys to where an executive from the same building had just opened his umbrella and stepped into the street. When Virgil got to the scene the guy was lying dead in the snow with the bronze figure buried in his skull. The dead man had a vacant look on his face, which was understandable considering there was a desk ornament where his mind used to be. The bronze statuette was submerged so deep in his head nothing was visible above the pulverized scalp except a single gloved arm raised like a drowning man going under for the last time. An umbrella lay nearby with a neat, Ali-shaped hole in the top. The umbrella looked expensive.

Virgil processed his pictures at the Majestic and delivered

64

an apology to Larry while they were fixing. The old man had a sketch pad in his lap and was doodling a Doré illustration from *Paradise Lost* while he listened to a baseball commentary. Larry could have been a good artist but never had the drive to make anything of it. Pissed his time away on three-card monte scams and ripping the change from toilet condom machines.

'I just wanted to say I'm sorry about losing my temper this afternoon,' said Virgil. 'I was tired and stressed out. It was wrong of me and I apologize.'

'Don't worry about it.'

'But I meant what I said. It's a bad idea to get mixed up with that Benny Fordice guy. Have you known him long?'

'A few months. He tipped me about the angel at the mall. Knows people who know people. That kind of thing.'

'He's an accident waiting to happen. A fuck-up. It's written on his face. Whatever he's into just don't get involved.'

'Do you believe in God?'

'No.'

'So why waste the one life you have being a zero like me? I work with machines all day. I get oil in the pores of my skin and scabs on my knuckles. You deserve better than that.'

'Sure, but I'm not going to get involved in this bullshit.'

'What other chance do you have? This photography thing is a dead end. You know that. You're heading for a straight job unless you do something drastic.'

'That's not true. I've got dreams.'

'Dreams cost.'

'I'll think about it, all right? I won't say any more than that.'

Virgil stepped into the street and suddenly knew with absolute clarity that he would take part in Larry's scheme. The knowledge hit him with the force of revelation. He was locked in the pursuit of easy money.

Good pictures. No story. The *Graphic* didn't take the pictures but at least the night editor came out to the reception desk and told Virgil to his face.

'The guy who blew himself up. It's not what I call a picture. Just blood on the walls. Nothing to draw the eye. The guy with the caved-in head is better, but I need the story. That's what you have to do, kid, if you want to sell your pictures. You have to turn journalist. Get the story. And make it current. Like this Vishnu Jones bomber thing. Get me something on those lines and I might be able to put some work your way.'

Virgil had to settle for fifty dollars from the *Village Advertiser* and went back to the cinema feeling he couldn't do anything worthwhile. As far as he could see he didn't have a future. No change in his life, no different textures to the day. Just the same four walls and the same hand-to-mouth existence.

Marcy had let Virgil keep the portfolio of pictures she showed him that afternoon, and when he got back to his room he jerked off as he looked through them. It took him a while to come. Marcy's sickness made him pull back from images of fucking her.

In all the pictures Marcy looked straight at the camera, but the expression of wide-eyed innocence she feigned as she wedged a foam penis up her snatch was as impenetrable as a kabuki mask.

Before he went to bed Virgil set roach traps around the skirting board. As he did so a single roach scuttled from under the bed, so he swatted it with his shoe. It was only a partial hit and the broken insect crawled slowly across the floor dragging its exposed guts behind. Virgil watched the dying creature's progress as he ate his supper and admired the insect's strength of purpose as it struggled to reach safety.

NAUGHTY NADIA (472) She's naughty, she's a life-size replica of the perfect woman, with moving eyes! If you need total satisfaction Nadia will please even more than you thought possible $99.99

BRAZEN BRIGITTE (473) Her silky hair, Curvaceous Hips and legs, two Luscious love tunnels and vibrating throbbing will drive you crazy with desire. She'll hold up to 250lbs before complaining $59.99

JUICY LUCY (474) Here she is! The Chinese Doll who will please and please again and again with her realistic ripe young breasts, pulsating vagina and eager open mouth $39.99

BLACK BESSY (475) Your very own coloured dark skinned lover. Three inviting holes for you to pleasure as much as you please $39.99

BIG JOHN DOLL (476) One for the ladies (or him). Inflat-able life-size, open mouth, open rear and 8" impressive penis $39.99

THE MILK MAID (477) 3 openings of love, moving arms & legs, real hair & ejaculating tits! Any position you want $99.99

Chapter Seven

M arcy's body was breaking down. No dementia or mela-
nomas, no spectacular eruptions of disease, but instead
a gradual weakening of the limbs that felt like she was ageing
a year every month. She recalled an image from the Chaucer
books she studied at school. A man so old and tired he walked
the countryside tapping his stick on the ground, begging the
earth to open up and give him a place to finally sleep. Marcy
felt like that man. She was no longer anxious to live.

> 'I'm going to fuck your brains out, baby. Split you wide
> open with my monster dick until it comes out of your
> mouth. You will be screaming for it, baby. I will show you
> what a real man is like.'

It had been the same three days running. Marcy got up at
noon and found an envelope pushed under the door. No name,
no address. Inside was a newsprint message pasted ransom
style on white paper and a Polaroid of an average-sized hard
on. The penis had a mole on it. Marcy wondered if she would
be able to pick out the dick in an identity parade.

The note didn't disturb Marcy, nor did the drawings and the
silent phone calls. She had been a pole dancer and an erotic
model for several years and during that time she had been
stalked and, on two occasions, raped. She was used to getting
threatening messages on the phone, deliveries of furniture and
pizza she didn't call for. One time she opened her door to find
two undertakers standing in the hall. They took off their hats

and said they were there to collect the body of Marcy Glass. She wasn't fazed. Men were as difficult to understand as a Labrador retriever.

The creep would have to be dealt with so she phoned the box office at the Majestic and left a message on the answerphone for Virgil to call her as soon as he could. She didn't want to ask for help, hated feeling vulnerable, but she wanted company that night as she killed time behind a barricade of inch-thick steel and dead bolts, waiting for her stalker to leave his next sinister calling card. Virgil was the only trustworthy guy in her address book.

That a prowling pervert had been outside her door, just a few feet away from where she was sleeping, made her mad. She had bought a big kitchen knife in Lechter's a week ago and gripped it in her coat pocket every time she stepped from her apartment into the hallway. She wanted to meet the guy, would take pleasure in slitting the fucker's throat. Or maybe she should invite him in and give the guy the screw of his life. Spread her gift around.

She burnt the note in the kitchen sink and left another message on the Majestic answerphone: 'Please give me a call as soon as you can.' Virgil called back at one.

'Sorry to wake you, but I really need someone to come round and sit with me tonight? I've got a creep leaving me notes and it's fucking frightening.' She knew an appeal to Virgil's chivalry would get results.

'Sure, whatever,' said Virgil and hung up.

Marcy wasn't going to let the creep or the disease break her routine. She remembered a story told by a guy at the Aids clinic. A Buddhist monk is sitting in a field with his master. They are playing chess. A guy runs past and tells them the world will end in five minutes.

'The world is going to end,' cries the novice. 'What shall we do?'

'Finish the game,' replies his master.

When she completed her stretch exercises, using the back of a chair as a *barre*, Marcy did a hundred sit-ups. She kept the carving knife within reach but tried to push the spectre of the stalker from her mind. He wanted to dominate her life. He wanted her to cower in fear. Every thought she wasted on this guy was a little victory to him.

She concentrated on counting sit-ups. Lying down she saw cracks in the ceiling. Sitting up she saw damp around the windowframe, like blue cheese.

There was a Gershwin tape playing on the deck. She bought it three years ago after seeing Woody Allen's Manhattan. If the sun came through her window just right, then the music put her in the same urbane, monochrome life. But that was when she had imagination enough to transfigure her room by effort of will. These days she was tired to the bone and incapable of seeing anything but drab walls. She saw the worst in other people and the worst in herself.

She checked her body weight on the scales and her shape in the mirror. The tool of her trade demanded a lot of maintenance. Once a model passes twenty-five she is a declining asset in the erotic picture business. Vigorous exercise had kept Marcy's ass and thighs free of cellulite dimples. Marcy would die in her prime.

There were track marks on her arm for the compulsory penicillin shot against the leptospirosis that was spreading liver and kidney failure around town via rat's piss. She had a photoshoot that afternoon and would have to take blusher to cover the needle pricks. Her soya oil breast implants looked good. She joked with her friends that she had nutritious breasts. Low in saturates, high in polyunsaturates. The skin wasn't stretched any more.

Some of the girls that started in the porn trade the same time as her had reached the big league. They were taking home a basic forty grand a year tax free from movies and making maybe twenty-five thousand a week on top, touring with a strip show. From photospreads the smart girls moved up to movies. Slick, soft-focus footage shot by a poolside in Reseda, Simi Valley or van Nuys, and shown on the Playboy Channel, picking up best anal scene at the Hot d'Or awards at Cannes. The girls worked out, ate right and milked their fame going coast to coast as featured dancers in an erotic revue. They spent most of the year living in a camper van, doing twenty shows a week, answering fan mail, selling videos at each appearance, signing posters. Five years of jiggling their tits for rednecks and they didn't need to work again.

Marcy never left square one. Still holding her cunt open for Chick, Foxx, Cock Riders, Double D Nurses. She was Ricki the horny dentist from Houston, or Terri the nympho stewardess from Minneapolis; whatever bullshit the caption writer thought up. Things could have been different. But her career stalled five years ago when she went jogging in Central Park and got struck by lightning.

It happened like this:

She was jogging around the perimeter of the park with five other runners. They didn't know each other but had grouped together to be safe from muggers. The sky darkened and there was a light drizzle. The drizzle turned to rain but she kept running because she was determined to reach the three-mile target she had set for herself that day.

Marcy had no memory of the lightning strike itself but could remember the moment before she was struck. The five joggers rounded a bend and skirted a wino sleeping on a park bench with a supermarket trolley full of soda cans next to him. Marcy broke her stride to jump a dog turd and found out what happened next when she woke in a hospital bed with blue spots dancing before her eyes and the taste of cold peanut butter in her mouth.

The wino got a direct hit. Judging by the photograph in the *Post* there wasn't much left of him. The bench on which he was sleeping was a mini Hiroshima. A crater, a smouldering duffle coat and a glob of metal that used to be a supermarket trolley. The sandy path was now a sheet of glass.

One jogger got his insides cooked like he was fried in an electric chair. Another had a coronary and couldn't be resuscitated. Another got fifty per cent burns and died a day later. One lady was okay, but all her hair fell out.

Marcy got ten per cent burns, mostly on the back, where her nylon tracksuit melted to her skin. She had burn marks under her breasts from the metal in her underwired bra which, in the instant of discharge, turned incandescent like a bulb filament.

She had burn marks on the soles of her feet where the current exited her body. She had minor haemorrhaging at the tips of her toes and fingers. But worst of all was the loss of memory and mood swings which lingered for months afterwards. The doctors said the electric charge scrambled her brains. She got depressed, she ate too much, she had panic attacks and sometimes would go to the shops and be unable to find her way home. She had waves of déjà vu, temporal lobe epilepsy; the present experienced as a memory.

The bodily symptoms cleared up but the disruption to her life was permanent. All her savings went on skin grafts for her back, feet and breasts. It was the first time she needed medication for HIV. She left hospital with her first prescription of AZT.

Marcy got dressed and waited for Lette Lipton to call. She sat on the windowsill and drank coffee. From her fifth-floor walk-up she got a barren, Stieglitz view of city rooftops: water towers and pigeons flocking on the brittle twigs of TV aerials; planes of slate and sky, shadow and light.

The radio said Broadway was down to single lanes despite the salt and grit because Nynex was digging up the road again. Fifth was clogged tight by a convoy of cabs protesting at mandatory spoken English tests the Taxi and Limousine Commission wanted to impose. Traffic was backed up around FDR Drive and all the horn honking and revving of engines had resulted in two guys shot dead and another bludgeoned comatose with a tyre iron. People were freezing to death in the gridlock. The news said one guy froze stiff in his driver's seat. His hands were stuck to the steering wheel so the emergency services had to snip his fingers with bolt cutters. He was zipped into the body bag still in a sitting position. His severed fingers were still curled around the wheel when they hitched the car to the tow truck. Marcy span the dial to find music.

When Lette arrived the girls walked across town to Eros Studios in SoHo.

'You seemed a little jumpy back there as you came out of your apartment,' said Lette. 'Anything wrong?'

'Don't worry about it,' sighed Marcy. 'There's nothing you

can do. Have you got your certificates?' It was Lette's first skin flick and she had asked Marcy to come along as chaperone and adviser.

'Yeah. PCR, ELISA and Western Blot.'

'Good.'

The studio was on the third floor above a bail bondsman's office and a Kung-Fu academy. The motto 'All words are lies. Everything is fiction' was sprayed red on the sidewalk, the letters bleeding through the snow. The slogan was spreading all over town like measles. It could have been a black call to arms but more likely it was situationist guerrilla art from the Village.

The studio was a cramped space with a bed and three electric heaters in it. The flick was to be called Sex Agent because the desultory script was a James Bond rip off. This involved the male lead dressing in a tuxedo for each scene and fucking women who each wore different national dress. It was a Japanese co-production, which meant at some stage the guy had to fuck a geisha. Lette was to be that geisha. She wasn't oriental but she had caramel skin and black pubic hair. Slit-eye make-up and she could pass for Japanese. When she arrived, the faggot doing the make-up painted kessho foundation on her face and neck and slowly turned her into a slant-eyed china doll. In the meantime a video camera was set up and the illusion of a Japanese setting was created by spreading a bamboo mat on the floor and hanging a picture of Mount Fujiyama on the wall. The picture was borrowed from a noodle shop two doors down and they wanted it back by six.

This was Marcy's life. The life that killed her. A world in which men want to be fourteen inches and spraying come like a firehose and women get what they want by exploiting this desire. She had seen so many pricks and cunts the genitals paraded before her seemed utterly alien, like a word repeated over and over becomes a strange noise devoid of meaning.

Lette's costume was a black satin dressing gown which could pass as a kimono. She used blusher to mask razor rash around her bikini line and suture marks under her breasts from recent saline implants. A puff of breath spray. Once she had greased her vulva with olive oil and rubbed ice cubes over her nipples she was ready to go.

The male lead, a jock with blond curly hair and dead eyes, stood in a corner concentrating on hardcore and squeezed his dick to firmness. Steroid muscles, sunbed tan, baby oil. He grunted in acknowledgement when Lette showed him her Aids test certificates. She was cleared by a quarterly polymerase chain reaction test, a week old enzyme-linked aminosorbid test, and a day old Western Blot test.

'Mine are on the table,' said the stud, and Lette checked his certificates with care.

When the guy was fully inflated he rolled a small elastic band down his dick until it was hidden in his pubic hair. The rubber band strangled his penis like a tourniquet, making it retain blood and bloat to the thickness of a beer bottle.

'Let me run you through the scene,' said the director. He was young, possibly a film student paying the rent. 'John comes in through the door and says: "Where's the micro film?" You say: "I don't know what you are talking about." And then he says: "Yes you do. The Russian bitch gave me your name." And then you say: "They will kill me if I tell you." He says: "If you don't tell me I will fuck you to death." At that point he pulls out his dick and you say: "Oh it's so big. Fuck your seed into me." Then you kneel down and he fucks you from the rear. Got it?'

'Fuck your seed into me,' repeated Lette.

'Yeah. But with feeling.'

A Fugees CD played on the deck as they shot the fuck scene four times. Long shot, a close-up of his face, a close-up of her face, a close-up of the dick action. The blow job took longer. The guy's dick had been de-sensitized by the constricting elastic band and it took half an hour of sucking before he came in Lette's face. Lette kept steady eye contact with the camera, just like Marcy told her.

'Oh, you were so wonderful,' said Lette, semen dribbling from her chin. 'I'll tell you anything. The French girl has the micro film. Her name is Marie Dupont and she lives next to the Eiffel Tower.'

Lette wiped come and make-up off her face and the set dresser replaced Mount Fujiyama with a string of onions and a couple of baguettes. A blonde girl arrived and rehearsed being fucked while wearing a beret.

'Fuck me with your mighty cock, Monsieur,' she said, practising her accent.

Lette got five hundred cash for the work.

'How was it?' asked Marcy, as she escorted Lette part of the way back to her apartment.

'It wasn't so bad,' said the girl. 'But that band around his dick made it cold as ice. It was like sucking a popsicle. Funny. Even though it's work, I still wanted the guy to like me, you know? It's still personal.' She laughed and then she cried and they sat on a park bench in Madison Square until she stopped. 'I'll be all right,' she said, blowing her nose then counting the money. 'The first time is the hardest, right?'

'Yeah,' said Marcy. 'The first time is a motherfucker. After that it's nothing.'

'They want me back to do the full works next week. Double penetration and I have to blow some guy at the same time.'

'Are you going to do it?'

'Fifteen hundred dollars and my name in the credits.'

'I guess you will. You better practise, though. Get some big candles or a vibrator, or something, and practise pushing it up your ass. It will make it easier on the day. Remember it only hurts if you tense up. Just relax and let it slide in.'

For a while they watched dog owners bring their pets to shit in wood chippings. The park looked beautiful in the snow but pedestrians didn't stop to admire the icicles hanging from the trees. Vishnu Jones had issued a communiqué saying he was planning a big bang and nobody wanted to stay too long in a public place.

'If you really need some work,' said Marcy, 'then maybe you could call this number.' She handed Lette a business card.

'Willie Turkel.'

'That's right. He's a photographer. Does high-class stuff. Good money. I got an appointment with him in an hour.'

'Maybe I'll give him a call.'

'Do that.'

Marcy and Lette said their goodbyes. Marcy didn't want to go home to eat so she looked for somewhere to get a burrito.

Virgil was due later that evening and Marcy had to work in the meantime. She posed in a studio above a dance school on 47th Street. The picture was to be used in an advert for sex phone lines. She had to wear stockings and suspenders and lie on a bed with one hand down her panties and another holding a mobile phone to her mouth. She got into the posture and the photographer, Willie Turkel, set her limbs the way he wanted. Willie was a Gothic decadent. He wore riding boots, jodhpurs and a black velvet coat. He never took off his shades and always wore black nail varnish and lipstick.

'Hold it there, girl,' he said. 'Just keep that position.'

So Marcy lay still and looked up at the ceiling tiles and fluorescent strip light for an hour while Willie took pictures. She was used to this. It had been much the same experience modelling for a group of art students. She would be put in some contorted position and for the next hour would have to maintain the posture as her back ached and her arms and legs went to sleep. She was adept at turning inward, losing herself in dreams and memories while the artists worked.

Willie made it easy for her to relax. He had been her boyfriend in the days he kidded himself he was bi, and they stayed friends. Her back still showed traces of the surgeon's knife and she needed a patient photographer to let her choose positions and costumes which hid her scars. Willie helped her out and would be the ideal person to approach with her mission of revenge. But she already depended on him to line up photographic work and she swore she wouldn't let one guy become master of her fate. She didn't want to lean on anyone. That's why she chose to use Virgil. He was younger, greener, easier to manipulate.

Today, as she lay with her back arched, face frozen in a rictus of ecstasy, she thought about Virgil. Certainly he hadn't disguised the arousal he felt at seeing her naked in the photospreads she had given him, nor had he masked the lust he felt for her in the flesh. On the two occasions they met he struck her as guileless and rather sweet.

Willie Turkel paid her two hundred in cash and let her keep the panties and stockings. Maybe he thought a microscopic trace of body fluid on the fabric could transmit HIV.

'I met an interesting freak,' she said as she dressed.

'Do tell,' said Turkel.

'He photographs dead people every night. Hangs around accident sites. You heard about the priest that got his head cut off?'

'Indeed.'

'He got it full close-up. You want to meet him?'

'He sounds a very intriguing young man. Choose your moment. Wait until he is quite desperate for help then bring him to me.'

When she got back to her apartment Virgil was on the steps with an aluminium suitcase.

'Nice room,' he said, with heavy sarcasm, when they were inside. 'Bijou. Cosy. Interesting fungi you've cultivated on the walls.'

'Yeah. Right.'

'I like the bank vault thing you have for a front door.'

'I'd like to feel safe without turning my place into a fucking prison cell.'

'This creep's really got to you.'

'Yeah. What's in the case?'

'A surprise. My friend Johnny Ray. He lent me some of his industrial-espionage gear as a favour.'

'What is it?' asked Marcy. Inside the case, packed in foam, were a TV monitor and reels of fibre-optic cable.

'An endoscope. Surgeons use them for keyhole surgery.' A fine wire terminated in a lens smaller than a pea. 'We can use it to watch what's going on in your hallway.'

'Great.'

'Where can I plug it in?'

There was a spyhole set in Marcy's new steel door so she could see who was outside. Virgil unscrewed it and glued the little camera in its place with bubble gum. When the monitor was switched on they got a fish-eye view of the stairs and hallway in lurid, VHS colour.

'We should be okay as long as the hall light doesn't scare your prowler away.'

'Let's go into the bedroom,' said Marcy.

'Why?'

'He won't put anything under the door if he sees the light on in the apartment and hears voices. We have to make it look like I'm not at home.'

'Right.'

Virgil carried the monitor into the bedroom and set it up on the dressing table.

'Nice quilt,' he said, admiring the blue, patchwork bedspread.

'Thanks. My mother made it. She's kind of traditional.'

They sat on the edge of the bed and Virgil looked around. There were S & M magazines on the shelves and books about cats.

'What's your full name?' asked Virgil.

'Marcy Glass.'

'So where are you from, Marcy Glass?'

'Little Odessa.'

'Do your folks know what you do for a living?'

'They think I'm a secretary. How about you, Virgil? Your folks still alive?'

'Sort of.'

'What does that mean?'

'I'll tell you some time.'

'Do they know you take pictures of dead people?'

'I don't tell many people about it at all. In fact you and Larry Onions are the only ones who know outside of the profession.' Virgil pulled some pictures from a manila envelope rolled in the pocket of his overcoat. 'I got some great stuff last week. Look at these.'

Two men and a woman lying dead on the sidewalk. Smart clothes, briefcase, umbrella, no heads.

'This fire truck was answering an emergency call and the turntable ladder on the back came unstuck and swung out. These four business types got out of a cab and three of them were decapitated right there. The fourth guy was okay because he was bending down to pay the tip. And check this out.'

A shitty hotel room. The picture was taken from the corridor past crime-scene tape barring the door. A smart Samsonite suitcase, the big kind for trailing around airports on a leash, was open on the bed. Jars of eyes in close-up, pickled testicles, kidneys, livers, hearts.

'Damn,' said Marcy. 'Is that some serial killer collecting souvenirs?'

'A Chinese doctor's medicine. You know, eating a tiger's dick is supposed to cure impotence? Eating human organs is supposed to let you take on the strength of the dead person. The guy had twenty pairs of eyes in that case. The cops said the eyes were small, like they came from children. Who knows where he got them?'

'Who do you suppose bought this stuff? Some Fifth Avenue bitch trying to stay young?'

'Beats me.'

'I have a friend who would appreciate your art. You're both quite alike. You share a necrophiliac personality.'

'That's unfair. You're mixing up morbid with real. I mean, take a look at this.' He took a silver pill box from his pocket. It had a rose engraved on the lid and a white capsule inside. The white capsule had a skull and cross-bones on it. 'Know what that is?' Marcy shook her head. 'It's a cyanide pill. Friend I used to know worked in a warehouse near Newark. It's where the State stores shit they aren't going to use. Like they got ten thousand wooden penises in there from a company in Saskatchewan. They were for schools to teach kids how to roll condoms. Then the state got chickenshit and decided not to use them, so all these wooden dicks got stacked in the warehouse. Anyway, they also got seven million cyanide pills left over from the cold war. The only protection the State could offer citizens against a nuclear attack. So I got my friend to open a packing case and steal one.'

'You're telling me that isn't morbid?'

'Not at all. Because if you have the means to your own demise in your pocket then living isn't an on-going accident but a positive decision. Taking each successive breath is an active choice. So, in fact, you're more alive than you were before.'

'If I had a poison pill like that I'd swallow it.'

She got wine from the refrigerator.

They talked about Marcy's work in the skin trade and Marcy seized the moment to lean forward and kiss Virgil. He backed away and she pecked him on the cheek.

'Hold on,' she said. She switched on an electric fire which cast the room in a red glow and flattered her figure as she slipped out of her clothes. She pulled Virgil's dick from his trousers and massaged it to stiffness. She jerked him off and it took him an age to come.

'Relax,' she said. 'It's quite safe.'

She fingered herself with her free hand and when they came there were no orgasmic shrieks or ecstatic contortions. Marcy's climax was marked by a shivering sigh, and when Virgil finished a couple of minutes later it was a hissing exhalation through clenched teeth. Marcy scrubbed herself in the bathroom and Virgil wiped pearls of semen off the bedspread with a tissue.

Marcy lay Virgil down and gently stroked his back until the skin rose in goose bumps. He smiled with pleasure and his face gradually relaxed, his fist uncurled against the sheet and Marcy was in the room alone. She watched him sleep, satisfied that a sexual bond between them would keep Virgil malleable for as long as she needed.

She was reaching for a glass of water on the bedside table when she saw a monster on the TV screen. A figure in a raincoat with his face masked by a dark hat. The demon of her nightmares and masturbation fantasies. She shook Virgil awake.

'What?' He blinked and yawned.

'It's him.'

'Damn,' said Virgil, and pulled up his pants and buckled his belt. 'What's he doing now?' he asked, concentrating on tying his shoes.

'Nothing,' said Marcy. 'He's on the stairs. The hall light has him spooked. He doesn't know if it's safe to come up or not.'

'Motherfucker.'

Virgil took Larry's paintball gun and a pair of cuffs from his coat and crept to the front door. Marcy put her clothes on and joined him. They both tried to modulate their breathing. There was the gentle creak of a floorboard in the hallway. One by one Virgil silently slid back the dead bolts. Another creaking floorboard, but much closer. Virgil and Marcy looked down at their feet and, in the light shafting under the door, saw a white envelope slide on to the doormat.

Virgil wrenched open the door, seized the bending creep by the collar of his coat and pulled him into the room. Marcy hit the lights. The creep fell face down, rolled over and Virgil sat on his chest. A spotty kid. Early twenties, maybe younger.

'Kimberley,' exclaimed Marcy.

'You know this guy?'

'He lives in this building. He's got a first-floor apartment. We say hello now and then.'

'Kimberley is a girl's name.'

'Could you let me up, please?' wheezed Kimberley. 'It's difficult to breathe with you sitting on me.'

Virgil pulled the paintball gun from his pants and pressed it against Kimberley's chin. The gun looked like a chromed automatic and would convince anyone but an expert.

'I'll let you up when I feel like it,' said Virgil. 'What's in the letter?' Marcy ripped it open and read.

'It says: "I am going to grease my monster cock and feed it up your ass. You are going to scream and squirm and shit a gallon of come, baby." And there's another picture of his penis.'

'Get up,' said Virgil. 'Strip down.'

'It was just a little joke,' protested Kimberley. 'Just a bit of fun. I don't know why you're both making such a big deal out of it, I really don't.' And he meant it.

'You need fucking psychiatric care. You think this is some sort of hobby?' said Virgil. 'Jesus! Strip.' He clipped Kimberley over the head and the guy reluctantly pulled off his tie. He stopped when he was stripped to the waist.

'This is so childish,' he said. 'If you want my wallet then just take it. Let's not go through this charade.' Virgil slapped him again. 'Will you stop doing that? It's not exactly fun.'

'If you get a slap from me you'll take it and like it.'

Kimberley took off his shoes and pants.

'And the rest of it,' said Virgil, putting the gun to Kimberley's ear. 'The boxers and the socks.' Kimberley hesitated then slowly complied.

'Your dick ain't such a monster now, is it?' Virgil prodded the shrivelled organ.

'Well, I'm cold.'

'And you're going to get colder.'

Virgil cuffed the guy's hands behind his back and wound Kimberley's neck tie around his head to make a gag. He and Marcy frog-marched the man down the stairs. They passed the door to Kimberley's apartment on the way to the ground floor, and Virgil wondered what weird shit they would find inside. He decided it would be the usual loser's library. A bunch of books about serial killers and Nazis. Consolation fantasies for an inadequate, ineffectual dweeb.

They reached the atrium. Virgil pushed Kimberley into the revolving doors and flipped the latches top and bottom to lock him inside. The naked man was on display to the street. A couple walking their dog in the snow stopped to look. Another couple joined them.

'Give them a good show, Kimberley,' said Virgil, tapping the glass. 'By the way, you have one month to move out of this apartment block or I kick your ass.'

'What time is it?' asked Virgil as they climbed the stairs back to Marcy's apartment.

'Getting late.'

'I was going to hit the sheets but I think I'll skip it tonight.'

They levered the door to Kimberley's apartment on the way up. A small place with little furniture. The walls were papered with a strange floral pattern which, close up, revealed itself to be pouting vulva snipped from skin magazines and pasted to the wall with great precision. There was a fruitbowl of dildos and vibrators. Bookshelves were stacked with nothing but hardcore videos. A large teddy bear on the bed had a neoprene vagina glued into the crotch. A near empty tube of KY on the table nearby.

When they got back to the apartment they put Kimberley's clothes in a garbage sack and dumped them down the chute.

'I don't want to stay here tonight,' said Marcy. 'You can't tell what a nut like Kimberley will do when he's made to look a fool.'

Virgil led her down an exterior fire escape and back to the Majestic. By unspoken agreement they didn't talk about Kimberley again.

'What's it like, Marcy?' asked Virgil, as they lay together on his bed.

'What?'

'Knowing that you're going to die.'

'Aids is a motherfucker of a disease because you don't know when it will get you. A doctor says you have stomach cancer and eight weeks to live, then you have a timescale. You write a will, see your family, go through the process and die. But with Aids it's the waiting that drives you insane. A friend of mine with the disease said it was like being put in front of the firing squad. You get your last cigarette, your last look at the sky, then they put a blindfold on you and you're set to die. The sergeant calls out "ready" then "aim" but the order to fire never comes. So you're left there in the dark, cringing from the bullets you think will come any second. At that point you don't want to live. You want the fuckers to shoot you and get it over with. That's how I feel knowing I have this disease. I'm sick of dying by degrees. Did I tell you my sense of taste has gone? Anti-retroviral therapy, AZT, T-cell counts. I mean what's the fucking point? I'm tired to the bone. Right now I just want to sleep. For ever.'

Virgil didn't say anything, so Marcy made a big effort to change the subject.

'What about Mary Gollecky?' she asked, and Virgil sounded grateful to be talking of practical matters.

'I talked to my friend Johnny Ray. He made a few phone calls, rifled a few databases, that kind of thing. Seems your friend is a pillar of the community. Large house, kids, husband is big in the Republican Party. Johnny has set a fidelity tester girl on his tail. The girl will get him on his own, proposition him and maybe fuck the guy if she gets a chance. All the while she's wearing a wire. Mary gets a tape and so do her friends and work colleagues. She gets a taste of what she did to you. Justice is served.'

'I like it. Can I ask another favour?'

'Yeah.'

'I don't want to go back to my apartment in the next few days. Can I stay here for a while?'

'I'll see if I can smooth it with Larry.'

Virgil listened to the breathing of the girl lying beside him in the bed and wondered what was going on in her head. It was absurd to think anything could happen between him and a dying girl. But sometimes he got lonely and he would like a friend, if only for a little while.

CLOWN ARREST

A helicopter pilot of the US border patrol observed a strangely dressed man trying to climb over a barbed-wire fence near Tijuana, Texas. The man was wearing red pants, a polkadot shirt, pancake make-up, a blue wig and a red nose. When challenged by police the man claimed to be a professional clown from Honduras. He said he was disillusioned with life in the US and wanted to rejoin his family in Honduras.

Chapter Eight

Raoul Steiner, one of the richest brokers in New York, took his three-year-old son to see Fantasia on Times Square. When they emerged from the theatre Steiner hitched the toddler on to his shoulders to carry him through the milling crowds. He pointed out the full moon to his son. As he did so the child dropped a rubber pterodactyl in his father's mouth and he choked to death right there in the middle of people and traffic. The corpse was still in the street at 3 a.m. and Virgil got a good picture, but so did the paparazzi staking out a theatre premier across the street. The *Village Advertiser* gave Virgil fifty dollars for the picture, and as he slept towards noon the note stayed curled in his fist.

The alarm bleeped. It put him in a polluted half-sleep, spiralling down through sepia vapours of nostalgia and regret, and despite the cold his shirt was shrink-wrapped to his body by sweat. The exterminators rang and he snapped out of it.

As instructed Reynard had arranged a visit from the Sanitation Department. There were two exterminators and they suited up in the auditorium before clearing the basement of vermin. They wore head-to-toe protection like NBCP suits. They laid down Pyrethrum for the roaches and tossed methyl-bromide canisters into each room to kill rats. When the toxic gas had done its work they hoovered up dead rats with a big vacuum cleaner. The machine had been invented by an exotic pet dealer in Amarillo for sucking prairie dogs into a bag, and city sanitation guys used them to suck rats from pipes and wall cavities. They used methyl bromide on the vermin because the usual arsenal of tuna dosed with difenacoum, warfarin and other blood thinning agents was no good. This new breed of super rat just got high on the stuff. In a couple of generations the species would adjust to methyl bromide and there would be nothing left to do the job but .45 hollow points. Because this wasn't pest control. It was inter-species war.

They made Virgil stay in the auditorium as they worked. He paced the aisle kicking Raisinettes that littered the floor like rabbit droppings. Johnny Ray joined him after half an hour.

Johnny was short, with a short guy's temper. He was from Vegas and often talked of going back but never did anything about it. He wore polished boots and a bolo tie and walked half-speed like he was moving to a Ry Cooder soundtrack only he could hear. He was laconic and Virgil got the impression he was deep-down lonely. Johnny kept a regular income by driving a white, six-wheeled Lincoln Super Stretch with Vegas plates, but made most of his money in surveillance and counter-surveillance. He could sweep an office, PBX switchboard exams, mains checks and spectrum analysis, all in thirty minutes. The term private detective didn't quite convey the amoral attitude he cultivated. He preferred to call himself an information broker. He tried to carry himself with an air of Buddhistic detachment and made a virtue of being mercenary. Virgil supposed several years of shadowing husbands and wives to by-the-hour fuck pads, watching them screw and hearing them moan, had led Johnny to loathe the human race. Nevertheless, Virgil considered him a friend.

'You got my endoscope?' asked Johnny.

'Yeah,' said Virgil. 'Thanks for the loan. But we got to wait for the exterminators to finish before we get it.'

'I heard there was a two-year waiting list for these guys.'

'I got a special arrangement.'

'Here's your computer.' Johnny handed Virgil a cheap attaché case. Inside was a bunch of wires and circuit boards and a keypad. 'Seven hundred, as arranged.'

'The money is in the apartment.'

'And here's your tapes. Five copies.'

Johnny handed over a paper bag containing five cassettes.

'Is it hot?'

'The girl got wined, dined, sixty-nined with a mike in her bra the whole time. The mark was real talkative. We got him good.'

When the exterminators were done they emerged from the apartment with two sandwich bags full of dead roaches.

'We free of rats?' asked Virgil.

'For about five minutes,' said the sanitation guy. 'The plumbing here is so ancient I bet there isn't a rodding eye in the system. Best keep your toilet seats down and a brick on the lid. Here's your Vermin Clearance Certificate. And here's your complimentary pack of methicillin. Have a nice day.'

The basement rooms smelled sickly sweet. After a couple of minutes in his room Virgil was still alive, so he figured whatever gas residue remained was harmless. He handed over the endoscope and money and Johnny Ray was gone.

Virgil went upstairs to Larry's projection box to fix breakfast. Larry was in his favourite chair flipping a coin.

'Tails. Damn. You know I had heads twenty-seven times?'

'Glad to see you're keeping busy.'

'Twenty-seven times. What are the chances of that? Must be a million to one.'

'Depends how you look at it. I just met a girl who got struck by lightning in Central Park. Sounds incredible but people get hit by lightning every week. Mostly men on golf courses. If you look at it from a personal point of view the luck in your life seems weird. Take the wider picture and, well, shit happens.'

'I guess. So how the fuck are you this morning?' asked Larry when Virgil was seated with a steaming mug of coffee. It was the first moment of introspection Virgil had allowed himself in a while and he discovered he was sick of looking at dead people.

'I don't feel so good, actually. I need a vacation. I want to take photos of something with a pulse. I got a girl paying me three, maybe four thousand for some work. If I could get some more, a proper stake, it could be my ticket out of this crappy situation.'

'St Sophia's?'

'I'll do it. What the fuck. Three weeks shy of thirty. I've got to get out of here.'

'Excellent news. I'll call Benny and let him know.'

'What did you need me for?'

'A look-out.'

'There's a condition. I come along but I take pictures. I want the whole thing on film.'

'Pictures of us?'

'Put a stocking over your head. No one will recognize you.'

'I'll have to talk it over with Benny.'

'You're sure you can fence the gear?'

'Fuck, yeah. This is a seller's market. My connection in the Village is desperate for anything he can get.'

'All right. We'll get together with Benny and work something out. And the girl stays here.'

'Whatever. You can fix up a room.'

Virgil pulled the evening shift at the mall and supervised its transformation from consumer heaven to impregnable fortress. Come nightfall the streets were relinquished to gangs and crazies. Guards with shotguns stood sentinel in the pavilion lobby of Metropolitan Plaza beneath flags of all nations and a revolving abstract sculpture called *The Common Man*.

At seven o'clock a truck pulled up by the main steps and a group of guys entered the building. Virgil met them in the lobby. He had been told to expect visitors. He guessed they were exterminators here to renew the warfarin, but close up he could see the insignia of cops, city engineers and the Manhattan Cable Co.

'You know where you have to take us?' asked one of the cops. The sight of cops put the fear in him. He had been safe in the Metro control room when the angel was jacked from the House of Usher van, no way to link him to the job, but sirens and cops still made him want to run for cover.

'Zed Station?' said Virgil.

'That's right.'

'I'll lead you there.'

Zed Station was a myth, like alligators in the sewers. It got its name from an architect who explored the tunnel system and said it reminded him of the Zoologischer Garten station in

Berlin. Most of New York's utility records had been destroyed by fire at the beginning of the twentieth century and virtually all documents cataloguing underground development were lost. In fact the Sanitation Department was still mapping old sewer ducts by flushing radioactive dye into the system and monitoring the water flow. So the notion there was an abandoned warren of subway tunnels and stations didn't seem fantastic.

When the first subterranean scientific streets were excavated in 1870 many vaults and chambers were dug and aborted. Some suggested these tunnels had been converted to an underground monorail by the CIA and some suggested the derelict stations were lined with lead and turned to nuclear bunkers to shelter a select group of city officials. But most thought the fabled Zed Line, which ran down Third to Wall Street and was supposedly decorated with white marbled walls and zercon light fixtures, never existed. But Virgil knew better. He had seen plans of Metropolitan Plaza and the abandoned Zed-Line station nestling in the foundations. And tonight his supervisor had left him instructions how to reach it.

The cops, engineers and cable guys were suited up in chain-mail and football padding. They had flame-throwers like Uzis, with gas bottles where the magazine should be.

Virgil took them to the service elevator and put his key in the panel to make it operate. It was a new elevator and still stank of incense a Shinto priest had wafted when blessing the mechanism. The parent company in Osaka had sent a Feng Shui geomancer to confirm the elevator was in harmony with the elements of earth, wind, fire and water. It was.

'Going down.'

The elevator dropped to the bedrock of Manhattan. Sharp descent. Levels flashing by. Ancillary plant hall. Main plant hall. When they came to a standstill they could hear the faint rush of the pump tunnel drawing up water from the Hudson for the air-conditioning chillers and sewage system.

They were at the bottom of the shaft. The group put on gloves and hockey masks. They looked like astronauts and the impression was enhanced when they stepped from the elevator into a chamber like an airlock. The heavy steel door before them said: 'Typhoid Warning' and 'Extreme Danger. No Unauthorized Personnel Beyond This Point.'

'What exactly are you guys doing down here?' asked Virgil.

'You didn't watch TV last night?'

'I wasn't in.'

'At nine o'clock all the cable channels cut out. Some fucks put little bombs in all the cable junction boxes. Must have taken them weeks to do and all timed to detonate at once.'

'Vishnu Jones?'

'No. This is some bunch of art-school bullshit media terrorists called Los Banditos. Did you see how they scrambled the *Graphic*?'

'Yeah.'

'Same fuckers put subliminal shit in Santa Barbara. "All words are lies. Everything is fiction." Spraying it around town too. Cultural jamming.'

'You're going to fix it from down here?'

'A lot of the cable runs through these tunnels.'

Virgil cupped a hand over his mouth and nose, pressed Open, and the door slid aside. Nothing beyond but darkness and the earthy smell of stagnant water. The atmosphere was cold like a meat locker. There were tunnels lower than this, water tunnels eight hundred feet below sea level and built for the next century, and the air down there was so cold it burned.

The engineers let loose a couple of puffs of fire from their flame-throwers. Squeaking and scurrying receded to the distance. Flashlight beams hinted at marble walls, frescos and gilt fixtures; a cathedral space with a grand stairway and cobwebbed light fittings hanging from the roof.

There was the flickering orange of a camp fire far down one of the tunnels and Virgil caught a glimpse of what might have been tents, some sort of encampment.

The noise of scampering rodents got nearer so Virgil quickly shut the door. As he rode the elevator to the city surface he thought about tunnel dwellers living in the sewers, subways and Grand Central. He wondered why, if they didn't like people or urban life, they burrowed to establish a niche in the city rather than just get the next Greyhound west to vast, natural solitudes.

The evening's excitement was over and there was nothing to do but return to the usual routine. After a cursory patrol of the mall interior Virgil retreated to mission control. His vision bleached by white walls and two-thousand-lux lighting. There was nothing moving on the monitors but he couldn't shake the feeling of being watched, so he locked himself inside.

He phoned Marcy and told her he had incriminating tapes of Mary Gollecky's husband. The kind of thing that could blow the woman's comfortable life apart. Marcy said she was thrilled but sounded even more glacial on the phone than she did in the flesh.

Now, with eight hours of privacy to himself, he could experiment with the computer in the attaché case he had bought from Johnny Ray.

Virgil didn't know anything about computers and didn't want to. He got off on techno jargon but he knew he wasn't anyone's alpha geek. Playing games and dropping opinions into the vacuum of cyberspace seemed like a waste of time, but hacking had a David and Goliath romance. He could dream he was some protocol-spoofing super nerd like Kevin Mitnick hacking North American Air Defence Command to have ICBM launch codes at his fingertips. This had been the topic of conversation when he first picked up the endoscope from Johnny. Johnny told him how he paid hackers to access secret company files and happened to mention a few of the companies who were wide open to intrusion. One of these was Mercury Press which, in the past two years, had become the biggest wholesaler of raw news, third only to Reuters and Associated Press. Virgil seized upon the idea and demanded Johnny show him how it was done. Johnny went one better and commissioned some dedicated hardware with the sole purpose of hacking Mercury Press. It was Virgil's intention to make up news stories, file them with Mercury Press and see where they were printed.

He was itching to begin, so he unpacked the attaché case. A dissected mobile phone, a modem and a motherboard, studded with Fujitsu chips so advanced they were still big news in

Shanghai. He powered up the CPU in blind faith the machinery would do what he asked.

The machine scanned the airwaves and cloned the Novatel source code of a mobile used by an office furniture salesman returning home on FDR Drive. Using the Metropolitan plumbing system as a giant antennae it bounced a signal off Asia Comsat in geostationary orbit over the equator, surfed in on Netcom and convinced the Mercury computer three streets away on Second it was receiving a call originating in the Cambodian domestic phone system. All this while Virgil brewed coffee.

'Ready to transmit,' said the little screen, and the cursor winked expectantly. Virgil sipped from his mug, holding it with both hands like a chalice, and strained for inspiration.

He composed a tale about a sick nun who, having rejected all forms of conventional medicine to treat her injured back, drowns when her electric wheelchair malfunctions and drives into the river at Lourdes. After a minute's thought he deleted the text. It seemed too neat, too much like a moral. Freud disliked Dali paintings because they were clearly the product of conscious artifice rather than the dreamstuff they claimed to be. Weird shit has to be ambiguous to be believed.

Craig Timpson, the guard who pulled the shift before Virgil, had left more petty post-it notes on the CCTV consoles demanding people wash up their coffee cups and not leave them for him to do. Petty shit like that. Virgil cracked his knuckles and prepared to take his revenge.

'Government officials in the old Portuguese enclave of Macao revealed details of an incident in which a sewage worker was eaten by a twenty-five foot python while inspecting the drains beneath an apartment block in the east of the city. Chang Toi was inspecting a crack that had appeared in the foundations of the condominium when he was attacked by the snake, which throttled and ate him before anyone could come to his aid. Police moved in to recover the body and remove the snake but discovered the reptile was now too fat to be extracted from the foundations of the building. Residents of the apartment block had apparently known of the python's presence for two years and attributed the disappearance of several pets to the hungry reptile. Nevertheless they regard the animal as a source of good luck and have so far refused to let the police destroy the python in order to recover Mr Toi's body. A police spokesman said they would have to wait several weeks until the snake had sufficiently digested the sewage worker before it could be removed from the foundations of the apartment block. The city sanitation department and the deceased's family expressed little concern at the delay in holding a funeral. Several of Toi's colleagues are reported as saying, "Nobody liked him much, anyway." '

Mercury Press would need to attribute the story to an author so Virgil signed it Barrington Fingenbaum, which was the pseudonym he decided to use for all his little fictions.

He liked the idea of an alter ego. He liked secrets, disguises, false IDs. He wanted to be someone else.

CARJACKER FINGERED

Juan Alonzo, 41, has been charged with car-jacking in San Diego. The main evidence against him is his own finger, which was severed in a car door. He claimed the finger at a local hospital, where it had been handed in, and demanded surgeons replace the severed digit. However, when police officers arrested him for carjacking he said he was mistaken and the finger belonged to someone else.

Chapter Nine

Virgil blasted himself to consciousness with coffee thick as gravy and met Benny and Larry at Levy's Café.

'Larry tells me you're up for the job,' said Benny.

'Yeah.'

'He's a useful kid,' said Larry.

'How about it, Virgil. Are you fit?'

'Enough.'

'But are you lucky?'

'I'm a regular rabbit's paw.'

'Good. We reckon to do this tomorrow night.'

'You know the deal. I take pictures.'

'Why pictures?'

'I want a newspaper job. That's the only reason I'm up for this.'

'All right, but we get to vet the pictures first. No flash. No close-ups.'

'You got it.'

'Right. Let's put this thing together.'

Virgil could tell by the steel in Benny's voice that events had stepped up a gear. He was used to Larry bullshitting about his fantasy beach house and cocktails at sunset, but Benny was pure business. A man set on turning talk into action.

'How do you two get inside?' asked Virgil.

'You wait outside with a radio and let us know if the cops show up. I got a key to get in. On the way out me and Larry fake a forced entry.'

'Alarms?'

'Switched off until workmen finish repairs. Lots of rope and wire swinging in the draught. They would trigger the movement alarms the moment they were switched on.'

'The hole?'

'Six-foot drop into the crypt. A knotted rope should do it.'

'How do you dig up into the treasury?'

'Chisel and crowbar. Shift a couple of big blocks of stone in the support pillars and the treasury floor should cave in.'

'This is the bit I don't like, the bit where it gets all Mission Impossible. Either the floor doesn't fall in or the whole fucking lot comes down.'

'They got steel props down there. Any rock fall would be local.'

'Noise?'

'The area isn't residential.'

'Is there much stuff to carry out?'

'If me and Larry take a sports bag each we should manage.'

'How about it, Larry? Sure you can fence this shit?'

Larry was looking out the window trying hard not to listen. His face telegraphed how scared he was to be taking on a serious job.

'What?'

'Can you fence the shit?'

'Sure. But even at metal value it's still a good score.'

'All right.'

'Clothes,' said Benny. 'You go out today and buy a full outfit. Not from a local store but from a thrift shop you never used before. The clothes are worn for the duration of the job. You don't wear them beforehand and they get burned straight after, okay?'

'You've been thinking this through for a while.'

'These fuckers treat me like shit, kid. And each Sunday I have to listen to them preach all that first-shall-be-last bullshit. For ten years I've been working out how to get even. And this is it. We do it right, we do it quick and clean.'

'Yeah, I got it.'

From the cold burn in Benny's eyes Virgil could see the man was drawing on betrayals and disappointments from way back, long before he began work at St Sophia's. The job wasn't a question of money. It was revenge against the world.

'One last thing,' said Benny. 'We can't rent a car in our own name. How about it, Virgil. You got someone you can trust?'

Marcy had a modelling assignment that evening and invited Virgil along.

The shoot was for a sex-toy catalogue and was happening at Willie Turkel's place. There was a bed, lots of lights, Turkel and a guy from the sex-toy company making sure he got the pictures he wanted.

Virgil was preoccupied with the Sophia's job but didn't want to be alone. He needed to confide in Marcy but didn't want her involved.

Marcy stepped out of her clothes in the corner of the room. The catalogue guy affected boredom in the presence of nudity, but for Marcy the boredom seemed real. As she padded across the room to the bed she was her usual remote and impassive self.

They started with lingerie. A satin French maid's outfit shot from behind, the skirt hitched up to expose Marcy's pussy. Fishnet body stockings, nipple tassels, PVC corset. Then toys. Vibrators of different shapes and sizes. Some got hot, some spurted water, some pumped up and down. Marcy didn't use the dildos. She just lay on the bed and pretended the sight and touch of the objects drove her wild.

Virgil was deeply aroused to see her muscles and tendons tense as she assumed each ecstatic contortion. When she spread her legs her pussy lips parted and he could see wetness all the more arousing for being death on contact.

The presence of the other men in the room made Virgil uncomfortable. The girl was being exploited, so he should do something about it. Yet she was in control, manipulating her allure. The girl had no dependency upon him. She didn't need his protection. It made him feel boyish and useless.

Virgil checked out the pictures on the wall. A bunch of Mapplethorpe dicks. The picture over the fireplace was *Man in a Polyester Suit*; a huge penis flopping out of a zipper.

Turkel's apartment was a baroque salon, all red velvet and

gilding. The man himself wore shades no matter how dim the lighting and caressed his photographic equipment with black lacquered fingernails. Virgil was freaked out by Turkel's tattooed, pierced self, and the man noticed. Turkel bent close and pulled up his eyelid so Virgil could see the Celtic runes stencilled on the inside of the lid. Virgil shivered and backed off. Turkel struck him as a vampire, a decadent used up in pursuit of pleasure and pain.

'Marcy has been telling me all about you,' said Turkel. 'The work you do at night.'

'It's a living.'

'Is it?'

'Well, no, not really.'

'I thought not.' Turkel lay a consoling arm around Virgil's shoulders. 'I know a lot of people and I might be able to help you some day. I want you to take my card and when you have something to show me, something very special, you call, and we can talk business, all right?'

'Sure,' said Virgil, guessing it was the answer most likely to loosen the creep's grip around his shoulders.

When they got back to the Majestic Marcy jerked Virgil off and asked him to massage her back and neck while she rubbed herself. As she approached climax she said: 'Burn me.'

'What?'

'Here.' She gave him a Clipper. 'Burn my shoulder.'

'Fuck, no,' said Virgil, but she put the lighter in his hand and pushed his thumb to make a spark. He wafted the flame near her skin. She shivered and trembled and subsided. She instructed Virgil to cover the burn with a sticking plaster. She didn't explain.

Later Marcy cried without saying why, so Virgil held her and studied knots in the headboard until she stopped.

'Do you have a driving licence?' he asked before they slept. He didn't want her involved but there was no one else he could ask.

'Yeah. Haven't driven for ages, though.'

'I need to rent a car tomorrow. Could you do it? I'll give you the money.'

'Why do you want a car?'

'Can't tell you.'

'Why not?'

'Just can't.'

'All right. It will have to be in the morning. I'm meeting a friend for lunch.'

Virgil fell asleep feeling that for all Marcy's weirdness he had soiled something pure.

HE WENT BERSERK AND STABBED
HIS MOTHER 43 TIMES WITH A
12-INCH BOWIE KNIFE.
WHEN HIS 11-YEAR-OLD BROTHER
TRIED TO INTERVENE, HE STABBED
HIM 25 TIMES BEFORE CLUBBING
THEM BOTH WITH AN IRON BAR.
LATER, HE SAID: 'IT WAS
INEVITABLE.'

Chapter Ten

The night of the raid Virgil and Benny sat in the projection box listening to Charlie Parker while Larry powered down the cinema. The three huddled around an electric fire and drank cheap cola that tasted like chlorinated water. Benny played patience, laying out each card with slow precision. Larry talked.

'You know when they gassed Carson at Sing Sing, the wife of that security guard he killed was there to see it. She was on TV saying Carson was pure evil and killing him was no more than shooting a mad dog. But people have to think like that to throw the switch. I mean, I knew Carson. He was my buddy and I lost count of the times he helped me out, covered for me at the fish plant when I was too stoned to make it in. So try and imagine a guy you know and feel for sitting in a gas chamber. Try and think what he must go through when the cyanide pellets get dropped and he starts to spasm and arrest. That's why I didn't carry a gun when we jacked the angel and why I ain't packing now. Only reason I'd carry a gun is to put it to my own head if we got cornered. I mean it. Do or die. If I go to jail I'd be in my eighties before I was eligible for parole. No way I'm dying behind bars.'

They planned to do the job at two, and as the wall clock counted down Virgil watched his companions and the different ways they dealt with fear. Benny didn't say a word; Larry wouldn't shut up. Virgil took a shit every ten minutes until his guts were empty, then his body started to misinterpret the adrenalin dumping into his blood stream as sexual excitement and he had to jerk off twice. This must be how it is to be a soldier in war time. Skimming the jungle canopy in a Huey gunship, counting off the miles till the LZ.

At two Benny said, 'Let's do it,' and it was a relief to be up and moving.

They drove to the UN building in a Hertz Lexus Marcy hired earlier that day. Virgil was in the back seat. Adrenalin hit him like an amphetamine rush and the city lights and dash indicators scintillated so bright they stung like needles. He could change his mind, make excuses and bail, but he didn't.

They parked across the street, got out and locked the car.

Larry looked up at the sombre frontage of the church and the high campanile and murmured, 'A man can die but once; we owe God a death and let it go which way it will he that dies this year is quit for the next. Fuckin' A.'

Benny ran across the street and up the steps of St Sophia's. He unlocked the door and, when he was sure he was unobserved, Larry ran across the road to join him. Virgil skulked in the shadows of the parking lot. His camera was loaded and ready to shoot.

Benny and Larry left the door unlocked in case they needed a quick exit.

The church interior was dark and deathly quiet. Torch beams illuminated saints and martyrs. Effigies of dead men watched from the shadows.

'Keep your flashlight pointing at the floor,' said Benny. 'Don't let people see light through the windows.'

They hurried up the central aisle of the nave to the choir. Larry fought the urge to bolt, to throw down his equipment and flee the building. It was a war between a nervous system hard-wired for flight and a mind which needed calm.

The hole was in front of the sanctuary. A silver crucifix gleamed on the altar, and before it was blackness where the congregation would have knelt at the rail to receive communion. The hole was surrounded by yellow tape and wooden barriers, which Benny pulled aside. Larry tied a nylon rope around a pillar and threw the end into the gaping space. Benny stood on the lip of the hole and shone his torch inside.

The crypt was a low-ceilinged network of passages and pillars. It had a flagstone floor, except where the falling bell had crushed the tiles to powder exposing bedrock.

Benny slid down the rope into darkness. Larry hesitated then followed.

Outside, Virgil stamped his feet to keep warm. He would take pictures of Larry and Benny exiting the building. He would go inside the church and photograph the damage. He would photograph the cops working the crime scene. Tomorrow's front page: the heist laid out frame by frame like a *Spiderman* comic.

Virgil checked the street. No cars, but a man in the distance getting closer. He was on the church side of the street, maybe three hundred yards away.

'How you guys doing?'

'In the hole.' Larry's voice on shortwave.

'Hurry it up.' Virgil sunk deeper into shadows.

Larry's flashlight lit wall niches filled with rags and crumbling skulls.

'Who are the stiffs?' he asked.

'No idea,' said Benny. 'There was a brass name plate on a coffin they found down here. "Peter Van Hooft, 1697–1751." No records.'

'These guys must have seen the town while it was still New Amsterdam. When Manhattan was just Mohawks and fur trappers.'

They were standing on the schist bedrock of Manhattan. The stone glittered with garnets, amethysts, fool's gold.

Benny led Larry to an archway.

'Take the keystone from the top of the arch and it all falls. The treasury floor comes down with it.'

'How do you want to do this, again?'

'Chisel the stone loose, tie a rope around it and pull from a safe distance.'

They unpacked their tools.

There was no cement to chip at, just solid stone. Larry worked the left side of the block and began to chisel a passage for a rope. The impact of hammer against chisel stung his hands and the anvil chime echoed around the church walls.

Virgil coming through on the radio.

'Kill the noise. There's a guy walking past and he can hear you.'

Larry and Benny stood still, tools in hand.

'Are we clear yet?' asked Larry.

'He's right outside,' Virgil whispered.

'What's he doing?'

'Climbing the church steps. For fuck's sake get out of there. I think he's going to try the door.'

Larry hauled himself out of the hole and ran down the centre aisle. His heart was hammering. He was making demands his old body couldn't fulfil.

'He's checking the lock,' said Virgil. 'He is definitely going to try the door.'

Larry skidded to a halt and put his shoulder to the main door. The latch turned and Larry fought hard to stop the guy getting in. The pressure subsided.

'He's backing off. He's checking the windows.'

'Who is he?' hissed Larry into the radio.

'Forties. Suit. How the fuck would I know?'

More waiting. Virgil again: 'He's moving on. He's at the end of the street. He's gone.'

'Fuckin' A.'

'Lock the door.'

'Benny has the key.'

'Then hurry up. I'm going to listen to the police waveband. If I hear the name St Sophia's you guys get the fuck out of there.'

'Right.'

Larry swung down on the rope once more and joined Benny in the crypt. They finished chiselling at the arch. They had created two holes either side of the keystone. It had taken them ten minutes. When they were done Benny threaded a rope through the holes and they stood back ready to pull.

'On three,' said Benny. 'You ready?'

'Yeah.'

Larry tightened his grip on the rope.

'One.'

They braced themselves to heave.

'Two.'

Larry gritted his teeth.

'Trouble.' Virgil on the radio. 'You got made. Possible two-eleven at St Sophia's. Three cars on the way.'

'We're gone,' said Larry, and hauled himself out of the crypt. 'Benny. Time to go.'

'To hell with that,' said Benny and took up the rope. He pulled and strained and sweated and gradually the keystone began to move.

'No time, Benny,' said Larry. 'We are walking.' He would count to ten then fuck Benny, he was gone.

'Come on, Benny,' whined Larry. 'This is bullshit.'

The keystone came loose and was followed by the rasping, grinding sound of great blocks of granite starting to twist loose. Larry didn't see what happened next. The seismic impact of the treasury floor collapsing rippled through the building and mingled with the sound of breaking glass. His torch beam illuminated nothing but a broiling dust cloud.

'You all right, Benny?' he asked.

No reply.

Virgil didn't hear the floor of the church collapse but he felt the tremor shudder through the sidewalk.

'You guys all right?'

Just static from the radio.

'Larry? Benny?'

A cop car turned into the street. A second. A third.

'You have about thirty seconds to split, guys. Do you hear me?'

Larry was choking on masonry dust and couldn't see further than a couple of feet. 'Benny? You all right? Virgil is on the radio. He's saying something about cops.'

No reply from Benny, but the sound of a man scrambling over rubble. The dust began to clear and Larry saw Benny pulling gleaming trinkets from the debris and stuffing them in his sports bag. 'Benny, you dumb fuck, we are leaving right now.'

Benny zipped up the bag and threw it to Larry. His last find was a gold box, which he put in his pocket. He climbed out of the hole and shook the dust from his clothes and hair.

'You are so fucking stupid,' said Larry as they ran down the nave aisle to the main door.

They skidded to a halt and turned tail as blue cop strobes flashed in the stained glass above the door.

'That's it,' said Larry. 'We're screwed.'

'There's another way out,' said Benny. 'Feretory door.'

Benny ran back towards the hole but skirted its lip to reach the sanctuary. He ran up the altar steps to a wooden door flanked by carved panels depicting angels and apostles. The door was locked so he kicked it open. Larry was last inside and turned to see the main door at the end of the nave open and flashlight beams advance down the aisle.

The feretory was a small room behind the altar, containing ceremonial silverware, books and altar linen. There was a fire exit in the far wall and Benny started ramming the door with his shoulder. Larry joined in and when they hit the door simultaneously it broke open and they spilled into an alleyway bordering a construction site.

'Split up,' said Benny and vanished into shadows.

Larry found a break in a chain-link fence, squeezed through and ran, skirting garbage cans and boxes, heading towards the Hudson.

Virgil saw the first pair of cops enter the church and the rest taking off down a side alley. The obvious implication: Larry and Benny making a break for it from the back of the church. Virgil followed, camera at the ready.

He joined the cops as they ran across the construction site, stumbling over frozen clods of earth. A hopeless pursuit. Larry and Benny home free.

Pictures of cops hands on hips catching their breath. Pictures of the church interior. Pictures of a priest with a .38 midnight special tucked into his cassock belt. The universal cop response to Virgil popping his flash: where the fuck did he come from?

Virgil left when the crime scene was locked down and non-essential personnel were excluded.

He made his way home down deserted sidewalks, keeping

to the shadows and backstreets, and collapsed panting against the back door of the Majestic. Then Virgil felt scared. Like a driver running a red light the fear kicked only when the crisis was past. Virgil got the shakes and puked cola, then dry-retched until he was nearly coughing blood.

PHANTOM TWIN

An Indian boy who complained of stomach pains was found to have an undeveloped twin foetus lodged in his abdomen where it had been feeding off him for the past fifteen years. Doctors say they found a seventeen-centimetre-long foetus weighing nearly two kilos. The foetus had an arm, a head, a tongue and fully developed teeth.

Chapter Eleven

Virgil awoke in Marcy's bed and was working out the implications of the night's events even before he opened his eyes. He had to retrieve the Lexus still parked outside St Sophia's. By now the burgled church would be a crime scene and the cops would be interested in the owner of a car parked nearby all night. Better if Marcy recovered the vehicle because she wouldn't fit the description of the suspects. However, if he sent Marcy to St Sophia's for the car she would have to know what had been going on.

'I was in some pretty deep shit last night,' he said when she brought him coffee. Virgil thought he detected a thaw in her manner towards him as if, despite herself, she was starting to care. Her shoulder was still bandaged where he burnt her.

'Like what?'

'Like a burglary.'

'You're putting me on.'

'St Sophia's. It's near the UN building.'

'Fuck. Stealing from a church. That's pretty low, even for you.'

'Yeah. Can't deny it.'

'What did you do, exactly?'

'Larry ripped off some silverware. We met up after the raid and stashed the stuff here. Didn't get much. I took pictures.'

Virgil unzipped a sports bag and tipped the contents into his lap. A silver box. Two gold cups. A silver jug.

'Are they worth much?' asked Marcy.

'A few dollars for scrap. Larry says he has a fence that will pay more. Some kind of millionaire hoarder is buying this kind of shit off the street. Larry calls him the Tooth Fairy.'

'What about Mary Gollecky?'

'It's in hand. Johnny is still collating tapes. We'll hit her tomorrow, the day after at the latest.'

'So what now?'

'Pick up the car. You can help me with that. Then see if Larry is okay. He seemed pretty bad last night.'

Virgil stood at the end of the street and watched Marcy walk to the car. A couple of black and whites were parked outside St Sophia's and a cop talked to Marcy for a little while.

'What did he say?' asked Virgil when Marcy picked him up.

'Nothing much. Just wanted to know where I was last night and if I saw anything suspicious.'

'Let's drop off the car then go see Larry.'

Larry was in his projection box sipping coffee and looking very ill. The night's adventures had clearly driven his body close to breaking point.

'How you doing, Larry?' asked Virgil.

'Feel like shit.'

'Talked to Benny today?'

'Phoned him at his place on the East Side last night. He's okay.'

'How much for the stuff?'

Virgil emptied the church silver on to the floor and Larry examined each piece.

'Maybe a thousand if we're lucky. The stuff isn't exceptional. Benny has a gold box he put in his pocket last night. We'll go over there when I've finished my coffee, pick it up and take it all to the Village. You can play bodyguard. How about you, Marcy?'

'I've got things to do.'

They stood in the corridor outside Benny's apartment and knocked on his door. When there was no reply they shouted through his letter box. The door of the next apartment opened and an old black man shuffled out in slippers.

'You didn't know about Benny?' he said.

'What about him?' asked Larry.

'Took the dog for a walk first thing as usual. Got hit by a car. Killed stone dead.'

'You're kidding?'

'No, sir. Stone dead. You family?'

'Friends.'

'Stone dead, but ain't that life.'

The old guy turned and shuffled back inside his apartment.

'Got your penknife?' asked Larry.

'Sure.' Virgil handed it over.

Larry forced the lock on the apartment door and they went inside. It was a bachelor pad. Food cartons everywhere, no plants or decorations. Crummy furniture. The only touch of class was a pencil portrait of Benny's ex-wife. The picture was framed and hung in the bedroom, and was signed 'Larry Onions'. One of his better likenesses. It was the first thing Larry broke when he started tossing the place.

'What you looking for?' asked Virgil.

'The gold box.'

Virgil helped him look and found the box in a tennis shoe at the bottom of the wardrobe.

'Shit,' said Larry examining the lid. 'The stone is gone.'

'Stone?'

Virgil didn't get an answer. Larry paced the room for a while then ran out to the corridor and hammered on the old man's door.

'What happened to the dog?' asked Larry when the man answered. 'Did it get hit by the car as well?'

'Yes, sir. I saw it all from my window. Looked like his back was broken.'

'But it didn't die?'

'Not while I was watching.'

'What happened to it?'

'Somebody must have called Benny's ex-wife, because she came and picked the dog up in her car.'

'Thanks very much for your help.'

Virgil and Larry left the apartment.

'Are you going to tell me what's happening?' asked Virgil.

'Call Johnny. Tell him to bring his car and meet us at Levy's. I'll tell you about it when we get there.'

They took a booth and ordered coffee. Larry explained the situation.

'Benny came to me with the idea of the job. He said there was a ton of stuff worth stealing in St Sophia's treasury. He had this nutty idea about a little gold box with a relic in it. It was supposed to contain St Cecilia's knee, but he didn't give a shit about that. He researched the box and reckoned the big glass bead set in the top was a diamond. A big diamond with a name and a history. The idea was we would steal it and I would fence it for him. I thought the whole story was a load of horseshit, but I went along with it because I wanted my hands on the silverware. It's like *The Maltese Falcon*. A bunch of guys going nuts over nothing but junk.'

'When were you planning to cut me in on the deal?'

'I didn't think the stone was real. There was no point saying anything.'

'You saw the box last night. Was the stone genuine?'

'Seemed to be when I cased the treasury display, but what would I know? Benny was convinced it was the real shit.'

'So what has he done with it?'

'Benny used to have dealings with some pretty outside people. He boosted his shit wages by holding stuff for gangster types. Coke, junk like that. You see, these mobsters get raided every calendar month, so it made sense to leave their valuables with a neutral party for safe keeping. One day a guy turned up and dumped a briefcase on Benny. He told him to keep it safe for twenty-four hours. Benny looked inside the case and couldn't believe the stuff in there. Amethysts, diamonds, emeralds, you name it. Jewellery like you've never seen. I mean there were rubies, sapphires, pearls. It was a pirate's treasure chest. You could rake your hand through the case and it would come up dripping gold and jewels. The stuff was all jumbled up so Benny figured nobody had a list of the contents. He saw a ring with a diamond bigger than a pea and decided to keep it for himself.

'The next day the guy came by and picked up his briefcase. Within half an hour he was back with some goons demanding the ring. Benny said he didn't know anything about a ring, so they trashed his apartment. They dismantled the toilet cistern, crumbled up cakes of soap, smashed his stereo, but they didn't find the ring. They made an ultimatum. The ring in one hour or you're a dead man. They staked out the apartment in case Benny tried to run, but he never left. When the hour was up they knocked on his door and he handed over the ring. And they never could work out where in his apartment he had the thing hidden because they searched everywhere.'

'So?'

'So the story got around but Benny would never let on where the ring was hidden. Most people assume he had it up his ass, but one night he got drunk and told me the secret. He had hidden the ring inside his dog. He pressed the ring into a Doggy Num Num, Cruton's favourite chocolate snack, and popped it in his mouth. The ring was safe in the animal's gut for a day. It was a brilliant hiding place. The only drawback was he had to mash up a dog turd with a fork to get the ring back.'

'And you think that's where the diamond is hidden?'

'That's right. Which is why we have to find Mrs Fordice before the dog takes a shit.'

Johnny arrived and they took a ride in his thirty-five-foot stretch. The car had a mirrored ceiling, two TVs, whisky tumblers and decanters. The mini-bar was full of beer and spirits.

'Anything you drink you pay for,' said Johnny over the intercom. 'There's a camera in the ceiling. I can see what you're doing.'

Larry used the car phone and got Mrs Fordice's address from directory enquiries.

'Delancey Street. Near the Williamsburg Bridge.'

They rang the bell but she wasn't home. Larry buzzed one of her neighbours and shouted into the intercom.

'Could you tell me where Mrs Fordice is, please?'

A crackling voice said he didn't know.

'Did you see her with a dog this morning? I saw it get hurt and I was wondering if it was all right.'

The voice said she took the dog to the vet.

'Do you happen to know which vet?'

The voice said the St Francis Veterinary Surgery.

'Do you know it?' said Larry to Johnny as they got back in the car.

'Yeah. It's near here. Big place. Acts as a kennel as well. Celebrities leave their pets there while they're out of town.'

They parked across the street from the St Francis Veterinary Surgery.

'Johnny, you better stay here with the car. Me and Virgil will go inside.'

The waiting room was full of people sitting with pet baskets which mewed or barked. Larry gave the receptionist a wide smile which displayed his yellow teeth.

'Hi. I'm a friend of Mrs Emily Fordice. I understand she brought a white Afghan hound called Cruton in earlier today. I believe it got hit by a car. Could you give me any word as to the dog's condition?'

'I'm afraid Cruton passed away. He had a very bad back injury and Mrs Fordice didn't feel he should suffer any longer than was necessary. I'm sorry.'

'That's all right. Thank you for your time.'

Larry walked out of the surgery and head-butted a light pole. Virgil joined him.

'Fuck. Now what are we going to do?'

'Keep thinking,' said Virgil. 'Just because the dog is dead doesn't mean it's evaporated. The body is still around somewhere. What do you suppose vets do with pet carcasses?'

'Garbage?'

'Not ordinary trash. That would be a health hazard.'

'There's your answer,' said Larry.

A blue truck had pulled up at a loading bay behind the vet building. Guys with gloves and surgical masks were throwing white polythene sacks into the back. The truck had 'Franklin Special Waste Collection' written on the side. Larry and Virgil ran across the street to the stretch.

'Follow that van,' said Larry, and Johnny hit the gas.

They followed the truck for three hours as it made rounds of doctors' surgeries, dentists and undertakers. If the driver

124

realized he was being shadowed by a white stretch limo he didn't show it. Eventually it headed for the very south-eastern tip of Manhattan, near the coastguard building. They watched as the truck tipped its load into a barge.

Larry got out of the car and ran down to the pier. There were too many stevedores around to jump on the barge and start rooting around so he had to stand by and watch the barge pull out into the river and head south.

'Hundred and three,' he said, getting back in the car.

'What?'

'The barge number. Where do you think it's going?'

'City dump, I suppose,' said Virgil. 'Fresh Kills.'

'Where is that? Got a map in this car?'

'Pocket atlas in the glove box,' said Johnny. Virgil checked the index.

'Staten Island. Got to loop around through Brooklyn to the Narrows Bridge.'

'Step on it,' said Larry. 'We have to beat the barge.'

They sped through the polyglot cantons of Queens and Brooklyn and made the Narrows Bridge in thirty-five minutes. The turntable suspension groaned as the four-ton chassis leaned and torqued. Virgil navigated as they crossed Staten Island to Fresh Kills on the west side of the island.

The city landfill was an astonishing sight. Rolling dunes of garbage. Three thousand acres wide and a hundred and fifty feet deep. Four thousand tons of shit arriving daily. Any further expansion and the dump would be visible from space, like the Great Wall of China.

The air was full of the rich, yeast stench of fermenting organic waste, clouds of flies and seagulls spiralling overhead. Lawn sprinklers damped down the eye-watering, putrid stink with pine-oil deodorant. No snow cover, because the broiling refuse was warm like compost. Yellow diggers rolled the garbage flat under caterpillar tracks. Foul liquids seeped from trash thick with carcinogenic compounds and heavy metals: cadmium, phenol and toluene; cobalt sludge bleeding from corroded batteries. Pipes syphoned methane to a nearby smelting plant which forged confiscated guns into manhole covers. A million years hence this would all be fossilized. A strange geological strata of compressed beer cans and polythene.

There was a visitor's centre and a group of school kids were handing back umbrellas loaned as protection against seagulls. The kids bought brochures and T-shirts and paperweights with bits of authentic New York garbage preserved in glass balls. The kids licked ice cream and watched the bums at work.

Vagrants sifted through the junk, examining each article with a connoisseur's eye. They filled sacks with scrap metal. One guy found a half-eaten lettuce and bacon roll and started munching. The vagrants kept out of the way of the prison warders who were supervising a chain gang from Riker's Island. It was token work. Shifting garbage from one place to another, ankle chains snagging on broken lawn chairs and kicking up flies from used diapers. Scarves over the face against vomiting and dizziness. Worse than disinterring corpses at Potter's Field and better punishment because it was utterly purposeless. The guards didn't let them slack.

Sanitation Department personnel wore NBCP suits and trod amongst the rubbish with the exaggerated caution of astronauts. One of the sanitation people walked past Virgil and Larry on his way to the supervisor's cabin. He was carrying a clear bag with a pair of hands in it. It wasn't uncommon to find human remains at the dump. Two years ago they found an entire human skin. They never traced the owner.

Barge 103 was towed into harbour an hour later as daylight was fading, and a grab crane unloaded the contents. Larry watched polythene disposal sacks from the veterinary surgery get scattered down a slope of rotting vegetable matter and he was wading through the refuse to reach his goal before the sanitation guys loaded the sacks into a furnace, or whatever it was they did with hazardous bio-waste. Virgil followed at his own pace and Johnny elected to stay with the car.

They sweated for an hour slashing open each bag with Virgil's pocket knife, but no Cruton. All the sacks tagged 'St Francis Veterinary Surgery' were too small to contain an Afghan. Judging by the weight of the bags they contained guinea pigs and rabbits.

'Goddamn it,' said Larry when they got back to the car. He wiped his face with a handkerchief. 'Not a fucking thing.'

'To tell you the truth I can't see Mrs Fordice leaving this dog with a vet,' said Johnny. He was sitting on the hood of the Lincoln smoking a cigarette.

'Why not?'

'Women are sentimental about animals. A maternal thing. This might have been her ex-husband's dog, but she lived with it for a few years. She would want to see it properly buried.'

'Why the fuck didn't you give us the benefit of your psychological insight before we spent an hour digging around in hazardous waste?'

'Because you didn't ask.'

'Shit.'

They got back in the car. It was snowing again, but Johnny kept the windows down because Larry and Virgil were stinking up his car.

'If you want my advice,' said Johnny, lowering the partition between the driver and the passenger compartment, 'you'll get some of those doggy magazines. *Dogue* or *Vanity Fur*. They do funeral notices. I bet you'll find the dog you're looking for.'

'Aren't you going to ask us why we're looking for a dead dog?' said Virgil, discovering a sardine in his shoe and throwing it out the window.

'Because you're stupid,' said Johnny. Neither of his passengers could argue.

PROPELLER DEATH

A man whose wife organized a plane ride as a birthday gift to help him overcome his fear of flying panicked and forced the pilot to land his plane on a highway near Tucson, Arizona. Ron Soren, 39, jumped from the three-seater Cheetah as it came to a stop and ran into the still-spinning propeller. An eyewitness said Mr Soren's upper body was 'liquidized'. The pilot is being treated for shock.

Chapter Twelve

L arry had borrowed Johnny's stretch and loaded the trunk with polythene and a pick and shovel. He was ready to do some serious grave robbing. Virgil rode shotgun.

They climbed into the limo and headed for Newark via the Lincoln Tunnel. Suit-and-tie lemmings in the opposite lane were wasting a morning trying to reach offices iced, flooded and blacked out by a nocturnal chill factor of minus fifteen. Virgil and Larry were on their way to the Dog Gone Pet Cemetery which, according to the obituary column of *Dog Breeders' World*, was the last resting place of King Xosia Moncrief, AKA Cruton.

Larry's quest for the St Sophia's jewel had become an obsession. Virgil doubted the diamond's existence, but went along for the ride in order to keep Larry out of trouble.

Larry estimated the best time to dig up the Afghan was between six and eight in the morning. The industrial district which was home to the cemetery was patrolled by a private security firm until six, and the first pet interments started at eight.

They arrived at the cemetery at seven and got to work fast as they knew that within the hour the first cortège of golf carts would be setting out from the viewing rooms across the frozen memorial lawn to an open graveside. It was a large graveyard and it took them precious minutes to find the right headstone because all they knew was that Cruton was buried near the long, thin graves of the boa and miscellaneous snakes' section.

It was a fresh grave, but the earth was frozen and needed

breaking up with a pick. Virgil was too tired to give a fuck about a mythical diamond, but it was obvious Larry was too frail for heavy work. Virgil levered up clods of soil with the pick and Larry threw them from the grave with his hands.

At twenty to eight Virgil hit something solid. With Larry's help he pulled the object from the hole. It was a casket. Inside they saw a plaid dog blanket and, with the blanket pulled aside, a dead Afghan. The dog had rigor mortis and it was difficult to manoeuvre into the polythene sheet.

'Damn, that stinks,' said Larry. The dog smelt bad in its frozen state and he wondered what it would smell like when it thawed. They dumped the dog in the trunk of the limo and scattered pine air-freshener sticks over the corpse.

'What if cops pull us over because of the smell?' asked Virgil.

'Say we hit a skunk,' said Larry and they burned rubber just as a hearse laden with turtle-shaped wreaths pulled in the cemetery forecourt.

A room in the cinema basement was ready for the dissection. Virgil didn't want to cut up the dog down there because the awful smell would contaminate his room and cling to his clothes. But there was nowhere else to do the job, so they set to work. There were polythene sheets on the floor and a set of sharpened kitchen knives ready for the purpose. Larry had prepared a couple of cyclists' anti-pollution filter masks by sprinkling the inside with cologne.

The original idea was to pull out the dog's guts in manageable sections and fine chop them on a bread board, but Larry realized he could save time by using the RoboChef liquidizer he'd got for making milkshakes in the summer. He brought it down from the projection box and plugged it in. All they would have to do is drop a bit of Cruton's guts in the liquidizer bowl, start the blades, and pour the liquefied mess through a sieve. They would find the stone in no time.

In fact they found the stone on the third bowlful. As stomach tissue was turned to a frothing, pink milkshake by the whirling rotor a tick-tick-ticking sound became audible. It was the stone hitting the sides of the plastic bowl. Larry rinsed it under the tap and held it to the ceiling bulb. It was, as Benny had said, a diamond. A big one. Pink. Its perfect facets refracted beams of light around the room like a glitter ball.

'I am seriously rich,' whispered Larry. 'A pink diamond. Fifty times the normal carat price. Look at it. Flawless. No inclusions. An old stone, so it won't be on the gem appraiser database. We can sell it anywhere, and no alarm bells.'

Larry punched the air, but Virgil was more circumspect.

'Celebrations later. I've got a score to settle.'

The Kasbah department store was uptown on Fifth. The windows were already decorated with festive tableaux. Fairy lights winked in sequence around Sega consoles and power tools. A doorman doffed his top hat as Virgil and Marcy pushed through the revolving doors. There was a soft-focus picture of Mary Gollecky on the wall, which identified her as the current duty manager. She had a blonde bob and a high-collar power-dress. She looked like Hillary Clinton.

Virgil and Marcy walked the aisles looking for her. She wasn't in the toys section, she wasn't in the perfume shop, she wasn't at customer services. They found her at the jewellery counter, supervising a major refund.

'Hang back,' said Virgil. 'And look after my coat.'

Virgil slipped off his raincoat to reveal overalls stencilled NY Exterminators Inc. He chose a door marked Staff Only and pushed his way through.

Marcy watched her old enemy deal with the customer and remembered the night Gollecky ignored her pleas for help as she was stripped and fucked on the bed. Then, and every day since, Marcy felt her physical inferiority to men; the weakness that made her and every girl she knew regard subways, bars and offices each as a threatening male domain. She earned her pay serving the needs of men, needs she saw on every billboard and movie screen, and it made her feel like she was walking in a foreign land. She used to fantasize about lifting weights and turning herself into the personification of vengeance, like De Niro in Cape Fear. She resented relying on Virgil's help and contacts to see justice done.

Tony Bennett tunes stopped and the voices began. A woman's voice. Low and seductive.

'Hi. What's your name?'

'Ron Gollecky. Can I get you a drink?'

The tape was a montage built up from the recordings of several assignations between Mary Gollecky's husband and Johnny's hired girl. Snippets of dialogue intercut with the sound of vigorous fucking and the phrase 'Ron Gollecky. Can I get you a drink?' to give it a beat.

At the first mention of her husband's name Mary Gollecky looked up from the refund form she was filling in and glanced around for some explanation of what she was hearing. The tape continued and she heard her husband say:

'My wife's a frigid bitch. She won't do what I want.'

'Come on. Suck me.'

'Ride it, baby. Yeah.'

And gasps and moans and 'Ron Gollecky. Can I get you a drink?'

Mary's face blanched white and her eyes lost focus. She stood behind the counter with her pen in her hand. Mothers in the toy section covered their children's ears against the sound of animal fucking.

The recording cut out after a minute and the sudden silence jerked Mary Gollecky out of her trance. She ran to the bathroom and passed Virgil, who was emerging from the 'Staff Only' door.

'How did she take it?' he asked.

'Deep shock.'

'Is it enough for losing your life? Does it put it all right?'

'Oh yeah. I don't want to kill her. Just give her a taste of what it was like. This is the moment she will remember. The moment when it all fell down. And I was there to see it.'

'Worth a thousand?'

'Yeah. So what now?' she asked.

'Tapes get sent to local Republican Party officials and the newspapers. Tapes get sent to Mary's colleagues. Ron Gollecky loses his job and Mary either quits and starves, or swallows the humiliation of working amongst people who know her husband likes a thumb up his ass at the crucial moment.'

'Good enough.'

'And now Haas. We got to work out a way to hit a big-ass corporate lawyer. Not easy.'

'I got some ideas about that.'

That night Virgil visited Larry and invited him to Fontanes restaurant by way of celebrating his big score.

'Come on, Larry. Get cleaned up. Get a shave. I'm taking you to dinner.'

They met Johnny outside Fontanes. Virgil was dressed to kill in a Ralph Lauren suit from Bloomingdales. Credit card chic. Larry was dressed in the moth-eaten suit he kept for funerals and court appearances, but it got him through the door. He was high and his leg jittered throughout the meal.

The restaurant had muted piano music and gold leaf everywhere, like a Greek orthodox church. Virgil felt out of place and knocked back a couple of glasses of wine to relax. He ordered wild mushroom ravioli with spinach and deep fried sage and found it a delirious pleasure. He became so preoccupied with food he didn't make conversation until coffee and the bill.

'What have you been up to, Johnny?' he asked.

'Been doing a couple of hotels near the Park. Mini-bars. People do all sorts of weird shit to get free drinks from mini-bars. They drill through the base of soda cans and siphon the contents, and they do it in a five-hundred-dollar-a-night suite. Think about that. Some bigshot going from hotel to hotel with a little drill in his suitcase. "Don't forget to pack my gold cufflinks, honey. Oh, and don't forget my drill." Idiotic. Why don't they just pay for the soda? Miniature gin bottles re-filled with water. Whisky bottles tainted with gravy browning. Beer bottles filled with piss. You wouldn't believe the shit people pull. They caught one guy mixing a shampoo cocktail to get the right shade of green to fake crème de menthe.'

'So what do you do?'

'Install fibre-optic sensors in the refrigerators so if a drink gets lifted from the rack it gets added to the bill automatically. I don't put the cable in myself, of course. I'm an agent for the company that does. Nice commission.'

'Nice commission? How about fucking millions?' Larry was drunk.

'Millions?' queried Johnny.

'We dug up a dog and did an autopsy,' explained Virgil. 'Remember that dog we were looking for at the dump? Larry found a diamond inside. Sort of like a Christmas cracker.'

'You guys have way too much free time on your hands. Did you see this diamond?'

'I saw a stone. But I wouldn't know a diamond from a piece of glass.'

'I could sell it for you.'

'Larry has a buyer lined up.'

Larry laid his head on the table and started to snore. Other diners frowned their disapproval but Virgil savoured a Cognac and was too high to care.

'This is it, Johnny,' he said, sitting back and patting his full stomach. 'This is my dream. I've worried about money all my life. And here I am in this razor-fucking-sharp-suit with champagne in my glass and a new job tomorrow.'

'Job?'

'I got a bunch of pictures in the *New York Graphic*. A robbery at a church. They offered me a job. Staff photographer. I start tomorrow.'

'Fuckin' A. Two weeks shy of your thirtieth as well. Made it just in time.'

'A toast. Success.'

They touched glasses.

'Success.'

* Sonny Delgado was killed when he fell face-first through the glass ceiling of a bicycle shop he was attempting to burglarize. When he hit the floor the pen torch he placed in his mouth punched back into his brain.

– Dade County.

Chapter Thirteen

Virgil's first night on the job. He clocked on at seven-thirty
in the evening. His laminated pass got him past the receptionist and into the offices of the *New York Graphic*. Virgil liked
having an official-looking pass and wore it on his lapel like a
sheriff's badge. No longer an outsider, he had a role, a purpose.

The night-shift photographers were tooling up in the muster
room. Fresh film, fresh batteries, strong coffee. Virgil put spares
for his camera in a metal locker. In the periphery of his vision
he could see the old-timers checking him out. First-day-at-
school-nerves.

'Hi, I'm Ferris,' said a fat man in a raincoat. 'We use a buddy
system here when a guy starts the job. I'll be showing you the
ropes for a few days.'

'All right.'

A pool of black Lexus sedans in the underground car park.
Ferris threw film in the trunk.

'I got my shit all laid out here,' he said, gesturing to the
cardboard boxes jostling for room with the fifth wheel. 'Spare
camera parts, flashbulbs, typewriter, fireman's boots, sand-
wiches, coffee, change of underwear, change of shoes and socks.
It's the emergency kit, kid. They'll give you a car, and if you
don't carry this shit you'll regret it. We are tuned to the police
frequency at all times, but I heard you're used to that shit
already.'

'Yeah.'

Up the ramp and into the street.

'First stop, Mr Devlin. You know who he is?'

'The editor.'

'That's right. The Big Enchilada. He has an office in Metro Plaza, but he's never in it. Weird place. Pictures of Napoleon all over the wall. He likes to think he and the spirit of Napoleon have a sort of psychic bond on an astral plane somewhere. He holds court at the Tsukiji, listening for celebrity gossip. He likes to give new guys a little pep talk. Enjoy it. It's the only time you'll ever meet him.'

Tsukiji Shushi-Ya had a doric façade and big windows so that street walkers could see chic diners, crisp linen, candle light enflame crystal and silver. It was a direct challenge. Are you rich enough to dine here? Are you good enough to get in? Virgil climbed the steps, rain dripping from the brim of his hat, and felt like lowlife scum.

The dining room was three quarters empty. Lepke Devlin squatted on a chair in the corner like a malevolent toad. Fifties, quite bald. A wide gash of a mouth that seemed it might hide a whip-lash tongue to snare flies. Six settings at the table, five of them empty. Karosomen and sake in front of Devlin. A chef slicing cuttlefish beyond the glass kitchen doors.

Virgil and Ferris sat down.

'This is Virgil Strauss, Mr Devlin.'

Devlin looked Virgil up and down.

'You Jewish?'

'No. It's just my name.'

'You take pictures.'

'Sure.'

'Art school?'

'No. I do weird shit. Street life.'

Virgil kept good eye contact. He wasn't going to let the big guy intimidate him. He wouldn't let the gilt opulence make him cringe.

'The street. Good. The street is the best school. I got to have men on my payroll, understand? Not boys. Not students. Men. Men who can bag the picture. Is that you?'

'Absolutely, sir. I won't let you down.'

'You're paid on commission. Fuck up and you let yourself down.'

'Understood.'

'Get a grip on what the *New York Graphic* is about. The *Graphic* is Manhattan's oldest and most successful tabloid. Tabloids are a visual-entertainment medium and that's what we give people: visual entertainment. Because I don't care how rich and cultured a guy is, he is still governed by his balls, by daydreams, by envy. That's the holy trinity as far as we are concerned. Power. Ass. Money. In close-up, as-it-happens colour. I'm not interested in objectivity. It don't sell. You see people used to be real passive. If there was nothing in their daily paper they would say, "Gee, nothing much happened in the world today." These days if their paper doesn't have tits, death, cheap sentiment, a moral crusade, then they buy a different paper. We turn trials into soap operas with stars, plot twists and daily cliffhangers. We put the lurid and appalling on Joe Public's breakfast table. It's more than a freak show. It's a complete fucking cosmology. It's Valhalla where the rich and famous live out their epic passions and tragedies. We give little people a glimpse into a world of ready sex and fine living. Consolation fantasies for losers. Because we, papers, TV, magazines, are the central nervous system of the entire fucking world. The trivia, the noble dreams, the dirty little thoughts; we aren't some college élite grading news, creating a hierarchy of facts. We are the id, the whole fucking chaos, uncensored. And we never sleep, understand? The phrase "slow news day" became extinct in 1980. No bank robbery to photograph? Fuck you. Rob a bank yourself and take pictures doing it. No news? Make news. Deliver. No excuses. Remember the mantra of every guy working on the *Graphic*. "Money. Power. Sex. Decay." Bring it home. And pictures, kid, pictures.'

Devlin turned away. Virgil watched in revulsion as the fat fucker shovelled noodles into his mouth. A nudge from Ferris told Virgil he was dismissed.

Virgil and Ferris cruised the city listening to the police band. Street lights streaming over polished bodywork, neon cascading over hood and fender. Empty avenues viewed through a blurred windscreen. The soothing, metronomic squeak of wipers. Fat, spattering rain drops refracted brake lights; Walk/Don't Walk becoming iridescent rubies and emeralds.

Virgil leant back on the headrest and let his eyes half close. Ferris gave him the guided tour.

'Up till midnight it's misdemeanour shit. Female impersonators, bar brawls, shit like that. You have to have an instinct for those kind of calls, tell which will be a picture, because you could chase around town all night and see nothing but cop tail lights. Midnight till two is stick-up time at late-night grocers and liquor stores. Bullet wounds a go-go. A headshot for a Magnum and the picture ed will be kissing your ass for days. Two till four is kicking-out time at the bars, so you've got auto wrecks and bad domestics. Prime-time stuff; it's where the money is. Some lost soul always takes a dive from a window around five, and we are always there.'

They drove past a burnt-out tenement near Harlem.

'I was there when it went up,' said Ferris. 'Place stank of ammonia. Sure sign of arson. Some amateur trying to mask the smell of gasoline. I was pulling bodies out of the rubble and taking pictures all the while.

'Say you got an arm sticking out from under a pile of bricks. It looks okay but you don't know if the sap is breathing or died of smoke in the fire. What's the quickest way to tell if the guy's alive?'

'Burn marks?'

'The skin is clean.'

'Cold?'

'Cold doesn't mean dead.'

'Pulse?'

'Too slow. Too easy to fuck up. You got to be quick. There's other injured people crying for your help.'

'What then?'

Virgil didn't like playing the novice. He'd seen more sick shit in his life than Ferris ever would, but he kept quiet and let the guy make like an old pro.

'Rub the skin. A body that's been near a major fire sheds its outer dermis like a lizard. If the skin comes away in your hand you know it's a roast and move on.'

The first call of the evening: the Two Mules nightclub in the Village.

The story went like this:

A burglar climbed inside a wooden box and mailed himself to the Two Mules in the hope of cracking the safe when they closed for the night. But the club had been prosecuted for health violations, and when it closed that night it closed for good. When the burglar crept from his box he found himself locked inside a deserted building. The forensic guys said that must have been about two weeks ago judging from the bloated and rat-nibbled corpse. Some brewery people doing late calls arrived at nine to collect unsold beer stock and found the burglar dead from what appeared to be a combination of starvation and alcohol poisoning.

The cops were helpful. A purple, balloon body amongst a litter of beer bottles. Ferris got good pictures.

An A train at Delancey station.

A fifteen-year-old kid had been holding up liquor stores using grenades his Viet-vet father picked up in Da Nang. The kid would walk into a store wearing a raincoat and rubber Frankenstein mask, open his coat and reveal the bombs. He would threaten to blow himself up if he didn't get the contents of the register. The money went on records and computer games. He was featured on America's Most Wanted. A star. The cops wanted him bad.

The kid was on the way to his next raid, riding in a subway carriage on his own, when a grenade pin became dislodged. Blown-out windows, a big, sooty blast mark against the wall of the carriage, and beneath it a pair of jeaned legs still casually crossed.

'She's all yours,' said Ferris. Virgil shot a roll in sixty seconds and knew each frame was pure gold. He hated to think the pictures would appear with captions. The image should stay abstract. It didn't need a time and place.

Next stop, a dead hooker on waste ground. Black. Dismembered. Bisected. Beheaded. Cops kicking away rats driven delirious by the coppery tang of blood. Virgil recognized one of the ambulance guys.

143

'Any idea who she was?' he asked. The woman's jaw had been smashed with a hammer and her fingertips burnt. Someone didn't want her identity to be known.

'No clothes or ID but one of those cops there knows her from Port Authority. Part of her left ear-lobe is missing, you see? She was a hooker. Chickenshit porn actress. Name's Lette Lipton.'

'I think I heard that name.'

'Then you been keeping bad company.'

'Recognize the MO?'

'Sexual molestation. Major tissue loss at thighs and upper arms. Possible cannibalism. Fifth in three months.'

'You got yourselves a series.'

'Yeah, but different semen types each time. And two of the previous corpses carried bite impressions. Different teeth. Different people. This is a bunch of psychos acting in concert. Efficient. Methodical. Getting good at what they do.'

Flash painted body-fat white and muscle deep red like refrigerated carcasses in a 34th Street meat packer's. Virgil got close-ups.

Virgil clocked off at two and hit the streets on his own. He could see the lack of autonomy in this job could feel like a strait-jacket if he let it get to him.

He saw Robert De Niro step out of his Nobu restaurant in TriBeCa. De Niro was Virgil's favourite actor but he was too cool to ask for an autograph and shadowed the actor from the other side of the street.

De Niro walked around the block. He didn't seem to have a destination in mind. Maybe he was just catching some air at the only time he could walk the streets without being bothered. As he turned to re-enter the restaurant Virgil raised his camera to his face and framed a shot. At that moment De Niro turned to look at him and their eyes met through the viewfinder. Virgil lowered the camera, the picture untaken, and saluted the actor. De Niro nodded in acknowledgement and vanished inside. Virgil was elated to have had some contact with his hero.

He decided not to take the picture out of respect. He had watched Taxi Driver till the tape broke, but that wasn't the whole story. Virgil knew the futility of trying to take a marketable celebrity picture. He knew the pressure paparazzi lived under. Press-pass photographers got in to events with no trouble. They were like wedding photographers. They dressed in a tux, sipped champagne, waited for the stars to pose. Freelancers and tabloid crews were outside in the snow, chugging coffee and bullshitting with the doorman. Those few feet between the door and the limousine, those few seconds, were all they had to beat fans and bodyguards and professional autograph collectors to get the shot. He once saw a freelance paparazzo drop dead as he chased Sean Connery's car down the street. His job at the *Graphic* might drive him to the same frenzy trying to deliver, but he could take the pressure.

The *Graphic* was interested in two types of star pictures. Firstly, candid shots: an actress with her tits popping out of a ball gown, or a rock star groping someone else's wife. Secondly, generic shots: a picture which personified an actor's image and could be plucked out of a picture agency archives when a magazine wanted to run a profile. Both types of picture were almost impossible to capture. Better off snapping dead people. They kept still and didn't have bodyguards.

Virgil was walking home, feeling good about his job and a regular income, when Vishnu Jones fulfilled his threat to bring carnage to the streets of Manhattan.

Dawn was coming up and Virgil was longing to sink into his bed when he spotted the Dalmatian lady. She was at the end of the road standing in a cone of street light. He recognized her silhouette and her dog.

The dead bodies Virgil heard about on the news were almost always discovered by a person walking a dog, but it was only since he began to visit crime scenes in person that he realized it was the same person and the same dog. The Dalmatian lady. He didn't know who she was but she had an infallible nose for catastrophe.

He ran down the road after her, but she was gone. Virgil looked around and glimpsed her turning a corner down a side street and so resumed his pursuit.

No matter how fast he sprinted the Dalmatian lady always eluded him and was never closer than the far distance. It was like chasing a rainbow. She led him through a twisting route of back lots and alleys, and when Virgil eventually quit the game he was at the heart of the rag trade on 38th and 8th. Bleak warehouses.

A bum with an icicle embedded in his face staggered out of the shadows. He scared the shit out of Virgil. Either somebody had stabbed the vagrant with an icicle, or it fell off a roof and speared him as he was lying asleep. The guy tried to speak but the blood in his mouth turned his words to spray and bubbles. Virgil lined up the shot. He depressed the shutter and the premises of Lyle Fashion Inc, clearly visible in the left of the frame, were vaporized in a fireball that lit the street like daylight. Virgil worked his finger like he was pumping a trigger and made frozen moments of the approaching shockwave, cars flipping over and a juggernaut of debris roaring towards him like an express train. When the cyclone struck, Virgil hit the sidewalk and the vagrant flew like a bird.

The blast brought down a couple of empty warehouses. Deaf, mute, Mexican textile workers had been chained to their sewing benches and working round the clock. Their body parts were jumbled amongst the bricks. Some Jews working late in an adjoining building were also amongst the dead. Police, fire trucks and ambulance crews reached the scene, and behind them were a bunch of volunteers wearing yarmulkes, who picked up pieces of the dead. Under normal circumstances the emergency services flushed remains smaller than a golf ball down the drains, but a Jew must be buried as near intact as possible. Israeli émigrés used to the carnage of Tel Aviv bus bombs scraped flesh off the asphalt and sopped blood in wads of cotton wool. They went about their sacred duty with exquisite tenderness, and Virgil got it all on film. His hands were shaking. He was euphoric to find himself alive.

Air support arrived turning the site into a little Vietnam. A searchlight burned Virgil's hands as he lifted his Leica to shoot. The PA commanded bystanders to clear the area. Virgil pulled down his hat to mask himself from the 32× lens and thermal-imaging gear swivelling in a gyro-stabilized camera pod under the chopper's thorax. The cop camera was so powerful it could inspect the pores of his skin.

There was a girl amongst the debris. Her body was charred to the bone, little more than a skeleton in rags, but a pane of glass had melted over her head, preserving her face like she was sleeping.

The Dalmatian lady watched Virgil from the other side of the crater. They were separated by smoke and flames and wreckage. The girl's eyeballs were sunk and quite black, haemorrhaging associated with severe cerebral haematoma, a symptom exhibited by the extremely dead. The lady turned away and the dog followed with a charred foot in its mouth.

The first of the fire marshals showed up and began securing the crime scene. Cadavers shipped to Quantico for FBI/FAA X-ray checks for volatile solvents and fragments of the detonating mechanism.

Half an hour after the blast the police had the area locked down and excluded press, but Virgil was already heading uptown to his Majestic darkroom. The *Graphic* could have pictures of the blast. The cadavers would be his own to sell.

'Why so early?' asked Willie Turkel.

Virgil was peering into the gloom of Turkel's apartment. Somewhere beyond the pool of light thrown by a table lamp the man himself sat smoking a cigarette.

'I got some hot shit for you.'

Virgil held out a sheaf of photographs. Turkel's hand, with the signature black nail varnish, emerged from the shadows to take them.

'These are body parts in the rubble of the Vishnu Jones bomb site. The pictures were taken a couple of hours ago. The *Graphic* will run them but I'm thinking maybe you pay more. You mentioned you might act as an agent if I ever had anything good. What do you think?'

'Marcy told me you have a lot more material like this. She mentioned a decapitated priest.'

'I got boxes of good pictures I can't sell.'

'According to Marcy you described yourself as a connoisseur of weird shit. Well, I know some people with the same appetite. Rich people, seekers of the bizarre. I could arrange private sales of your art. Make you a lot of money.' Turkel produced a wad of hundreds from a breast pocket. 'This for the Vishnu Jones pictures. A lot more for the rest.'

'What's the deal?'

'I become your sole agent. You sell no pictures except through me. When you sell a picture you sell the full rights. You don't meet the buyer. You just hand me the negatives and I own everything you do.'

'That's hard.'

'No fucking around. Yes or no before you leave the room.'

Virgil hesitated.

Fuck it.

'All right.'

'Excellent. Shall we drink on it?'

'I got to get some sleep.'

'Bring me all your pictures, decapitated priest included, and I'll make you a wealthy young man.'

Seven in the morning. Virgil went back to the Majestic to share his news with Larry and found the old man awake at the bathroom sink bandaging a bullet graze on his left shoulder.

'Shit,' said Virgil. 'What happened?'

Larry's face had the blank, wide-eyed expression of absolute despair. It worried Virgil. Maybe a doctor told Larry he had terminal cancer, or something.

'I was taking the diamond and silver stuff to the Village. I was going to meet my connection. I got mugged on the subway.'

'What happened to the diamond?'

Larry turned away without speaking. He leant on the sink for support and his tears mingled with the bloody water spiralling down the drain.

BIRTHDAY BOY DIES JUMPING FOR JOY

Jim Brewer, 9, died in a Newark hospital yesterday evening about the time he should have been enjoying a birthday party with his friends.

Mary Brewer, his mother, woke him at seven in the morning and sang 'Happy Birthday'. She fetched Jim's gifts from the stair cupboard and while she was out of the bedroom Jim, in his excitement, jumped up and down on the bed using it as a trampoline. He fell off the bed and broke his neck.

Chapter Fourteen

Virgil awoke to music from his clock radio, and for no reason remembered a sunny day at the funfair, an incident he had not recalled for twenty-four years. He was six years old and wandering alone between the big wheel and the ghost train. He came upon a booth where you could pick an envelope and maybe win a teddy bear. Virgil was lonely and the bear had a friendly smile, so he spent his last pennies on an envelope. The card inside said 'Sorry, better luck next time'. So he had to leave the bear behind and find his way home with empty pockets. Virgil felt heartbreaking pity for his younger self and wanted to protect him from all the harm that would come his way.

He got up, drew the blinds and let the sun lift the heavy cargo of sad memories he carried through each day.

Virgil had a new place to live. He had got an advance on his wages and rented a suite at the Mayflower Hotel. All his worldly possessions fitted in the trunk of a taxi.

The Mayflower used to be high class when he worked there years ago but had now fallen on hard times. It gave discount rates for long-term residents. Virgil's room was painted red, but a Japanese lampshade created a blue, subaqueous murk. The plumbing rattled. Decades of re-decoration had gummed stopcocks tight with a sclerotic accretion of paint. The wall-paper was blistering and leprous. Tangles of lead wiring hung from wall sockets in arachnid knots. But Virgil liked his new home. It had separate rooms: kitchen, living room, bathroom, bedroom. A place he could decorate and keep clean. Live like a normal person.

Virgil's first big purchase was a widescreen TV. It was positioned in the corner of the living room, surrounded by drifts of bubblewrap and styrofoam beads. He sat in an armchair and checked out his reflection in the black glass. Marcy came in from the kitchen with coffee. She had stayed the night.

'Remind me to buy Apocalypse Now on laserdisc,' said Virgil.

He switched on the TV. All newscasts were about the bomb. A thousand-pound nitrate fertilizer charge surrounded by propane cylinders for accelerated combustion and shrapnel. The bomb was so big Vishnu Jones must have been assembling the device in the warehouse basement for weeks: a busy self-storage place, guys loading palletes with fork-lifts, but none of the workers could remember what Vishnu Jones looked like. They had seen him clearly, but his face was so average they could recall nothing about him.

Virgil's pictures had been syndicated and were shown on the news. He thrilled to see his work next to the CBS logo. TV: the big time.

Virgil punched the remote to see if his pictures were shown on any other stations. He got cable reception but the other channels were down.

'This thing isn't tuned in,' he said.

'Those lunatics blew up a bunch of TV masts this morning,' explained Marcy. 'Those info terrorists. Los Banditos. The Everything is Fiction guys that did the *Graphic* and the cable junctions.'

'More bombs. Just what we need. Why can't these people get jobs?'

Marcy shrugged and checked out the decor in daylight.

'Nice old rooms,' she observed. 'Kind of retro-furnished. Life-as-a-movie kind of place.'

'That's right. "Reality is something to be risen above."'

'Nietzsche?'

'Liza Minnelli.'

'I wouldn't mind a place like this.'

'Why not move in with me?'

'Here?'

'Yeah.'

'With you?'

'Yeah.'

'Don't get hung up on me, Virgil. I won't be around long.'

Virgil sighed. He had a mental picture of him and Marcy living like normal people. The pedestrian but wonderful routine of cooking, ironing and evenings in front of the TV. He didn't want to be alone all his life.

'Why can't we talk about this? I like having you around. Think about it. I can make a difference to the time you got.'

Marcy looked out the window and down five storeys at the quadrangle below. The little square of etiolated grass, surrounded on all sides by high walls, was sick yellow. It got one hour of direct sunlight a day, a few feeble rays when the sun was at its zenith. At night TV gunshots and sirens merged with domestic arguments and echoed around the walls, bizarre acoustics melting individual words to a constant, hellish cacophony. But Marcy was used to screening out noise. Virgil gave her a warm double bed, food, attention. For all his talk of the solitude of heroes he wanted to set up a domestic scene and play happy families. It was better than facing death alone, but it might get suffocating.

'I'm in the mood for a walk,' she said.

End of the working week and Virgil was determined to take it easy. He and Marcy strolled to the waterfront. They held hands.

Workmen were demolishing the front of a house, chipping at bricks, trying not to bring the whole thing down. Virgil sometimes walked this way on Sundays and wondered who lived in the old brownstone. It stood alone on a patch of waste ground, the last intact structure amongst the debris of levelled housing projects; a here-be-monsters blank on his street map. The house reminded him of newsreel footage of post-war Berlin. A freakish survivor in a city smashed to rubble by artillery barrage and aerial bombardment. The side of the house showed phantom traces of the building that used to adjoin it: floors, chimney, staircase. A fireplace-turned-bird's nest fifty feet up; chintz wallpaper defaced with graffiti tags. The curtains of the house were always drawn, and Virgil sometimes saw boxes of groceries delivered to the door.

'They're finally moving the fat man,' said a neighbour, as he stood with Virgil and Marcy and watched the action. Something pink and whale-like was being lifted into the sunlight by a crane. 'Seventy-five stone he weighs. Wonder he lived so long.'

The guy was bloated beyond belief, a cartoon character inflated to bursting. Just a pink blob with dainty hands and feet protruding like flippers, and a helpless, bearded face. His penis was lost beneath rolls of fat. A seagull flew in from the river and perched on the guy's head.

Virgil wondered what it was like to be that man. He tried to imagine the days, the years sealed in that bedroom. Nothing to do but listen to traffic and watch shadows move up the wall. How much would you have to eat to sustain seventy-five stone? A week's groceries in a day. Constant munching, barely pausing for breath. How did he shit? Who cut and washed his hair? How did he reach for food? What horror to be locked behind those eyes. A living hell. Better off dead.

Virgil didn't take pictures. His camera was ready at his apartment and loaded with film, yet he contained himself. He could have fetched it in a couple of minutes but decided to resist the urge to possess this atrocity.

Lunchtime.

'Where to now?' asked Marcy.

'The Majestic. I'm worried about Larry. He hasn't been right since that diamond got stolen last week. I hope he's OK.'

They walked through the auditorium to the projection box. There was paper all over the floor. Drawings of faces. Larry sat in his chair rounding off a chin with a flourish of his pencil.

'What the fuck are you doing?' asked Virgil.

'Making a wanted poster. I'm going to take it down the city shelters and see if anyone recognizes the guy who mugged me, the guy who stole my diamond.'

Virgil leafed through the drawings on the floor. Composites, like an FBI forensic artist would create, but these pictures could have been anybody. Some faces looked young, some looked old. Some looked oriental, some looked caucasian. Every possible feature and shape.

'Think people will recognize this guy?' asked Virgil.

'Sure. Once I get the resemblance right.'

'Johnny said something about work he might have for you.'

'He wants me to give him a few forgery lessons. Get the benefit of my experience.'

'Forge what?'

'Money. Today I'm going to show him how you treat cotton paper with sun block to make it pass an ultraviolet test.'

'Why?' asked Marcy.

'I don't ask and he don't tell me. But you know he's mixed up with those Los Bandito types. What could be a better way of fucking with reality? Subvert the money supply. Remind people they got nothing in their pocket but paper and metal. Anyway, I got to finish these pictures before I get into any of that.'

'Big waste of time.'

Larry made coffee and Virgil scanned the spines of his current reading. The life of Cecil Rhodes, the history of De Beers and the CSO, geology books for kids, diamond leaflets from jewellers. Larry's wanted posters pinned all over the walls.

'This is getting fucking obsessional, Larry. You lost the stone. It wasn't your big score. Learn and move on.'

'It's my rock. The Onions' diamond. I'll find that fucker who robbed me. I'll go to every needle bank. Every methadone shop. Every soup kitchen. I'll find him.'

'What's the attachment? You were going to sell it the moment you got your hands on it, anyway. Wasn't as if you would keep it.'

'I have never done anything right my whole life. Sometimes a guy has to draw a line. The plan was that I would get the rock. Sell it, get the beach house, cocktails at sunset, happy ever after. That's it. That's all. The plan hasn't changed.'

'Has anyone seen your drawings?'

'Yeah. Showed one to a couple of beggars on Third. They said they knew the face.'

'They'll say anything for a dollar,' said Marcy.

'It's a lead. I'm going to find the guy. I'm going to go around every Salvation Army place, every rehab centre.'

'Waste of time.'

'It's a learning experience. I've found out a lot. You know diamonds aren't worth much? The price is kept artificially high by stock-piling the surplus. And the idea that you get a diamond wedding ring is new. All down to De Beers advertising. People think diamonds are the best collateral there is, but it's all a big lie. A rogue mine dumps its share on the market and it all falls down.'

'Paint a landscape. You were good at those.'

'I'll find that stone. You see if I don't.'

A burrito lunch then a taxi ride. Virgil told the driver to stop outside the hospital.

'Why are we here?' asked Marcy.

'To meet my mother.'

'Is she a nurse?'

'You'll see.'

Another part of Virgil's scheme to keep Marcy. Show her as much of himself as possible. Involve her in his life.

They walked through the reception area to the elevators. There was a flower shop inside and Virgil bought a bunch of plastic daffodils. The receptionist knew him by name, as did the owner of the flower shop. Virgil and Marcy took an elevator to the top of the building and he led her to a private room overlooking the street at the back.

The room was white and bare and contained nothing but a grey-haired woman lying in a bed. She was being fed through a tube in her nose. The sedentary bleeps of an ECG conveyed the tempo of her pulse. On closer inspection Marcy saw the woman's eyes were open but unfocused. There was little that could be said about the face. It was slack and didn't convey any qualities like happy or sad, pretty or plain. Although the woman appeared to be in her sixties there were no crow's feet at the corner of her eyes. Laughter and tears had not made a mark. Instead there was just a single crease where the eyelids opened in the morning and shut again at night. Marcy lifted the woman's wrist and read the tag.

Jane Doe.

'So what's this all about?'

She and Virgil sat on the edge of the bed and he stroked his mother's hair.

'This is my mother. She is like this all the time. The nurses turn her over, wash her, exercise her muscles, change the bed-clothes. That's it.'

'How did she get like this? Is it senile dementia?'

'Nope. Act of God. In nineteen sixty-nine she stepped in front of a bus outside Lincoln Centre and got knocked down. She didn't die but she got a bump on the head and has been here ever since.'

'Who was she? I mean who is she?'

'No idea. No identification in her wallet. No missing person reported. Chain-store clothes. No dental record. All she had on her was a lottery ticket bought the previous week in Dallas. I hope she wasn't trying to kill herself over money, because when the cops tried to find out where she bought the ticket they discovered she had won a half-million share of the jackpot.'

'Damn.'

'That's what pays for all this. The money is held in trust. She can breathe on her own, so there's no question of turning off a machine. She will just stay like this until she dies or the money runs out.'

'What happens when there's no money?'

'They'll probably want to stop feeding her. I think they can do that if I give my permission.'

'Will you?'

'I don't know. Though I suppose I should think about it. There isn't much money left. A couple more years at most.'

'How do you fit into all this?'

'They had her in a New Jersey shit-heap hospital for a while. Some place near Atlantic City. One of the orderlies fucked her and she got pregnant. They didn't have DNA tests or any shit like that in those days, so they never found out who the father was. It was a Catholic place and they didn't want to terminate. She carried the baby to term and here I am.'

'How come you have an English accent?'

'I had a bunch of different foster parents. One couple were English and I picked up their way of speaking. When you've been just a number in an orphanage you exaggerate anything that makes you special. So I worked on the accent.'

'You never knew her? Never heard her voice? Never saw her smile? She doesn't even know you exist?'

'The nurses used to get me to read to her. They wondered if there was some sort of mystic bond between mother and son, that maybe if she heard my voice she would recognize it, sort of by instinct.'

'Nothing?'

'Didn't twitch a muscle.'

'Do you think it got through to her?'

'Beats me. The doctors say no, but they don't know shit. You should see them test her for conscious thought. They clap their hands in front of her face to make her blink, stick pins in her hands and feet. It's fucking medieval.'

Virgil stroked his mother's hair and thought how it would be if she simply opened her eyes and sat up. The rhythm of the ECG would quicken and her hand would grip his. It wasn't impossible. He often read about cops who got shot and woke up thinking Nixon was president. One cop took a shotgun blast in the chest and was clinically dead for five minutes. Damped his mind to the most basic brain activity. He was a vegetable for ten years then one day sat up and talked non-stop for twenty-four hours. Went home and had to deal with the future-shock of ATM machines and pierced nipples. The article mentioned the guy had been given a shot of antibiotics the day before he awoke. Virgil secretly gave his mother shots of tetracycline and streptomycin in the hope of replicating the miracle, but nothing happened.

There was a ten-year-old boy in Tulsa who suffered from Sturge-Weber syndrome, which meant he couldn't speak and kept throwing fits. The kids at school gave him a ton of shit, so eventually he shot himself in the head with his father's shotgun. Blew the entire left side of his head off; half his brain splattered up the wall. The ambulance attendants were loading him into a body bag when he opened his eyes and said, 'My head hurts.' He could speak fine after that, though he was none too bright. Not college material.

People pronounced brain dead sometimes sit up and ask for a glass of water. One guy was lying in bed after a car wreck. The doctors said there was no brain activity and were pushing the guy's wife to let them have his body for parts. This was all happening in the same room as this guy and he could hear every word. He couldn't see anything. Said it was like being suspended in whiteness. Kind of cosy, like snuggling up in bed. But he could hear every word. Luckily, he snapped out of it in time and started moving his hands. It made Virgil wonder if brain-dead donors are aware of being cut up and are trying to scream as the scalpel goes in.

Every form of scanning the hospital could provide was tried on his mother in the hope of finding brain activity. PET scans, CAT scans, magnetic-resonance imaging and sonography all drew a blank. They polluted her veins with radioactive tracer, N13 ammonia isotope, to observe the blood flow around her brain and body, but saw nothing except a tenacious heart that refused to stop beating.

Specialists explored a graphic of her mind. The rotating, polychromatic, wire-frame model of his mother's head should have been lit up with a firestorm of sparking synapses, like aerial footage of Dresden bombed at night, but the electrical discharge that was his mother, her thoughts and memories, was missing, and there was nothing but inert tissue.

'This must have made for a shitty childhood,' said Marcy. Virgil wondered if he could detect a softer tone to her voice.

'All childhoods are shitty. Fact of life. No use feeling sorry for yourself. But it is kind of difficult to have this half and half situation. I can see her and touch her but have no idea what TV she likes, her favourite food, if she's Republican or Democrat. Shit like that. It's a sort of parallax effect. She seems close but actually she's a billion miles away.'

'This is such bad shit.'

'I've done my crying.'

'Do you love her?'

'Don't ask me questions like that. So do you want to see a movie, or what?'

*　　*　　*

159

That night Virgil phoned Larry to make sure he hadn't taken an overdose. Larry said he was okay.

Virgil and Marcy sat in bed listening to the radio. He liked to feel Marcy's body next to him under the duvet. He liked making cocoa for her.

Virgil flipped through the papers. He cut out weird stories and pasted them in his scrap book. Marcy didn't understand his need to keep a random collage of weird stories and hot images. He tried to explain it to her.

'You can understand things better if you jumble them up. It makes you see things fresh. Let me show you.' He opened a section of the paper. 'All these lonely-hearts advertisements. If you want to know about the people sending in ads you can read each little message individually or you can randomize it and see what that tells you. Like if we just read the words in heavy type at the beginning of each ad. The first words say a lot because they tell you what was at the forefront of the person's mind when they wrote the message. Listen:

'"Affectionate, affectionate, Aries, autumnal, caring, caring, Christian, creative, help, lonely, lonely, lonely, middle-aged, plump, romantic, romance, Rubenesque, serious, shy, talkative, tall, Taurus, wanted, wanted, warm, warm-hearted, widow, yearning." See?'

'See what?'

'It tells you all about these people. Far more than a single advertisement. That's why I cut out stories and pictures. The news makes better sense if you scramble it up.'

'You're fucked.'

It was taking a lot of self-control for Virgil not to hit the streets in search of weird shit, but he resolved to stop photographing dead people for a while just to prove he could do it. Instead he unpacked his computer and sat in bed with the machine balanced on his lap. He got ready to send a new story across the airwaves to Mercury Press.

'Which towns do you know have a big Chinese community?' he asked.

'Here, of course. And LA.'

'Yeah. But apart from us and LA. The kind of place too remote to bother checking the story.'

'I don't know. Anywhere. Most places have Chinese people.'

'Wichita Falls?'

'Yeah, why not?'

Virgil began to type.

'Two men have been arrested in Wichita Falls following a spate of grave robberies at an exclusively Chinese graveyard in the north of the city. The men were arrested following a routine check by traffic police which revealed the corpse of a long-dead woman wrapped in a roll of carpet in the back of their vehicle. Over the past year the bodies of four women have been dug up and removed from the graveyard. The deceased were young, single women and it is thought they were exhumed in order to be married and reburied with dead, single men. One of the four was exhumed but dumped back in the grave later the same night. The deceased woman was born in 1966, the year of the fiery horse, a year of ill omen, and therefore possibly regarded as an unsuitable mate. The arrested men originate from the Shaanxi province of northern China, where it is regarded as shameful for a man to be buried without a wife. It is therefore the custom to provide a wife for a dead man in order that he should not remain a "bare stick". Relatives of the missing women said they hope police inquiries will reveal the location of their loved ones.'

'How's that?' asked Virgil. 'Weird enough?'

'Yeah. Creepy. Where did you pick up this stuff about Chinese customs?'

'*National Geographic.*'

Virgil signed the story Barrington Fingenbaum and committed it to the ether.

Marcy peeled off her night gown and said, 'Let's play. Get your camera.'

Virgil stood at the end of the bed and Marcy peeled back the duvet.

'Come on. Make me a star.' She switched to erotic mode and he found himself sharing the bedroom with a stranger.

She squeezed her breast, put a nipple to her mouth. She

spread her legs, spread and pushed fingers into a vagina wet with spit. Virgil took pictures. *Memento mori.*

Marcy toyed with herself and demanded Virgil pull her hair as she climaxed. Virgil turned up the music, lay on the bed and let Marcy suck him. The intercom next to the bed buzzed. He picked up the handset and Marcy continued to suck.

'Hello?'

His dick wilted.

'Who is it?' asked Marcy.

'The cops. They're here to take me down the precinct.'

MERMAID ARRESTED

Coastguards found a woman living as a mermaid three miles off the coast of Florida. When they fished her out of the water she said, 'You only caught me because I came up for air.' She said she was 'transitioning' and couldn't live on land any more. She wore slacks, a black T-shirt and tennis shoes, but said she had been eating lots of seaweed and expected to grow a tail soon.

Chapter Fifteen

S gt Anspach put Virgil in an interview room and forget about him for an hour. Virgil sat very still, breathed slowly, got his galloping heart under control. He wanted to be a machine.

It was a small room for sweating suspects down. Bars on the windows. Table and chairs. Ashtray. Cup of coffee. A succession of bored hoodlums had carved the table top with keys and pocket knives, turning it to a palimpsest of graffiti: tags, fuck-the-pigs bravado, sexual drawings as crude as Neanderthal cave pictures, stick people sucking dick.

Sgt Anspach was bald and black and had priestly detachment.

'This is about a theft that occurred a few weeks ago. Wondered if you might be able to help us in any way.'

'Sure.'

'Can we record this interview?'

'No.'

'The House of Usher van. Two guys held it up as it left the Metropolitan car park. Took an antique angel from the rear. Worth a few thousand dollars. You were the security guard that shift. Asked to work some extra hours that morning. Is that right?'

'Yeah. I can always use some overtime.'

'How long have you worked there?'

'Three years.'

'Like the job?'

'It's all right.'

'Pretty boring, huh?'

'Gives me space to think.'

'Shitty hours.'

'You get used to it.'

'Doesn't exactly pay much, does it?'

'Makes the rent.'

Anspach moved from behind the table to take a seat next to Virgil, thus establishing a mood of openness and trust. Virgil made good eye contact, kept his body language locked down.

'You remember the theft, don't you? It was on your shift at the mall.'

'I heard about it afterwards. I was inside the mall at the time.'

'You didn't know what was happening?'

'I heard cops called by for the security tape, but that was after I went home.'

'It was a pretty slick score.'

'Is that right?'

'Oh yeah. The guys knew which van to hit. They knew what was on board. The flex in every phone booth in a two-block radius of Metro Plaza was snipped with bolt cutters either before or right after the job. Police response time was tripled as a result.'

'Really?'

'What I'm trying to say is, those two guys seemed to know a hell of a lot about when, where and how the angel was leaving the building.'

'Good at their job, I guess.'

'Let's run some tape.'

Sgt Anspach led Virgil to an office equipped with a TV and a VCR. It was security tape of the car-park ramp. Nothing moving but the date/time read-out. Anspach pressed fast forward and the numbers blurred. 'Look at this,' he said. '06:57 and the camera is set to give us a grandstand view of the raid. That position hasn't shifted for five hours. Now look. 06:58.' The camera position shifted to a section of wall. When the House of Usher van drove out of the underground car park and stopped on the ramp all that was visible was the left rear tyre. The raid occurred out of sight. 'You moved the camera position, is that right?'

'I guess. I don't recall. You have to change the picture now and again to stop from falling asleep.'

'Just bad luck you changed the position ten minutes before a robbery.'

'Yeah. Damn bad luck.'

Anspach seemed to lose interest in his line of questioning.

'St Sophia's church,' he said.

'Yeah?'

'A big theft, lots of silver missing. You were right on the scene.'

'Got lucky. I'm a journalist. I work the streets. It's not such a long shot I would trip over a B & E now and then.'

'The thieves had keys to the structure.'

'What's that got to do with me? You've checked pawn shops, second-hand stores, known fences?'

'You know a lot about cops.'

'I watch TV.'

Virgil's confidence was rising. Anspach had pulled him in for an interview but hadn't laid out any evidence of Virgil's involvement in the crimes. The man had circumstantial evidence in spades but no physical clues or corroborative testimony. The interview was a last effort to break the case. Keep his nerve and Virgil was home free.

'Got anything else you want to say to me?'

'No.'

The two of them sat quietly for a moment, each contemplating the situation. Virgil was cool. He looked the cop in the eye. He wasn't going to be psyched out.

It was obvious Virgil had set up the score. They both knew that. The circumstantial evidence left no doubt. But circumstantial evidence wasn't a case, and Virgil would walk.

'All right, Mr Strauss,' said Anspach in a reflective tone of voice. 'I'll get an officer in here and you can make a written statement. Thank you for your time.'

'Not at all.'

When Virgil left the station he walked out of the building trying not to run.

CELEBRITY SAYS 'HAIR TRANSPLANTS SAVED MY CAREER'

CSI patient Caspar Hotchkiss (left) is a professional Michael Jackson impersonator who felt his career was in jeopardy because his receding hairline was taking away his youthful appearance.

Solution: CSI's Super Follicle program during which 988 small grafts of one to three hairs each were densely transplanted into just the first half inch of his hairline.

Price Range: $8 to $22 per graft
* Celebrity quality
* Affordable prices
* Discount programs
* Easy financing
* Free grafts after 1600 (single session)

1–800 COOL HAIR

The California Scalp Institute, A Medical Group

Chapter Sixteen

Johnny and Virgil climbed three flights of stairs to reach Mathias Haas' apartment. They were both wearing overalls. Johnny knocked.

'Exterminator.'

Haas opened the door.

'Yes?'

'New York Exterminators. The landlord asked us to check you over for roach infestation. Some of the other tenants have complained.'

Haas led them inside. The apartment was Japanese minimalist. Space. The smell of citrus. The oppressive hush of money. An unambiguous statement: I'm rich enough to own nothing.

The man himself was small and fit. The clearly defined tendons and veins of his neck suggested he ate well and worked out. He wore an oatmeal shirt and baggy pants and padded around the apartment barefoot. He seemed pleasant and calm. Virgil concentrated on the lawyer's wealth. He stoked his envy to see the job through.

'I'm sure we haven't seen any roaches,' said Haas. 'My wife would have mentioned it if she had. She hates bugs.'

Haas knelt on the kitchen floor and Johnny showed him how bugs bred in the cracks where the tiles met the wall. Virgil said: 'I'll check some of the other rooms if that's okay,' and headed for the bedroom.

He slid shut the oriental paper screen that acted as a bedroom door and looked around. A plain room with a large, pine bed and a wardrobe and dresser. Lipsticks and brushes on the dresser. Female clutter battling Bauhaus austerity.

This was the kind of trouble Virgil could live without. Hauled in by the cops in the middle of the night. Saw the stairs down to the cells. Smelt puke and disinfectant. He just wanted to keep his head down, vanish from the streets. But Marcy needed revenge, so here he was putting it all on the line for her sake.

Virgil put his tool bag on the bed and took out a remote video camera. The camera was a black, low-range transmitter and battery pack the size and shape of a paperback book. From it snaked twelve inches of fibre-optic cable tipped with a glass bead lens. He fixed the body of the camera to the back of the dresser with duct tape and positioned the tiny lens to give a side elevation of the bed. He taped a second camera to the top of the wardrobe and arranged an aerial perspective of the bed.

Virgil crept into the living room. Lively conversation happening in the kitchen. He looked around for a place to hide a camera. He settled on a matt black, fifty-watt speaker cabinet in the corner and taped a camera to the back at floor level.

He walked into the kitchen and coughed. It was a signal for Johnny to make excuses and leave.

'Doesn't look like you have a problem,' said Johnny. 'But we may check again in the next couple of days just to be sure. Thanks for your help.'

'Not at all,' said Haas. Virgil was close enough to smell the man's cologne and look him in the eye. Haas seemed to be an amiable guy. Maybe he suppressed the memory of the night he raped Marcy. Maybe he never knew her at all. Maybe Marcy had some kind of persecution complex. Virgil willed himself to believe in her. He would get the job done.

Johnny unscrewed a plumbing inspection panel in the wall of the fire escape stairwell and wedged a receiver and a twin tape VCR amongst the pipes and stop-cocks.

'Let's hope he doesn't fuck in the dark,' he said.

'And let's hope he doesn't have a normal sex life,' said Virgil.

'I've been spying through windows for years. Believe me, nobody has a normal sex life.'

Working the *Graphic* nightwatch. Cruising with Ferris. They patrolled the dockside. It was a rough place. In the past few weeks a lady acting as a school-crossing guard got busted for selling crack on duty. She was helping kids across the road and selling rocks in twists of coloured paper like candy. On the same day a tottering grandmother got busted hustling tranquillizers on a street corner. She was selling all kinds of prescription candy: ephedrine distilled from nose drops, and a potent mixture of steroid nubane and pharmaceutical cocaine. Both women were dumb enough to get busted for possession and intent to deal a couple of minutes after they started taking money. The old women broke under questioning and revealed details of a drug manufacturing outfit operating from old people's sheltered accommodation. A couple of eighty-year-old guys were faking prescriptions for cough mixture and travel sickness pills. The mixture of scopolamine and dextromethopham created a heroin substitute nicknamed Super Buick and explained a sudden spate of ODs amongst regular users in the district. It was getting that way on the streets. One big psycho-pharmacological experiment.

They bought coffee and doughnuts to go at Levy's. Ferris scarfed bearclaws like someone was timing him for a record. Virgil watched and blew on his coffee. He felt it was his turn to tell a war story.

'I once saw a dealer get busted here on the waterfront. This black guy was dishing out rocks of crack from a plastic bag. Cops appeared out of nowhere and started closing in on all sides. The guy had nowhere to run so he triggered a ship's distress flare scotch-taped to the side of his crack bag. The rocket went shooting up and over the Hudson. He and the cops stood with their hands in their pockets and watched the rocks float down on a little parachute and sink. The cops walked away without saying a word and the dealer just pissed himself laughing at them, even though he'd just torched several thousand dollars' worth of stock.'

Ferris chuckled, spat blobs of food on to the dash.

'No fucking shit. Did you get pictures?'

'Not that time. Didn't have my camera.'

'You should always have your camera. Take it to your fucking coffin.'

'Right,' said Virgil, nodding at the wisdom of Ferris's words. In fact the crack dealer story wasn't true. It was an exaggerated version of an incident that happened to Larry. But Virgil needed his anecdotes and scars. He was on a team now. It was expected of him.

That night Marcy stayed at Virgil's new place and they sat up in bed watching Psycho II on TV.

'What did you do today?' she asked.

'We set up Haas. Cameras in the main rooms. We're ready to fuck him good.'

'When do we go?'

'Johnny is tracking his movements, getting his routine. We'll be set to move at the end of the week.'

'Outstanding.' Marcy snuggled deeper into the duvet. The radiators weren't functioning and the room was starting to freeze.

'How was work?' she asked.

'All right. Me and Ferris went to Brooklyn. This ex-cop called O'Mally was having a birthday party when this thug jumped through the window dressed in black. O'Mally got his wife's Ladysmith from her purse and shot the guy twice in the chest and once in the forehead. Turns out the intruder was a Kung-Fu-ogram his wife ordered as a surprise. Good pictures. A ninja face down in birthday cake. Brains spilling out like scrambled egg and Happy Birthday Walter in blue icing. Real cool.'

'Steven Seagal was a Kung-Fu-ogram.'

'Had things been a little different we would have been spared that fucking ponytail.'

Screams and agitated violins from the TV. Norman Bates was getting creative with a kitchen knife.

'What makes someone kill like that, do you think?' asked Marcy.

'TV is bullshit. Psychopaths aren't frenzied, they just can't empathize with people; don't understand the difference between a man and a chair. They like to take humans apart to see how they work, like a kid with a clockwork toy.'

'How do they get that way?'

'Genes. Shitty childhood. How do I know? There's some sicko on the streets right now. I saw a girl in bits a couple of days ago. Her name was Lette Lipton. Arms and legs cut off.'

'I don't want to hear details.' Marcy seemed distressed.

'Cops said she was a porn actress. Heard her name mentioned at all?'

'No.'

'Black girl. Part of her ear missing.'

'I said no.'

'Imagine that. Tied to a bed. Having a madman cut you up real slow. Maybe he'd hang you upside down, keep the blood at your head, keep you alive and suffering longer.'

'I bet he killed real quick,' said Marcy.

'What makes you think that?'

'I think some of the street girls are really looking for a good end. A way out. It's a blessing.'

'You think anyone wants to get sliced up? Is that what you're saying?'

'Back in the fifties there was a guy on the West Coast slitting women's throats. There was never a sign of a struggle. Maybe the guy offing these hookers is the same. An artist, in his way, and the girls know that.'

'You're saying these girls volunteered to be cut to pieces as an art statement?'

'Don't dismiss the idea. It could be the only chance these girls ever get to matter,' said Marcy.

'That's truly sick.'

Virgil made two mugs of tea and returned to bed. Anthony Perkins rented another room at the Bates Motel. 'Twelve rooms, twelve vacancies.'

'You know, as sequels go, this is pretty good,' he said.

'You never did serial-killer stuff when you were out taking photographs?'

'No. Though God knows there was enough opportunity. The cops seemed to take one down every few months. And for every lunatic they catch they reckon there are five too smart to get cornered. There's a guy around town at the moment who shoots taxi drivers in the back of the head and steals their socks.'

'Why?'

'There aren't any reasons. Ask Norman Bates.'

'But you never took pictures.'

'No. Well, sometimes, if I really needed the money. But I was more interested in sort of cosmic fuck-ups, you know? You've got to have a clear agenda when you hit the streets or you just won't get anywhere as an artist. Besides, all newspapers have their own staff photographers and they always make it to crime scenes. The only way to make money is to specialize in weird shit which nobody else covers.'

'A psychiatrist would say you do it because of what happened to your mother.'

'Well, that psychiatrist can go fuck himself. I mean give me some fucking credit for self-awareness. I know what I'm doing and why. I'm not a slot machine. I don't take in childhood trauma and dispense sicko art as a reflex. This stuff has meaning beyond my problems. I photograph shit that happens every day on the street. It's the way life is, and if other people don't want to acknowledge it then that's their fucking problem. I'm seeing things the way they really are. I'm awake. I got my eyes wide fucking open.'

'And you say you aren't a cynic.'

'I'm not a cynic. I like life. But how it really is, not some fragile, idealized version.'

'You've spilled your tea.'

The film ended with Anthony Perkins out of his mind once more and declaring the Bates Motel open for business. Virgil thought about the conversation he just had with Marcy. How his description of his photography kept slipping out of the past tense and into the present. He realized his brief holiday from taking pictures outside of *Graphic* business hours was over and that he would hit the streets tomorrow night like old times, follow his art, look for weird shit he could sell to Turkel. He felt good about it.

The Virgil Strauss Atrocity Show. Open for Viewing.

(387)	Climax solid vibrator	8″ long	1.2″ thick	$7.99
(388)	Big boy solid vibrator	10″ long	1.4″ thick	$9.99
(389)	Bully boy soft vib/dildo	7.5″ long	1.5″ thick	$12.99
(390)	Jelly feel soft vib/dildo	8″ long	1.7″ thick	$15.99
(391)	Large G-spot vib/dildo	9″ long	1.5″ thick	$10.99
(392)	King Mammoth vib/dildo	14″ long	2.5″ thick	$19.99
(393)	Anal plug vib with lube	7″ long	4.5″ thick	$9.99
(394)	Electric up/down vib	7–10″ long	1.2″ thick	$19.99
(395)	Finger and thumb vib	8/5″ long	1.1″ thick	$12.99
(396)	Vibrating cock ring			$7.99
(397)	Black Rambo	10″ long	3.5″ thick	$10.99

Chapter Seventeen

Virgil and Marcy were heading down to the Mayflower atrium and the street. Virgil stopped halfway down the grand stairs. It was a fine day, he had a job, a girl, his cop troubles had evaporated, but he felt a slight flutter of anxiety. It was like being a kid again. Enjoying the last half of the summer vacation, yet the prospect of a new year at school approached like dark clouds building on the horizon. Virgil couldn't pin down what was worrying him yet still he felt a gathering sense of dread.

He checked his mail box on the way out. Two letters. The first was from Mercury Press and was addressed to Barrington Fingenbaum.

In order to continue filing tall tales on the Mercury Press bulletin board Virgil had concocted a resumé for his alter ego. He even opened a bank account under the name and was drawing a pay cheque. He had used his home address at the Mayflower as a place to mail the money and it was to this address that Mercury Press sent an invite to its annual party. Virgil's python story had only appeared in the newspaper a couple of days ago but Virgil guessed the guys sending the invites would ask hacks who lived close enough to make it through a blizzard.

The second envelope contained the front page of yesterday's *Graphic*. Virgil's picture of the Vishnu Jones explosion under the headline BLAST HORROR: MORE REVELATIONS! and the baseball scores. Over the top of the picture were pasted the words 'Fast falls the eventide' and 'Loved the picture'. The page was signed 'Vishnu Jones' in magic marker.

'What do you think?' asked Marcy.

'Unimaginative hoax. Didn't you see the news? Nuts queue round the block at police HQ all saying: "I'm Vishnu Jones. I surrender."'

He folded the note and put it back in its envelope. He wanted to spend a morning walking around town with Marcy. He didn't want to think about inadequate bombers outside of office hours.

'Someone went to the trouble of finding your address,' said Marcy.

'This bomber has been so fucking methodical, so fucking smart. You don't think he's going to give it all away by writing fan letters to nobody hacks? This carnage is his art. His masterpiece isn't finished yet. He wouldn't jeopardize that.'

'You going to throw it away?'

'No. I'll drop it off at the precinct on the way to the subway. Show that Anspach fucker I'm a good citizen.'

Virgil dropped the note at the precinct house, accompanied Marcy to Turkel's studio and watched her push a tennis racket up her snatch. He made his way to Metro Plaza and got jumped by cops and FBI as he walked into the offices of the *Graphic*. He never knew how they responded so fast.

Virgil was marched into a side room. He thought he was about to be busted for complicity in the angel heist, for the St Sophia's raid. He couldn't understand why it took so many cops to bring one guy in.

'You are Virgil Strauss?' asked a suit.

'Yeah.'

'Resident at the Mayflower Hotel?'

'Yeah.'

'Working as a photographer at the *New York Graphic*?'

'Who the fuck are you?'

The guy laid a Polaroid picture in front of Virgil. The Vishnu Jones letter. 'Loved the picture.'

'I'm Special Agent Irving. Tell me about the letter.'

'I got it in the mail this morning. Didn't think anything of it but I handed it in at the station anyway.'

'Have you ever received any communications like this before?'

'No.'

'You're sure?'

'Yes.'

'You were present at the first major explosion. How come you were there when it happened?'

'Good luck. What the fuck is going on?'

'We believe this communication to be genuine.'

'Why?'

'The phrase "fast falls the eventide" has been used in ransom demands and bomb warnings sent to City Hall. It's a codeword.'

'Fuck.'

'This information does not leave the room, understand? We get thousands of letters every day. This phrase is the only thing that sorts the real messages from the dross.'

'What do you want from me?'

'I'm going to tell you something in confidence. The chief is talking this case up like we got imminent busts, but we don't have a single lead. Pulled in every extremist and known subversive. *Nada.* You are our only lead and we think Vishnu Jones will be in touch again.'

'What makes you say that?'

'He needs a media outlet.'

'Why me? Why not Norman Mailer or some Pulitzer prize winner at *The Times*?'

'Because you're an unscrupulous fuck who takes pictures of the sickest events imaginable, and your paper prints these pictures without question.'

Virgil didn't get offended. Veteran *Graphic* photographers would take 'unscrupulous fuck' as a compliment.

'I don't get it.'

'Vishnu Jones gets his rocks off creating chaos. It's not enough to cause chaos. He has to see the destruction he creates. But he can't visit the bomb site in person because he knows we'll be looking out for him. So he needs a pair of eyes to view the carnage on his behalf. You are his eyes.'

'Which means what exactly?'

'If you're going to be on site when the next Vishnu Jones

bomb goes off the guy has to give you advanced warning. That's the best chance we've got of minimizing casualties and maybe tracing the bastard. We've got taps on every phone and fax line into this office, people monitoring the mail, people watching your apartment and your phone. Agents Dieter and Bains will be assigned to protect you.'

He gestured to two guerrillas in the corner. Buzzcuts, mirror shades, sober suits.

'These guys are going to follow me?'

'They will be with you wherever you go.'

'Do I get a choice?'

'You're not an observer of events any more, Virgil. You are a participant.'

'I got to talk to my editor.'

Virgil went looking for Ferris and found him in the muster room strapping on his Kevlar vest.

'Can you take me to the sushi place? I got to see Devlin.'

'Devlin is here and he wants to speak to you right away. He's in his office.'

Lepke Devlin was in his office striking Napoleonic poses in a full-length mirror. He was annoyed at the interruption but brightened when he saw it was Virgil.

'You heard about the FBI,' said Virgil. (A redundant statement. There were cops and special agents crawling over the office dismantling every telephone junction box they could locate. The picture editor's office was being emptied to make a place where Virgil could receive calls.)

'I can't tell you the things you have done for this paper, Virgil,' said Devlin. 'First the Vishnu bomb and now this. You're a fucking horse-shoe. A lightning rod for fine disasters.'

'Meaning what? When you let the FBI in here what was your price for co-operation?'

'I'm going to put you on page one.' Devlin held up a dummy front page. THE MIND OF VISHNU JONES. A blank space at the centre of the page where Virgil's picture would go.

'I've lined up a psychiatrist and you and he are going to put a story together. What Vishnu Jones is thinking, his motives, his background, that kind of thing.'

'His message was three words long.'

'We'll use general FBI profiles and flesh it out. It's not a problem.'

'I don't want my picture in the papers.'

'It's your job. You signed the contract. We own you. They're setting up lights and make-up right now.'

The FBI equipped him with a pager and a locator device which they strapped to his wrist. There was no buckle on the locator device. It would have to be cut loose. They strapped him into a white Kevlar vest and taped a microphone to his chest with duct tape.

'From now on wherever you go, whatever you do, we'll be listening.'

Virgil's face was powdered, his eyebrows smoothed, his lips painted. He sweated under studio lights. He hated being photographed. Facing the lens was like staring down the barrel of a gun.

The *Graphic*'s staff photographers hit the streets and Virgil was left alone in his new office.

'Can't I go out too?' he asked.

'No,' said Agent Irving. 'You have to stay where we can reach you.'

'Must I stay in the office?'

'No. You can move around the building, but you mustn't leave Metro Plaza.'

Virgil checked up on Aubrey. Aubrey manned the *Graphic* darkroom. He was running off prints from Virgil's old negatives. Virgil had been trawling through every drawer and cupboard for old product he could sell to Willie Turkel.

'How long is this going to take?' asked Virgil.

'All night,' said Aubrey. He fixed himself a coffee and sat down to work with the enlarger.

'Well, I appreciate your efforts.' Virgil peeled off a couple of hundred-dollar bills and dropped them on the counter.

Virgil wandered through to the newsroom and watched a *Graphic* hack edit a weather report.

A hurricane had levelled large sections of Mexico, drifted out to sea once more and was heading north along the US Gulf coast. A geostationary weather satellite showed the imminent landfall of a beautiful vortex, like water swirling down a plug hole only four hundred miles wide. Ten billion dollars of damage waiting to happen and likely to bankrupt insurance firms already on the brink after a year of inexplicable meteorological catastrophes. The National Hurricane Center in Miami was calling the twister Pablo according to a pre-agreed list of male and female names chosen to reflect the cultural diversity of the United States. However, the millionaire Marcel Barnum who owned the Weather Watch Network had decreed the tornado should be called Victoria in honour of his daughter. Neither party would back down so the papers sided with the National Hurricane Center and were referring to the twister as Hurricane Pablo, while the hourly bulletins on the Weather Watch Network were referring to it as Victoria. Some TV stations tried to compromise by referring to Hurricane 'Pablo-dash-Victoria' or 'the hurricane formerly known as Pablo', but gave up because it was too much hassle. In the meantime the tornado and accompanying tropical storms had left twenty-seven Mexicans dead and hundreds homeless.

So many stories. So much random death. New tales, same details. Virgil was tired, and when he rubbed his eyes he saw in the kaleidoscopic phosphenes the infinite repetition of serial killer atrocities and war crimes. Knives and guns, power and control.

He had once read a thesis from a Toronto professor suggesting folk myths replicate and spread in the manner of a virus. For example, the oft told tale of the man who, while sitting alone at a bar, is approached by a beautiful girl. She offers him a drink. He accepts. From the moment the drink touches his lips he remembers nothing until he wakes in a hotel room with an IV in his arm and a kidney missing. Computer modelling suggests this kind of story adapts from host to host, mutating to new strains and variants, like the rat-born contagions infecting New York.

Time for drastic surgery. Book burnings and toppling radio masts. Virgil could understand what motivated Los Banditos. Too much fucking information.

Virgil closed the door to be alone in his office and thought about his mother.

As he got older Virgil understood there were advantages to not having parents. It was good to be blank. He liked being self-invented, not having the burden of a family history. No duty of taking over the family business, playing football or enrolling at West Point. No parental expectations to judge himself against and be found wanting.

Biology is destiny and most guys Virgil's age were trying to cope with the first horrifying signs that, despite their hopes and dreams, they were turning into their fathers. Same kind of job. Same kind of paunch. But Virgil couldn't make a comparison, and so enjoyed at least the illusion of freedom.

He had chosen his own name, Virgil, because it sounded clever and unusual; Strauss, because he used to hang with Jewish kids and admired their business sense even if he couldn't emulate it. So he was Virgil Strauss, a kid with no family, and that was the way it would always be.

ARMED RESPONSE

Law enforcement advisors to the movie industry

Former NYPD vice sergeant expert in rules & procedures, undercover investigation techniques, supervision, body/verbal language, uniform & set designs and firearms & tactics, and crime scenes. Advisor for season three of Hill Street Blues and Emmy episode of Cagney and Lacy.

Call Rudy on 212–46–74688 and leave a message.

Chapter Eighteen

Hallowe'en. Virgil's thirtieth, and the city on alert. Rats, snow, and now a lunatic bomber. Habeas corpus was suspended and the cops had stop-and-search blocks every couple of hundred yards. All to find Vishnu Jones. People got frisked on the subway. A sweet little girl riding next to Virgil got busted for a pocket of gamma hydroxy butyrate. Virgil passed unmolested. His two guardian angels walked a step behind wherever he went. Dieter and Bains had their agency badges to flash him out of trouble. People stared at the two androids.

Virgil and Marcy arranged to meet at the cinema and sort through Virgil's old pictures to see which could be sold to Willie Turkel. He told the FBI guys to wait in the auditorium while he visited Larry. They sat in the back row. Their mirror shades reflected swinging scrotums and the relentless, industrial piston thrusts of monstrous dicks. Their mouths betrayed no flicker of emotion.

This was how it was for Virgil. Constant surveillance. The double click of a tap going active when he answered the phone. A close escort as he pushed a cart around the supermarket. At least he didn't have to wear a wire any more. That was the price of his co-operation. The feds had to give him a little space to himself.

Mercury Press had Virgil's address and were still mailing him about the press party. The cops had him down as the prime suspect in the House of Usher angel heist. The FBI was all over him as the only lead in the Vishnu Jones situation. Virgil was tempted to pack a suitcase and vanish, but he had cut and run from so many things in his life.

Virgil and Marcy arranged the photographs in piles of ten and put them in envelopes.

They worked hard and kept out of the way of two guys in hard hats who were touring the building. Larry said he didn't know who they were but they were carrying blueprints. Larry joked that maybe they were going to turn the building into a shopping mall, and there was an edge in his voice which suggested he half believed it.

'So how would you feel about an early retirement?' asked Virgil. 'Suppose the place was bulldozed. You could put your feet up. Watch boxing, or whatever. Meet some people your own age to talk to.'

'With my lungs I would end up in a nursing home,' said Larry. 'And I got no money, so it would be a shitty nursing home at that.' His laugh sounded desperate.

'Relax,' said Marcy. 'They are probably looking to decorate, that's all. You get enough customers, don't you?'

'We pay our way. Or so the accountant says.'

'There you are, then. If it ain't broke don't fix it. They won't want to mess with you.'

'This is a big plot of land near Times Square. Worth a shit load of money to the right corporation.'

'That stuff takes decades to happen. Architects build little wooden models and city officials do surveys and shit. If they started the process now you would be long dead by the time they got round to doing anything about it.'

'That cheers me up.'

'You know what I'm trying to say.'

'Yeah. But you can always count on the worst to happen. If you guys could look out for a cheap apartment I would appreciate it. If there is money to be made these shits would kick me on to the street in an instant.'

When the envelopes were done they boxed them up and stored them in the basement.

Marcy and Virgil went for a walk in the park. Their escort followed. Virgil could cope with the intrusion but Marcy was getting stressed out.

It was a clear day but Virgil's shades turned blue skies to

rain. They walked through town. People stared. Anyone with two bodyguards must be a big shot. Virgil got asked for his autograph three times.

Kids were skating at Wollman Park and Rockefeller Center. Virgil hadn't the temperament for spontaneous gestures of affection but as they leant on a railing and watched kids play snowballs at Hecksher ball fields he took Marcy's arm. Things were going well between them. They never argued or found any subject about which they widely disagreed. Virgil didn't understand why she wouldn't think of him as a long-term prospect. He didn't want her to die alone. But today everything was fine so he enjoyed the crisp air and the snow. The snow was grey with exhaust pollution, but that was all right because car fumes induced nitric oxide, a vasodilator used in impotence creams, to help New Yorkers keep it up.

'What do you think I should do about the press party?' he said.

'When is it?'

'Couple of days. Maybe we should invite Haas. Use the occasion to our advantage.'

'Yeah. Rent a tux and go for it.'

'All right.'

They went in search of hot dogs. Later on they went to the Bronx Zoo to watch the keepers feed the penguins fish-flavoured lollipops. The birds had barcodes stuck to their beaks with epoxy resin to deter penguin snatchers.

In the evening they went back to the Mayflower and pleasured each other in their unique way. They made love in silence. Dieter and Bains were in the corridor outside. Afterwards Virgil lay on his stomach checking the papers for weird shit while Marcy massaged his back.

Pete Hernandez, an electrician from Queen, had been busted for killing his girlfriend's parrot following a domestic dispute. The bird was a sulphur-crested cockatoo called Sammy, which had an extensive vocabulary of Hispanic swear words and had been trained to repeat the phrase 'Pete Hernandez is a cunt' over and over again. The final straw came when the wheezing and incontinence Hernandez had experienced in recent weeks was diagnosed as psittacosis otherwise known as parrot fever. Hernandez poured aftershave over the parrot and threw a lit match into the cage. Interviewed on the court room steps his only comment was, 'I never could stand that damned bird.'

Lisa Lasarow was under arrest following a shooting incident at Grand Central Station. Apparently Mrs Lasarow felt frustrated that her husband's legal work meant he was rarely home, so she sought to have an affair. Having decided not to approach any of her colleagues at the public relations firm where she worked, she took, from a close friend, the number of the exclusive Ryecart male escort agency, which charges a hundred and fifty dollars an hour for the services of its urbane and highly sexed men. Mrs Lasarow decided to meet her escort in a public place and so arranged a rendezvous at the bottom of the main stairs at Grand Central Station. The escort would identify himself by carrying a bouquet of flowers. Following her friend's advice Mrs Lasarow went to her assignation with a Derringer pistol for personal protection. When she arrived at the station she found her husband standing at the bottom of the stairs in a dinner suit and holding a bunch of red roses. She shot him once in the chest and once in the groin. His condition is said to be critical.

Marcy was cutting her life to the bone, sweeping away the junk. In keeping with this radical mood she had given Virgil a bunch of old paperbacks, which he was glad to have because they were good titles, but he also wanted to empty his life of clutter. He wanted the monkish existence heroes led. A rented room with no decoration. A hat, a raincoat and a gun. Maybe a pack of cigarettes and a bottle of bourbon for the weekend. Yet every time Virgil looked around his own room he couldn't single out anything which didn't have sentimental associations or a fun use, like his records and videos. There was a china cat on his mantelpiece but it was a gift from a friend who died in a car wreck, so he couldn't ditch that. It was the same for his Bible. It was a big King James. His first girlfriend had given it to him and written an inscription inside, so he had to keep it.

*   *   *

Another shift doing nothing at the *Graphic*. Virgil took Marcy for company.

'What underwear have you got on?' asked Virgil.

'Black suspender and stocking set, as requested.' The FBI guys thumped the coffee machine and jabbed the refund button. Marcy and Virgil took the opportunity to slip out on to a fire exit and down to the mall. They ran around the concourse, screams echoing from the vaulted mall roof, shoes squeaking on polished tiles.

Virgil caught up with her on the fourth floor. He straddled her head and she sucked him with an audience of mannequins in a Gap window display. When he was done he put on a glove and fingered her off. Marcy wiped herself with tissues and sponged an area of the floor.

'If we leave this wet patch here the maintenance people will think they have a roof leak,' she said. Virgil smiled.

'Promise me something,' said Marcy. 'If I have to leave before the job is done you will see it through. Take care of Haas no matter what.'

'We do him tomorrow or the day after. Not going anywhere before then, are you?'

'Give me your word.'

'You got it.'

Virgil wanted to say how much Marcy meant to him and beg her to stay, but he didn't have the words. He looked away and for the briefest instant he saw the figure of a man watching them at the far end of the walkway. Then the figure was gone.

Virgil and Marcy ran after the man and found a fire door gradually swinging shut. They stepped into the fire stairwell. There was no one there. They leant over the banister, looked up and down, but there was no sign of the intruder.

'Stay down here,' said Virgil. 'Tell the FBI guys I'm taking a shit or something.'

He ran up the stairs, determined to confront the ghostly figure.

There was nothing above the mall but suites leased by lawyers and investment bankers. Virgil jogged up each flight of stairs and scanned the open-plan office space. Moonlight shafted through the blinds and lit dozens of partitioned work stations humanized with fluffy gonks and stickers. Mugs, family pictures, Far Side cartoons.

When he had surveyed each department he climbed to the next floor and repeated the inspection. It made him tired and out of breath. It also made him scared. More than once he thought his footsteps on the stairwell were mirrored by a second pair of feet, but every time he stopped to listen the sound ceased. He decided his footsteps must be echoing back at him.

The wind was up outside and the super-structure creaked and swayed. Light fixtures swung casting wild shadows up the wall. Doors swung open and shut. Water in toilet bowls shivered and rippled.

Sometimes, as he walked down a corridor, he felt someone was behind him, but when he whipped around and focused his torch beam there was no one to be seen.

Virgil decided to end his grand tour on the thirteenth floor. He was getting frightened.

A breath behind him. An aching sigh.

Virgil span around and was confronted by a huge figure in an anorak. A hood covered the figure's face like a monk's cowl. Virgil vented his fear in a blood-curdling roar and ran at the guy to bring him down and get a choke hold. Virgil missed, he didn't know how, and hit the carpet. The intruder vanished up the fire stairwell and Virgil took off in pursuit. No matter how fast he ran he couldn't gain on the footsteps up ahead.

The express elevator: an ear-popping ride through the building, through the Metropolitan Experience skydeck, past the tuned mass damper – a four-hundred-ton concrete block shimmying on hydraulics to counter the wind – past elevator cable drums big as a truck and up ladders to the roof. Nobody to be seen. Virgil stood alone amongst a forest of plant equipment. Two great telecone masts encrusted with transmitter dishes and signal boosters. Steam blowing from the chillers. Anemometers whirring. Wind sails and turbine funnels. Aircraft warning strobes turning the scene blood red at two-second intervals, and above them a gargantuan, opaque clock face illuminated from within. The clock could not be seen from the street. Like the Chippendale top of the AT&T building it could only be appreciated from adjoining skyscrapers. Up close Virgil could see the clock hands were coated in pigeon shit. Window cleaning cranes hung off the parapet like life-boat davits.

No one around. Virgil looked over the parapet and watched people, small like ants. He once read about a monkey raised by an anthropologist. She taught it a sign language vocabulary of four hundred words. One day she took the monkey to see the chimpanzee cage at the zoo. It was the first time the monkey saw other members of its species. She asked the monkey what it saw, and it signed, 'I see black bugs.'

Another phantom. Another shade that lived in the periphery of Virgil's vision. Citizens of a spectral city that co-existed with Manhattan, and only Virgil manned the gateway between the two worlds.

It was a clear night and the stars scintillated. Virgil looked across a vista of roofs. New skyscrapers. Red-brick ziggurats from the previous century. Water towers and TV aerials.

Mohawks walking high steel were silhouetted against the moon as they watched a girder rise to meet them.

A little fire flared on the roof of the office block in front of him. A shabby man waved his burning torch in salute. Virgil waved back. He looked from roof to roof and saw torches receding to the distance. A legion of cloud-borne mendicants solemnly marked Nocturne.

DOUBLE DISASTER

Six people were killed yesterday when the floor of a government building in Cebu, the central city of the Philippines, collapsed. The second-storey room was being used for an inquest into a ferry disaster which occurred earlier in the year. An overloaded ferry capsized in the harbour killing twenty-two passengers. When the ferry captain stepped into the courtroom to give evidence concerning the ferry disaster the weight of people became more than the floor could bear and it collapsed into the unoccupied room below. The captain and relatives of those who drowned in the ferry disaster were amongst the dead.

Chapter Nineteen

When Virgil rolled out of bed at noon Marcy was in the kitchen fixing lunch.

'Snowing again,' remarked Virgil. He was looking out the window. Marcy joined him at the window and looked in wonder as if she were seeing snow for the first time.

'Forty hours of tape,' he said. 'And I still have nothing on this Haas guy. Tell me about him.'

'Republican, country-club-type parents. Father was in the Air Force. Haas was always talking about honour and duty and shit like that, but he was the most spiteful, shit-stirring creep around. Total hypocrite. Wouldn't know honour if it bit his ass. He wanted to be a doctor but he got turned down by all the colleges. They could tell he didn't have a compassionate bone in his body. So he became some sort of corporate lawyer working for tobacco companies.'

'And you fucked him.'

'He spiked my drinks. I was near comatose. He raped me. You remember what we said? No violence? Well, it doesn't apply to Haas. Whatever it takes.'

Virgil watched afternoon TV while Marcy bathed and painted her face. At six he had a shower. At seven they changed into the formal wear they had rented for the evening.

'How do I look?' asked Virgil.

'Real cool,' said Marcy.

'You look beautiful.'

He got his camera, balanced it on a shelf and set the timer. Virgil and Marcy arm in arm in front of a stepladder and dust sheets. The timer clicked. Virgil held his grin. He thought about a Hispanic graveyard in Queens he once visited. Smiling photographs of the dead set in glass panels on the gravestones. Every college graduation picture, every wedding snap, spattered with rain and gravedirt, every image of youth and optimism, so fucking poignant it hurt.

Flash.

They processed down the corridors with Dieter and Bains in tow.

A blue mist of cigar smoke hung above the tables in the banqueting hall. Talking, laughter, gleaming silverware, spotless napery. Echoes of past grandeur.

Fifteen hundred clip-on bow ties, fifteen hundred sets of paste jewellery. The wind outside was so strong it wormed through the cracks in the windowframe and set the curtains wafting. Wine butlers oiled the corporate revelry and silver service staff brought food. A mermaid ice sculpture melted to a puddle.

Virgil's rented tux was as uncomfortable as his mall bodyarmour. He was flanked by two English war correspondents with a fund of anecdotes. He listened to their stories and laughed at their jokes, and thus made himself immensely popular with those at his table.

'You're a bloody good bloke,' said one of the war hacks, dribbling wine down his chin. 'Ought to be more like you working in the field. Not these office Johnnies knocking up stories over the phone from some hotel suite miles from the action. We need people with balls, people who get out there and grapple with life.'

'Absolutely,' said Virgil, and re-filled the man's glass.

Virgil was trying to look at ease. He sat back in his chair and affected an air of boredom. A cigarette would have been useful to play with. Instead, he toyed with the stem of his wine glass. Marcy seemed more animated, more involved than she had in a long while.

'Ladies and Gentlemen,' a PA-enhanced voice rumbled around the banqueting hall like the voice of God. 'The band are playing and the drinks are on the house. If you could make your way to the Orchid Room and the opening dance.'

The first song was a smooch number, so Marcy leant against Virgil and they swayed beneath a glitter ball.

'Stay with me,' said Virgil. 'I don't want you to go.'

'Remember me this way.'

Virgil felt her body heat and tried to imprint the sensation upon his memory. For a moment the crowd of dancers parted and he saw a familiar figure cross the floor and take a bar stool.

'He's here. Mathias Haas.'

'Where?'

'By the bar.'

Haas was on his own, looking pissed off. Virgil had sent an invite and a letter from a fictitious Dr Schone, hinting at major deals for a libel lawyer looking to get into the newspaper business.

'Do your thing.'

Marcy headed for the bar. Virgil saw her take a stool next to Haas, signal for champagne. She put a cigarette in her mouth and touched Haas' arm. Read her lips: 'Do you have a light?'

Dieter and Bains stood in the corner. Their mirror shades refracted beams of light from the glitter ball like death rays.

'I'm done,' Virgil told them. 'Let's go.'

It was a simple plan. Haas wouldn't recognize Marcy in her new, glamorous guise. He would take her home and fuck her. Maybe contract HIV. Pictures of the assignation would be printed in the *Graphic* during the upcoming Phips trial. Phips was a waiter with throat cancer. He blamed passive smoking and decided to sue the tobacco manufacturer. Haas would defend the tobacco company. It was a test case, big news, and Haas was likely to pitch his closing statement as a defence of free trade, come on like an earnest evangel of individual freedom and the American way. Virgil would bring him down. He would see Haas lose his job and his wife. Haas would experience disgrace and maybe the same illness as Marcy had done.

Virgil couldn't sleep. He didn't like to think of Marcy with another man. He didn't like to think of Haas fucking his life away. He decided to visit his old room at the Majestic to pick up the last box of his possessions. Dieter and Bains followed him to the subway.

Virgil always thought his room at the Majestic was austere, but he hadn't realized how much junk he actually owned until he started packing it in grocery cartons. He had every letter written to him in the last decade. Not bills and tax forms, just personal stuff. He was making up for an emotionally deprived childhood by hoarding affection. He didn't need a shrink to tell him that. He understood his motivations very clearly but still he wasn't about to throw the letters away. He filed them in chronological order and packed them in shoe boxes.

Before Virgil left his room he took a last look around. Since he gave up cigarettes nostalgia was his chief vice. If there was a constant theme to his life it was a re-occurring sense of time lost and opportunity missed. When riding on a train or Greyhound he might sit next to a person and, through the duration of the journey, learn something about them from the way they dressed, the way they spoke, what they read. At the destination they would vanish into the crowd and Virgil would feel a slight pang of loss to think he would never see that person again.

So although the basement he was leaving was only the most recent of a succession of rooms he had briefly occupied, Virgil couldn't resist a backward glance. He contemplated the sights and smells of the place. Then he closed the door and was gone.

The Majestic was set for demolition. No warning. Just CONDEMNED nailed to the front door one morning.

When Larry returned to his new place in Harlem from the cinema each day he brought with him another box of pilfered stock. He stole shrink-wrapped packs of light bulbs: sixty watt, forty watt, twenty-five watt, fifteen-watt pygmy, fluorescent strips, giant projector bulbs. He had fuses, spanners, screwdrivers and hex key sets. He had strange tools and spare parts, the purpose of which was hidden from anyone not steeped in arcane cinema lore.

Larry was hoarding this stuff because news was out the Majestic was to be demolished. A Bahrain-based company backed with Persian Gulf oil money wanted the site for an office development. On hearing this news Larry had reacted like a man told he was dying. He went through the full grieving process. He

202

tried to pretend it wasn't happening, contrived not to see the architects and demolition surveyors walking the corridors. Then he tried to reason with the lawyers representing the mob that owned the land. Offered clever money-making schemes, tried to demonstrate the Majestic could still pay its way. Finally he accepted the inevitability of the cinema's destruction and began looting the building in lieu of redundancy pay. He took anything that wasn't screwed down and a lot that was.

His new apartment was turning into the clutter-filled nest Virgil associated with mad old women who live alone with cats and piles of newspaper.

Virgil walked back to the Mayflower with his box of possessions and two bodyguards in tow. An overcast night. Low cloud reflected street light and shrouded the city in tangerine murk.

Virgil passed a payphone. It was ringing. The ringing receded behind him, Dopplered to a minor key, and stopped.

He walked up the street and approached another payphone. It too began ringing and ceased when Virgil passed.

He crossed the next street and saw a payphone at the end of the block. Each footstep brought him closer, but the phone didn't ring.

He reached the phone booth. It started to ring as he drew level. Virgil dumped the box he was carrying into the hands of Dieter and picked up the receiver.

'Hello?'

An electronically distorted voice like a record played at half speed: 'The day after tomorrow. Times Square, midnight. Bring your camera. Because fast falls the eventide.'

'Who the fuck is this?'

'Death. The reaper. The guy that will tear down New York. The guy that will have blood running in the gutters. I am Vishnu the destroyer.'

'Vishnu isn't a destroyer.'

'What?'

'In Hindu mythology Shiva is the destroyer.'

'So what's Vishnu?'

'A sort of holistic oneness type of god, I think.'

'Damn.'

The phone went dead.

'Who was it?' asked Dieter.

'Vishnu Jones.'

Bains on his mobile shouting for reinforcements, for phone-company records, any kind of trace. Virgil trudged on home because Vishnu Jones was too smart to be traced through a digital switching system, and even if he was snared someone would soon take his place. It was the nature of the times. Jones was a symptom of a growing fuck-shit-up metaphysic out on the street. There were thousands like him, sick of rats, disease and bullshit TV. People ready to bring Gotham a cleansing fire. He felt that way himself.

2 HEARTS BECOME 1 – Warm, kind-hearted woman with lots of love to give seeks sincere Christian male 40+ to share the joy of life and help mend a broken heart. Loves folk music/gospel music/poetry and takes the road less travelled. N-smkr.

Newark area.. Box 437

Chapter Twenty

Marcy went out early and didn't say where she was going. Virgil didn't know what to say after pimping her to Haas. She didn't describe what went down. She stuck to her routine.

'Finish the game.'

The spiral stairs leading down to the street were difficult to negotiate. An old Muslim woman who lived in the apartment above Virgil and Marcy had cut into a cantaloup and found the name of Allah spelt in pips. The faithful flocked to her room from all over town to see the miraculous cantaloup. She charged five dollars a peek. The queue currently ran down the stairs and out of the main door. An enterprising street hawker was hustling cold drinks to those waiting in line. He was selling Diet Cokes by the hundred but Budweiser wasn't shifting so well.

Virgil had taken pictures of the cantaloup for the *Graphic* but felt he was treading water since the Vishnu Jones explosion. The FBI wouldn't let him hit the streets. All he could do was admire the pictures Ferris was bringing in: an old lady who died in bed and lay undiscovered for seventeen years in a ground-floor apartment that looked out on a busy street; a mummified corpse tucked up in a patchwork quilt; a guy dead in a phone booth near the waterfront – a bullet hole in the glass, the guy slumped on the floor, the receiver still in his hand. He had been there two weeks and nobody noticed. Blow-flies fed and laid eggs in his eye sockets. His skin writhed with hatching maggots.

Virgil thought about Marcy and the way their sex life was

in decline. Marcy didn't like to be touched any more, unless there was pain involved. When Virgil rubbed her back with the lights on, he saw old cigarette burns between her shoulder blades.

It turned him off sex and it turned him off pornography. A couple of weeks ago he was looking at one of his favourite spreads. Twelve pictures of a girl with a black bob of hair, good nipples and muscular thighs. The magazine was nine years old and he had looked at the pictures so often he regarded the model as an old girlfriend. He was looking at the first picture, an establishing shot in which the girl was dressed in a ball gown and leaning against a mantelpiece, when his attention was drawn to her left wrist. Half submerged in shadow, but visible if you held the page close, were criss-cross scars. The inside of her wrists were not shown in any subsequent pictures, but there was no doubt she had tried to cut an artery at some point in her life. He looked at her smiling face, then down to the slash marks, and wondered about the girl. He knew he would never find out anything about her and would never jerk off to her picture again.

Virgil wondered at Marcy's relationship with Willie Turkel and tried to read the man by the decoration of his apartment. The collection of intricately carved ivory condoms from China, some jade dildos of Mayan design and three John Wayne Gacy clowns.

Turkel presented himself as an antiquarian, a dealer in high-class erotic art objects, yet Virgil sensed the dynamic of the man's trade meant he would inevitably have become a procurer of sexual services. Virgil could imagine the guy ministering to the needs of his millionaire clients, visiting their palaces and enquiring as to their very particular needs. Young, lean Oriental boys. Amputees. The blind. Mastectomy cases. Every peccadillo catered for. Cleanliness and discretion guaranteed. Virgil pictured Turkel in the role of priestly confessor as he took drinks on the yacht of a bored tycoon, but the mental image was wrong. Turkel wasn't the priestly type. He exploited, he didn't empathize. His manner was closer to the unctuous solicitude of an old-style gentleman's outfitter taking an inside leg measurement. But Virgil could see the attraction that working for Turkel held for self-hating whores. He wouldn't judge. He would turn no one away. His smile was a kind of absolution.

Turkel wanted more pictures to sell to his clients. Virgil saw his atrocities blown up poster size on water-colour paper, treated with platinum emulsion instead of silver. It gave the images a velvet, burnished feel. He ransacked old portfolios for more horrors.

It was lean times for weird shit. No real horror going down. The *Graphic* was depending on Virgil's Vishnu Jones connection for copy. Pile-ups on FDR Drive and a bunch of mafia guys floating to the surface of the Hudson, as one generation of hoods succeeded the next, but it was all stuff the networks could cover with more immediacy than the *Graphic*.

Ferris spent an entire night at a hostage situation but didn't get anything that wasn't broadcast live on prime time.

The gunman's name was Morris Diller. He stood three foot nine and was sixty years old. He worked in the optician department of a large uptown department store. He had taken shit about his height all through his working life. He coped by playing the clown but finally snapped when he discovered that, unlike his colleagues, he was not to be given a retirement party. So on his last day at work he packed an Uzi in his briefcase and held his fellow workers hostage. His demands were simple. He wanted a big cake and party streamers. He wanted the managing director of the company to enter the department store and present him with a watch. Not any old watch but a gold Cartier.

The stand-off lasted most of the night. The SWAT commander wanted to take Diller down, but the deputy chief had tactical command and the resigned expression of one who knew whatever decision he made it would be the wrong one.

At four o'clock the managing director of the optician company was fitted with a Kevlar vest and sent into the store with the watch. Minutes passed. A sombre rendition of For He's a Jolly Good Fellow was faintly audible from within. Then one by one the hostages were released. Morris Diller was last out of the building. He was wearing a party hat and a look of triumph.

He didn't want the watch to be repossessed so he smashed it under his heel before he was cuffed.

Ferris got pictures, but so did everyone else. The *Graphic* needed scoops. It needed Vishnu Jones.

How to seduce every woman you meet

Do you wish more women saw you as sexually attractive? Do you wonder why other guys get the best-looking girls? A new publication, *How to Seduce Every Woman You Meet* is now available and explains how you could greatly increase the number of women in your life. Compiled from years of experience and interviews with dozens of women, *How to Seduce Every Woman You Meet* overthrows the common stereotype that you need lots of money and *Baywatch* looks to get the girls you want. Check out our confidence-building techniques. She will be putty in your hands!

'After reading *How to Seduce Every Woman You Meet* my life has been one long orgy! I can't thank you guys enough.' – GD, Delaware.

'Women that ignored me now hang on my every word.' – DS, Tulsa.

....

Please rush me *How to Seduce Every Woman You Meet* at the special price of $19.99.
I understand that if I am not amazed by the results within thirty days I am entitled to a full refund, no questions asked.

Barnum Publications
Dept NYG
Box 8765
Brooklyn
NY 10036

Chapter Twenty-one

The streets were busy as Virgil and his FBI escort made their way to the Majestic. The public was unaware of an imminent detonation. It was Virgil's secret.

A hotel near the park was holding an international conference for conspiracy theorists, and intense-looking guys were handing out leaflets all over town. If there wasn't a God they could at least believe the CIA pulled strings. Magic bullet theories and Roswell filled the airwaves. Virgil's favourite theory came from a bunch of fundamentalist Christians, who not only believed hell was real but that a Russian oil exploration crew drilled down into it near the Finnish border and that the incident was hushed up by the KGB.

Streets on the West Side of town were full of animal rights protesters converging on a bowling alley which was having a tournament in which the competitors threw frozen chickens instead of balls. The bowling alley manager protested that the tournament was not cruel because the chickens were already dead, but the protesters said the contest demonstrated a grave disrespect to animal life in general and should be cancelled. The Humane Society refused to comment.

The Majestic stood alone on a patch of waste ground. The surrounding buildings had been levelled by controlled demolition and replaced by eight support cassions moulded to underpin the planned superstructure. Three weeks with a wrecking ball, and all that history erased. The site of the Majestic would be an ornamental water garden at the front of the building, and so demolition could be deferred a week or two without delaying construction of the megalith.

The interior of the Majestic was as cold and empty as a church. The walls were stripped bare, the projectors and sound equipment were gone. Just dark and shadows. Contractors were due to seal the place up the following day, as a prelude to demolition. Dieter and Bains stood guard in the foyer.

Virgil wasn't used to the silence. Every time he visited the place the projectors were working and he was cloaked in heat and noise. Now there was just Larry sipping from a tin mug and wrapped in a long coat to keep warm.

Larry was entertaining a vagrant in his projection box, some wino he brought in off the street and fed Scotch and pumped for information about the mugger that stole his diamond. The vagrant dropped hints to keep the Scotch coming and Larry lapped it up like gospel. Larry pushed for specifics and got angry when the vagrant couldn't follow through. Virgil had to intervene. If he hadn't been there Larry might have got physical.

'Cool it, for fuck's sake, Larry,' Virgil said, sending the vagrant on his way with the rest of the Scotch to shut him up. 'That guy would tell you anything, and it would all be shit. The last thing you need is cops. Sgt Anspach has my address. He makes a connection with us and the St Sophia's job and we have serious heat. So just relax.'

'I'm cool,' said Larry, with a shit-eating grin. He looked manic. 'Get any good pictures?'

'Fuck pictures. I need money. I need that diamond. I need to get out of this fucking town. It's killing me. Bend your mind to it. Let's get the fucking diamond back. Got another bottle?'

Larry poured. He pulled some old and musty ledgers from under his seat.

'Know what these are?'

'Course not.'

'These books contain summaries of personal correspondence addressed to the Antwerp Diamond Export Company. These guys are not part of De Beers' Central Selling Organization. They're independents that deal in crumbs from the table. Leakage from Canada, Siberia and Namibia. They do sights twice a year and sell good ice if you don't care where it's come from.'

'No shit.'

'Two assholes raided their office. They heard it was one of the biggest Manhattan dealerships of cut and uncut stones, and must have pictured a jewellery store the size of Macy's. These fuckers get inside and find nothing but a vault door that can withstand a nuclear blast. They rifle some filing cabinets so they don't go home empty handed. I made them an offer on the paperwork.'

'So?'

'So, last week the Antwerp Diamond Export Co. entered into correspondence with an unnamed party about the disposal of a pink diamond. Four point ten carats, internally flawless, no inclusions. They advise such a stone would be worth four hundred thousand dollars per carat. An exact description of the stone we boosted from St Sophia's.'

'Someone has it.'

'Tooth Fairy. Got to be.'

'How do we find him?'

'That is the motherfucker of all questions. On my mother's grave I'll track it down. Think I'd blend in with the 47th Street Lubavitchers wearing a yarmulke?'

'You're goyim, Larry, to the core. Come on. Realistically, what's the plan?'

'Right now? Buy some Jack and get fucked.'

'I mean long term.'

'So do I.' Larry's mood took a down turn. 'I see it as a serious career option. I mean what kind of life is it for me in this town? I would be better off riding box cars. Fresh air. Travel. What the fuck. I don't want to go out in a hospital ward. What is the last thing you want to smell? Fresh mountain air or shit and disinfectant. Die with your boots on. That's my advice. Die with a gun in your hand. Let the cops take you down. Fuck them all.'

'Would I be correct in saying you've already renewed your acquaintance with Mr Daniel's today?'

'You very well might.'

'Come on. Let me get you out of here.'

Larry leant on Virgil's shoulder as they took one last tour of the building.

'It's a shit hole but it's been my life these past few years,' said Larry. 'I've spent entire weeks in that projection room. I wouldn't know what the weather was like or anything. I only knew it was raining when the air-conditioning started blowing an earthy smell into the box.'

The silver screen from the main auditorium had been rolled up and taken away. Nothing now but the stage, as it was when the Majestic was a burlesque theatre. Larry and Virgil climbed up on to the stage and looked out across the empty seats. The seats were too threadbare and come-stained to be of use to anyone. The back of the stage, a storage space for ten years, was taken up by hoardings for *Cock Sucking Babes* and *Sally's Sweet Awakening*, a dusty glitter ball, flyers for black soul and comedy nights that never happened. The airbrushed girls bore no relation to the raddled hippies that took it up the ass in the films. Larry took centre stage with melon-breasted cut-outs behind him like a chorus line. He pulled a half bottle from his coat pocket and took a swig.

> 'Tomorrow, and tomorrow, and tomorrow,
> Creeps in this petty pace from day to day,
> To the last syllable of recorded time;
> And all our yesterdays have lighted fools
> The way to dusty death. Out, out, brief candle!
> Life's but a walking shadow, a poor player,
> That struts and frets his hour upon the stage,
> And then is heard no more; it is a tale
> Told by an idiot, full of sound and fury,
> Signifying nothing.
> Through death and birth, to a diviner day.'

'Mawkish, Larry. Cheap sentiment. Place is a shit hole. Always has been.'

'Fuck you very much.' Larry took a bow. 'I could have been a good actor.' He toasted the stalls. 'Did I tell you I acted in prison?'

'You would have made a great clown, Larry. You have the heart.'

Balmer arrived at the cinema and Virgil led him down to the basement rooms.

'Just checking the plumbing,' he explained to Dieter and Bains.

Balmer was the owner and manager of Levy's Café. He was also a good connection to the street. A call to Balmer and a wad of hundreds got Virgil a .45 auto at short notice. Virgil might be going out tonight to face Vishnu Jones alone. He needed protection.

'Check it out,' said Balmer, handing Virgil the gun. Balmer was a muscular guy, white hair, black suit.

'Sturdy little number but of dubious provenance. Don't sell it on. Bring it back to me.'

The .45 was a mess. It had a crust of dust caked in oil, a cracked butt and a bent sight. The sight didn't matter. Nobody used .45s for sharp-shooting.

In the silence of the basement Balmer cleaned the pistol. He used swabs soaked in nitro-solvent and carburettor scrub and soon the .45 had the blue sheen of well-polished gun metal.

'Sorry it's so fucked up,' he said as he worked, 'but you know how it is at short notice.'

For ammunition Virgil got a box of round-nosed, full-metal jackets. Twenty-eight rounds: enough for a back-up magazine. The bullets had cross-slits hammered in the nose for extra spread. The previous owner must have been looking to do serious damage.

Balmer screwed a silencer to the muzzle. It wasn't part of the package, just a way of test-firing the weapon without bringing the FBI guys down to investigate gunshots.

When Balmer was finished Virgil got ready to fire the gun at a plank and dustsheets at the other end of the room.

'Both hands,' advised Balmer. 'Get close up and don't raise it until you need it. It's heavy. Raise it too soon, your hands start to shake and you don't get a proper sight.'

Virgil assumed a killer mentality. 'I'm a machine,' he said to himself. 'Activate me.'

He pulled the trigger. There was little recoil and no muzzle flash. Just a quiet crack and splintered wood.

'There you go,' said Balmer. 'Ready to rock.' He gave Virgil a holster to fix to the back of his pants. 'On the house.'

Virgil got a table in Fontanes. A window seat. The gun loaded and digging into his back. Sheer bravado. He sat alone and saw in the wall mirror his hair was slicked to his forehead by sweat. Other customers stared. He hid behind a menu. He ordered at random and called for a bottle of Muscadet. He got methodically drunk and tried to smother the fear and self-loathing that made his skin crawl. This is what he asked for. This garbage. To be sitting in a fancy restaurant in a good suit. King of New York.

That evening at the *Graphic* Virgil set Aubrey, the darkroom guy, to make prints of his remaining atrocity pictures. Time to settle his account with Willie Turkel.

This year's crop of santas and elves were being drilled on the mezzanine. The chief Santa was a gruff guy who looked like a teamster and had a thick Brooklyn accent. He summed up.

'Elves are crowd control and photos. Santas are santas. You must know all the verses of Rudolph. You must know the names of the reindeer. Don't wear trainers. Don't flirt with the mothers. Shower. Use breath mints. Know the floor plan. Know the location of vomit buckets. I know it's weeks away, but don't forget any of this shit. That's all. You got homes to go to so clear out.'

As the Christmas crew departed they got a xeroxed elf guide.

'Congratulations,' said Santa, wearily shaking each applicant's hand. 'You're now an elf.'

Virgil locked himself in his office and played with his gun. He jumped and span around, shooting down mirage foes, hammer clicking on an empty chamber. After a while Virgil sat down and put the pistol to his head. When the hammer fell he jumped. He rolled a bullet between his fingers. He thought about Lee Harvey Oswald, he thought about changing history, and understood the maxim: a bullet has nothing but a big future.

*   *   *

Nine in the evening. Time to rendezvous with Dieter and Bains in the *Graphic* newsroom.

The FBI team was all set. The bomb squad was ready with their explosives-containment vehicle, a bank vault on wheels, and cryogenic equipment ready to freeze any device once it had been located. Medivac choppers were on standby. SWAT, the Fire Dept and NYPD Emergency Service Units were all ready to roll. Secret service guys were in the background being obtrusively unobtrusive.

The *Graphic* staff were implementing the doomsday plan: checking insurance cover, down-loading all software to hot back-up sites in Newark, clearing nonessential personnel. A commercial centre like Metro Plaza could be a prime target.

All the *Graphic* photographers were tooling up in the muster room. They would be riding out with the emergency services. They drank coffee, played cards. They were waiting for target. A target Virgil would supply.

They stripped Virgil and wrapped his upper body in a Kevlar vest. He wore a locator, a wire, a back-up mike. Devlin made sure Virgil had his camera.

'Do me proud, lad.'

They stood in the cold, stamping their feet to keep warm, watching the flickering neon paint Times Square red and green. There were snipers up there on the roofs and in the dark behind open windows. Virgil was surrounded by at least two hundred personnel with crackling radios. He was stationed next to a phone booth. Half-past eleven.

'Back off,' said Virgil. 'Give me some room to breathe, for Christ's sake.'

There she was at the corner of 41st and Broadway: the Dalmatian lady. Virgil didn't try to chase her. He simply followed her lead. Dieter and Bains flanked him.

'Where the fuck are you going?' asked Agent Irving.

'For a walk. Follow me. Bring the paramedics.'

Once again the lady remained elusive. Every time he turned a street corner he saw her disappear around a bend. She never came within reach. Sometimes she seemed solid as life. Other times her clothes and flesh seemed little more than vapour, and

Virgil could see bone and wispy intimations of organs packing the thoracic cavity.

Virgil found her sitting on the steps of a brownstone. He was a hundred yards away and approaching slowly. The cops were behind him but gave no indication they could see the woman. He expected her to vanish, but she stayed quite still. She stroked her dog. Twenty-five yards away and she turned her gaze on Virgil. Black, dead eyes and the ghost of a smile.

The explosion vaporized the frontage of the building. The delicatessen across the street soaked the blast. Every car, fire and burglar alarm in a radius of twenty blocks tripped and rang.

Virgil hit the asphalt and covered his head as debris rained down. The heat pulled his facial skin tight like sunburn.

There was screaming. A guy dressed in the remnants of a suit ran from the smouldering basement. His arms were missing and his face was gone. The guy staggered across the road shrieking and waving his stumps before he fell dead in a pile of garbage sacks and rats tore into him. He must have been holding the bomb when it went off. He must be Vishnu Jones. Virgil got it all on film. He approached the ruined building.

Smoked cleared and Virgil scoped the interior. The floor separating the basement from the rooms above had been knocked out and shored up with scaffolding. The void was filled by a massive bomb. A mixture of fuel oil, ammonium nitrate, sodium chlorate and sugar, all packed in large, plastic drums. The drums were surrounded by propane cylinders for accelerated combustion. The bomb, if detonated, would have the force of kilotons. A little Nagasaki waiting to happen. Twelve blocks turned to a smoking crater.

The detonating charge must have exploded as it was prepared and ripped up Vishnu Jones. A splintered table and chair in the corner. Blood. The epicentre of the blast. How the primary had blown without initiating the main charge would forever be a mystery.

There was a camp bed in the apartment, shelves and books. Nietzsche. Thoreau. Conrad. Intellectual dressing for little-guy rage.

There were quotes on the wall in magic marker:

He was a force. His thoughts caressed the images of ruin and destruction. He walked, frail, insignificant, shabby, miserable and terrible in the simplicity of his idea calling madness and despair to the regeneration of the world. Nobody looked at him. He passed on unsuspected and deadly, like a pest in the street full of men.

Virgil took pictures because he knew these words were as close as anyone would get to the mind of Vishnu Jones. Virgil could read the man's obsession, feel his wilful descent into shadows.

A voice from the rubble outside. A guy was lying on his front with a girder across his back. Maybe he was a resident of the building. His body was twisted at the hips so his ass was facing forward. It was as if invisible hands were wringing him out like a dish cloth. Yet the man stretched a hand and said in a calm voice: 'Could you pull me out of here? I'm stuck.'

'How are you feeling?' asked Virgil.

'Not too bad. Damned lucky, really.' The guy had no idea his body was broken.

'What's your name?'

'Marvin Copeland.'

'Afraid I can't help you, Marvin. You look a little tangled up there. Best wait until the cops arrive. They should be able to help.'

'Could you undo my tie? I can't breathe properly.'

Virgil cut the tie with his pocket knife. It was a silk Dior.

'This is so embarrassing,' said Marvin.

'Shit happens. Don't sweat it.'

'This suit is ruined.'

'Forget the suit.'

'I'll be late home. I should call my wife. Can you call my wife?'

'What's her name?'

'Catherine.'

'What's her number?'

221

'I can't remember.' The guy was sliding into shock.

'Hang in there, Marvin. Cops will be here soon.'

A paramedic scrambled over debris to reach them. He checked out the situation.

'What's the guy's name?'

'Marvin,' said Virgil.

'How you doing, Marvin?'

'I don't feel so good.'

'Is there anyone we can call?'

'My wife.'

'He can't remember her number,' said Virgil. 'I looked for a wallet but his jacket is ripped to shit. I don't know where it is.'

The medic knelt down so he could get closer to Marvin.

'Can you still hear me, Marvin?' he said.

'Yes.'

'You're dying, Marvin. You're badly hurt. You can't feel it because your back is broken. When the firemen and cops arrive they will pull you loose and when that happens you will die. Do you understand what I'm telling you?'

'Yes,' said Marvin. He was fading fast. His face was blue. The medic took out a pad and a pencil.

'Are there any messages you would like me to pass on?'

'Tell my wife I always loved her. Ask her to forgive me. And tell my children I love them too. Tell Anthony to look after his mother.'

The firemen arrived but were holding back out of respect for the dying.

'Anything else you want to say, Marvin?'

Marvin looked around. He looked at Virgil and the medic. He raked his hand through the dirt. He was saying goodbye to life.

'Can we pray?'

The three of them said the Lord's Prayer.

'Okay,' said Marvin. Virgil and the medic stood back and firemen took over. They lifted the girder with hydraulic jacks. Marvin's internal organs shifted in his shattered ribcage and a brief sigh indicated his heart had stopped.

Virgil walked away from the devastation in a daze. Pedestrians caught in the blast were wrapped in blankets and sitting at the back of ambulances shivering in bloody shirts and dresses.

Ambulance guys caught Virgil and steered him towards help. They wiped blood from his face, bandaged and stitched a wound in his forehead. Ferris came by and took pictures of Virgil and his injury. Multiple flash shots had Virgil blinded with a hand in front of his face.

Medics made Virgil stand up and get out the way as they doped a pregnant lady on pethidine and laid her on a gurney.

Virgil picked his way through the bedlam, firecrews unreeling hoses, debris, the buckled wreckage of cars. He reached a payphone and dialled Turkel's number.

'Vishnu Jones,' he said. 'I got the whole thing. Have the money. All of it.'

empty hell

'When thou art scorching in thy flames,
when thou art howling in thy torments, then
God shall laugh, and His saints shall sing
and rejoice, that His power and wrath are
thus made known to thee.'

'Annihilation might be
a truer picture of damnation
than any of the traditional images
of the hell of external torment.'

Chapter Twenty-two

❧❧❧

L arry's new apartment was on the top floor of a Harlem brownstone. As he cleaned his teeth in the morning he could look across rooftops to the trees in the park.

New York had changed during his time at the cinema. Great sections of street grid were developed and sanitized by corporations. The red brick offices of pre-war nabobs were bulldozed aside for new structures shaped in wind tunnels and earthquake pads. Each building was a city state and the road between was ravaged no man's land. Sheer, smoked-glass façades made Larry feel shut out and obsolete.

Change was most noticeable around Times Square and 42nd Street. The Majestic Cinema was the last structure to fall to the developer's hand. Larry had watched the cinema get boarded up. Workmen hammered sheets of plywood over the doors and windows. Soon the boards were covered in fly posters for a Metallica double live album. Larry wondered what it was like inside the derelict building. Silence. Shadows. Motes of dust. He didn't go past the Majestic if he could help it. He always took a detour to avoid looking at the site. Some day soon he would go back and there would be nothing but a bare patch of earth. He couldn't imagine how it would feel to see it.

He met Virgil at Levy's. By unspoken agreement they made easy conversation like old times.

'How come you never come up to Harlem?' asked Larry. 'What's the point waiting around Wall Street and Lincoln Center for shit to happen? I bet you'd be skipping over dead bodies just walking down the street in Washington Heights. Turn every corner and there is a Pulitzer snap waiting for you.'

'I don't do social realism. I do abstract. Shit in Harlem and the Bronx is man-made. People queueing for food stamps like third-world refugees. It demands things of the observer: moral outrage and action. It's too real. Too close to the bone. Besides, the place scares the shit out of me. I like the beat-poet approach. Rhapsodize the place as primitive cool but never actually go and get your white ass kicked.'

'So what instead?'

'I went down to the river last year and did an inventory of garbage washed up on the shore. Surgical gloves, dead fish, food cans, beer bottles, hubcaps, lighters, shotgun cartridges, running shoes, batteries, newspapers, tyres, and a whole continental shelf of supermarket trolleys heading out to sea. Might do it again when the ice breaks. So what have you been up to?'

'Fuck all. But I got an idea. A good one. Call Johnny and we'll talk it over.'

Johnny arrived at eleven-thirty. Johnny was subdued company at the moment because his mother was ill. He was born in New Jersey. His parents split when he was about fifteen and he went with his mother to live in a trailer park. It was a nice place but the stigma of living in an Airstream made problems at school. His mother hadn't expected the parting and took it hard when her husband set up home with a waitress from his favourite bar. She filled the empty hours buying stuff she didn't need from the home-shopping channel: junk jewellery, self-heating motorcycle gloves, zebra-pattern car-seat covers, a bedside lamp shaped like Johnny Cash, which played I Walk the Line every time it was switched on. In the end Johnny had to confiscate the credit cards and arrange for the alimony to be paid to him and then give his mother an allowance. She was also fixated by tropical diseases and was laid low by a touch of beriberi and dengue fever at least once a month.

Johnny said he felt guilty for not visiting her more often, and worried to think of her alone in her trailer. Then she had a stroke. It looked bad at first, but she recovered well and was just a little clumsy with her left hand. She slurred when she talked, but since her husband left she was juiced by midday anyway so friends were used to it.

'I should go home. Stay with her for a while,' was Johnny's constant refrain. 'You never know how much time you have left with a person. You wouldn't want them to go with things still unsaid between you. I should go home and take care of her.' But he never did.

Virgil quizzed Johnny about the computers built to hack Mercury Press.

'Exactly how many of those were made?'

'About a dozen, to my requirements. But I didn't make them. A friend of mine knocked them up. He could have had a production line going for all I know. But I asked for twelve, and that's what he delivered.'

'But why? What advantage is it to you to have newscasters spewing garbage?'

Johnny shrugged. 'I like fucking things up. People believe newscasters. Mess with that and you're messing with the fabric of reality.'

Virgil looked out the window and dreamed of fleeing the rat race. The experience of watching Marvin Copeland die made him want to quit the city and the life he had built for himself. But his dreams of escaping the overload of New York were imprecise. Whenever he got stuck in a crowded elevator or a supermarket queue he would picture himself standing alone in the Utah salt flats or the frozen wastes of Alaska. His idea of heaven didn't include other people. When Buzz Aldrin described the surface of the moon as 'magnificent desolation' Virgil thought it might be his kind of place. Which is why he dismissed the idea of living in any other town than Manhattan. It would be swapping one urban shit hole for another.

Larry had been waiting for an opportunity to reveal his new scheme.

'I've been thinking how to change our fortunes and I have had the brainwave of the fucking century, even if I say so myself. Come back to my place. I'll show you.'

Virgil and Johnny found a seat amongst the clutter of Larry's apartment and watched him lever up a floorboard. He took a

Bloomingdales bag from out of the hole. Inside was a silver box ornamented with cherubs, angels and a double-headed imperial eagle holding a wreath. Larry set the box on the table. It had four legs and a round hole at the centre. It was left to Virgil to state the obvious.

'It's a clock case,' he said.

'Yep,' said Larry.

'Where's the mechanism?'

'Thereby hangs a tale. I was in this spiel one night about ten years ago playing blackjack. I was flush, upping the ante by hundreds, when Devo walked in. Devo was a housebreaker. Wore shades even at night. Kept bumping into things. Total asshole, but his money was good so we dealt him a hand.

'He plays a few rounds and loses. Then he gets these fucking hot cards and nearly wets himself. You could always tell when he got a good hand because he got excited and you could feel his pulse shaking the table.

'Everybody folds except me, because for the one and only time in my life I'm sitting on a royal flush, so whatever this guy puts on the table I match. He starts to sweat because I'm bidding him out of the game. He puts down his Rolex and rings as collateral. I raise the stakes. He takes the Gucci shoes from his feet and puts them on the table. I raise the stakes. So in desperation he shows me the clock case. Solid silver. He adds it to the pot, which by this time is looking like a yard sale. I call him. When Devo finds out he's lost he screams the place down and they throw him into the street. I gave him his shoes back because I'm a charitable guy.

'As soon as I got the clock home and checked it out I knew it was special. It was in fucked-up shape because Devo, asshole that he was, wanted to sell it for scrap, so he smashed out the mechanism and face. There was a letter of provenance taped to the bottom. That fuckhead Devo probably thought it was a till receipt. Probably thinks Fabergé is a department store on Madison.'

'Fabergé? The egg guy? Those things are worth thousands.'

'Millions. I don't know where Devo got it. Some Fifth Avenue place probably got ripped down the line, and a guy found himself with shit too hot to fence. Went in looking for a VCR and boosted the clock because it's silver and sparkles.

'I've had the clock for ten years because I couldn't sell it. Hotter than plutonium. But things have changed. The Tooth Fairy is on a spending spree, buying up any antique shit on the street. Nickel-and-dime fences could shift the crown jewels of England right now. They want antiques, the weirder the better. Especially stuff with religious connections.'

'So?'

'So we let this clock lead us straight to the Tooth Fairy and take it from there. We put a chicken leg inside this thing and say it is a casket containing the sacred bones of St Tweety Pie. Our mystery buyer will want it. Religious shit plus the Fabergé connection. He couldn't resist.'

'And?'

'And we get Johnny to put a homing beacon inside this thing and send it on its way. It leads us right to the diamond. That's the deal. I get the stone. You two split whatever else we find.'

Virgil lit a Camel. He had started smoking again.

'Yeah. All right. Let's try it on.'

'There are those who are well and truly "programmed" before departure. These are the "heroic" or "lucid" suicides. What they seek is a place of exceptional beauty in which to die.'

In their case, he said, the chosen method was likely to be a cocktail of barbiturates and alcohol.

Chapter Twenty-three

They met at Larry's place. Larry poured drinks. Virgil sat with his .45 on the table in front of him. He didn't go anywhere without it.

'We're going to do this shit, are we not?' he said.

'Yeah.' Johnny and Larry kept their eyes on the gun. They were both tensed to run if things got ugly. Virgil enjoyed their discomfort.

'I want both of you to say yes and I want both of you to say why. This is going to take a hundred per cent and we have to be committed.'

'I want to do it because I'm out of this Los Bandito shit and the snow,' said Johnny. 'I want to be back in Vegas and I want money in my pocket when I do.'

'I need a pension and a house on a beach,' said Larry. 'Something I can say is mine. Nothing big. Just my own space.'

'I need an escape fund,' said Virgil. 'And I want to do it because I want to do it.'

They toasted the job.

'This is going to seem a little amateur,' said Larry, looking at the component parts of the holy relic they were about to construct. 'So we had better make a virtue of it being rough. This is the cover story: the bunch of bones we have here are the remains of a genuine, Vatican-approved saint. What saint did you pick, Virgil?'

'St Petroc of Cornwall, England. I looked him up in the library. He's big league but not enough to make it implausible we would have the remains.'

'Good. We'll say the bones were stolen along with a bunch of other antiques from an English church and shipped to New

York. That happens often enough to be believable. What bones did you get, Johnny?'

'A leg bone from Cruton and a couple of ribs. There's nowhere in the box to hide the transmitter, so I've drilled out the leg bone and hidden it in the marrow. Sealed the hole up with putty. The bone is signalling as we speak. Lithium battery. Should last months.'

'How do we track it?'

'This thing looks like a pocket calculator but actually it gives you a constant read-out of the distance and direction the box is moving. The display is easy to read. It takes regular personal stereo batteries but they run down quick, so bring a fresh set every time it's your turn to monitor the box.'

'Do you think the bones are convincing?'

'Not to a pathologist, but by the time anyone figures they're phoney the box will already be at its destination and it won't matter any more. As I said, the bones are lifted from Cruton's carcass in the park. They're messed up, and I rubbed a bit of wood stain into them so they look pretty old.'

'Right. So these bones got shipped to New York about ten years ago and fell into the possession of a religious nut who wants a suitable box to keep them in. He digs out the Fabergé clock case from God knows where and, hey presto, one saint in a casket. All right. Let's put this thing together.'

By the light of the bare bulb in Larry's apartment they watched him assemble the casket. He glued in a red velvet lining and dropped in the bones. He glued a scrap of perspex over the circular hole where the clock face should be and stood the case on its legs. Through the little window the bones could be seen nestling on red velvet.

'Think he'll go for it?' asked Larry.

'Sure to,' said Virgil.

'Okay, let's work out a shift pattern. Three of us. That's eight hours a day each. Virgil better take nights. You take mornings, Johnny. I'll do the afternoons. Odds are we'll have to follow the casket through traffic, so I've borrowed Vincent Palermo's new pizza-delivery scooter for a few days. We can weave through traffic in a way that's impossible with a car.

There is a bracket taped to the handle bars so you can use the tracker and keep your hands free. But most of the time you are going to be stuck outside a building for eight hours at a stretch with fuck all happening. Stay alert and stay out of sight. Anybody got a problem with that?'

Virgil and Johnny shook their heads. 'Okay,' said Larry. 'I've made the call. I've got an eight o'clock appointment at Levy's. Balmer has fenced shit for me before. After that the casket will be on its way and Virgil takes over. Johnny does four till twelve then it's me again. If the casket moves you use a payphone to call and let me know where you are. I've bought an answerphone so you can leave a message if I'm not available. Does anyone have a problem? Good. Let's go.'

It was the first time Virgil had been upstairs at Levy's. It was Balmer's private rooms and the premises of his taxidermy business. He didn't show a flicker of recognition when Virgil walked in. A pro.

Bear and zebra skins, butterflies, beetles and spiders under glass, an elephant-ear table, an iguana ashtray, whale teeth, a hippo skull, monkey-head paperweights.

The rooms smelt musty. There was an ultraviolet insectocutor on the wall. Moths fluttered and got zapped. Larry's conversation with the man was punctuated by the crackle of frying lepidoptera.

'How you doing, Balmer?' asked Larry. 'Got the merchandise, like I said?'

'Sorry to feel you up,' said the old timer. 'But you know how it is these days.'

'Sure,' said Larry. He turned to the wall, assumed the position and then Balmer checked him for a wire. He was thorough. Lapels, armpits, everywhere. Virgil next.

'Okay. What have you brought me?'

Larry opened the Bloomingdales bag and took out the box. The old guy examined the clock case and squinted in the little window at the bones.

'The dead saint?'

'St Petroc,' said Larry. 'Bits of him, anyway.'

'How much were you thinking of?'

'A thousand.'

'Five hundred.'

'The silver is worth a thousand at least.'

'So take it to a jeweller. Plenty around.' Balmer opened up a drawer, took out a cash box and counted out five hundreds. 'Money in your hand.' Larry made a big show of reluctance then took the bills.

The old man escorted Larry and Virgil to the street. 'Nice to do business with you,' he said. 'Keep well. And remember me next time you have something to sell.'

Johnny was waiting across the street with the scooter.

'Getting a reading?' asked Larry.

'It's gone faint,' said Johnny. 'What did he do with the box?'

'Put it in a desk drawer.'

'He must have transferred it to a safe. The signal is pretty weak, but it will do.'

'Well, now we wait. All yours, Virgil. Stay frosty.'

Virgil turned his collar up against the wind and snow and leant on the scooter. He wondered what he should say if a cop wanted to know why he was skulking in the shadows. He couldn't think of any reply except to say he was exercising his constitutional right to stand in a parking lot.

Virgil hadn't brought his police radio. Overexposure to atrocities soured him and he wanted a couple of nights as a normal person rather than an ambulance-chasing vulture. The newspapers had been full of death this week and the stories merged and oppressed him like a thunderhead getting ready to burst. Not moment-of-death pictures, like a suicide jumping off an office block or a bullet-riddled gangster twisted up on the sidewalk, but harrowing first-hand accounts of people facing oblivion. These were the nightmares, the point-of-death situations, which haunted Virgil since seeing Marvin Copeland die. Virgil's free-wheeling imagination converted terse prose to Cinemascope footage.

Today the papers printed sections of a diary written by an old lady living in a Brooklyn brownstone.

Mabel O'Shea was eighty-six and lived on the outskirts of Bedford-Stuyvesant. Her house had been fortified with steel front and back doors, triple mortise locks, and tough perspex in her windowframes instead of glass.

One day she stood on a chair in her hallway to change a bulb and fell breaking both legs. She broke the telephone as well. She dragged herself to the front door but couldn't reach up to undo the locks. She shouted for help but nobody heard. She crawled across the hall floor to the living-room doorway and threw a couple of ornaments at the window in the hope of attracting the attention of passers by. The ornaments bounced off the perspex without making a scratch.

By this time she was desperately thirsty so she crawled through to the kitchen and got some milk from the refrigerator. She passed out for a couple of hours and when she awoke her legs were so swollen and painful any further movement was impossible. For the next three days she lay on the kitchen floor eating and drinking from the fridge. When all the liquids ran out she pulled the fridge plug from the wall socket and collected the drips from the defrosting freezer compartment. There was a sink and faucet directly above her head but it was so out of reach it might as well have been on the moon.

To kill time she took a pen from her pocket and wrote about her ordeal on the card of a ripped-up cereal packet. She wrote about the indignity of lying in her own shit. She wrote about how nobody was neighbourly any more and even the priest didn't call. Her mouth gave her the phantom taste of sugar. Acetone. The sweet body odour of diabetics entering insulin coma. Her body was trying to absorb protein from her muscles and organs. Some time during the evening of the sixth day of her ordeal she expired of heart failure brought on by dehydration. She died of thirst to the distant sound of kids laughing in her neighbour's yard.

The stories put a chill on Virgil's bones. The phantasmagoria of blood and police lights Virgil lived nightly was turning him black inside. The bleak shit filled the airwaves, a steady, urgent tocsin. There was no escape. The milk carton he used for his breakfast cereal had the picture of a missing kid printed on it. Somewhere there were parents waiting by the phone, but the kid was no doubt already dismembered and buried in some psycho's cellar.

The morning news played the cockpit recording of a plane that crashed in Colorado. Not a transcript but the recording itself:

The Eagle ATR 72 turbo-prop is circling Denver at fifteen thousand feet.

'We got ice,' says the first officer. Then he and the captain bullshit for a couple of minutes about the female flight attendant.

'No word from ground yet?' asks the captain.

'Nothing yet. Still got ice.' The captain gripes about being based in Ohio and how he hates sitting in traffic as he drives to Cleveland airport each morning. Ground control gives landing clearance. The plane descends to thirteen thousand feet but alarms are triggered as the plane slides from a steep descent into a dive.

'Shit,' says the pilot. 'Totally iced. Pull up, baby. Level out.'

'Auto-pilot disengaged.'

'Come on, come on.' Heavy breathing. 'Goddam corkscrew. Up, baby, up.'

The pilots were fucked but they played out the emergency routine on the way down. Like Marcy said: finish the game.

The engines cut out. Restart. Nothing. Restart. Nothing.

'Oh Jesus fucking Christ.'

The crunch of impact.

The momentary smash stayed with Virgil all day. He heard it wherever he went, like a tune that got stuck in his head.

Virgil's mind was so full of fire and screaming he didn't notice the silver BMW outside Levy's until it pulled away. The beeper signal diminished as the car headed off down the street and he frantically tried to kick-start the scooter before he lost sight of the vehicle entirely.

The car went uptown and parked outside an antique dealership with Samurai armour in the window.

'Larry?'

'Yeah. What's up?'

'It's Virgil. The box is at Marchande Antiques.'

'Stay with it. The box probably won't move again until morning. I'll phone Johnny and let him know where to find you at four.'

'All right.'

SAFETY FIRST

* Arrange dates in public places, e.g., restaurants, bars, etc, not in your own home.

* Don't give your address until you are absolutely sure you wish to continue the relationship.

* Trust your instincts and don't meet again if you have any doubts.

* On your first date it is best to make your own way to the rendezvous. It is best not to accept any offers of transport.

* Leave details of your date with family or friends when meeting a respondent for the first time.

Chapter Twenty-four

Johnny arrived and Virgil left him standing alone beneath a street light. Virgil had no idea of Johnny's internal life. Sometimes he wondered if Johnny's talent for surveillance was spurred by a craving for intimacy, like the panty-sniffer that broke into Marcy's apartment a couple of years ago and jerked off into her shoes.

Johnny took position opposite the antique shop and drank coffee from a styrofoam cup. He watched the city wake up. Garbage trucks, delivery vans and the first trickle of commuters. He was too tired to think. He lost half an hour just staring at a yellow piss hole in the snow next to a hydrant. He broke his vigil long enough to get a newspaper and read about arrangements for the Pope's visit next month.

The guy left Marchande Antiques at five to nine. He was carrying a Bloomingdales bag. When his BMW pulled out Johnny followed on the scooter careful not to let a stop light get between them. He headed downtown and started winding through back-streets in a way that made Johnny wonder if he had been made.

The guy pulled into the parking lot of the St Francis Veterinary Surgery and Johnny ran to the nearest phone.

Larry was wheezing and on the point of collapse when he arrived.

'Has the guy moved?' he asked.

'No. The signal has been shifting around, but always inside the building.'

'Right.' He coughed up a gobbet of phlegm which hit the

sidewalk with a wet slap. 'These butts are killing me.'

At nine-forty things happened fast. The guy came out of the building and loaded the Bloomingdales bag into the trunk of his car. But the tracker unit indicated the box was still inside the building. Larry had the presence of mind to scrawl a payphone number on a cigarette packet and give it to Johnny.

'Take the scooter,' he said. 'Follow the fuck. Call me when he reaches his destination. I'm going to check out the vet.'

Johnny rode off on the scooter and Larry crossed the road to St Francis Surgery. The beeper was going frantic like a Geiger counter approaching an atomic pile. He walked up to the main door and the digital display told him he was within feet of the target but it was off to the right. He walked around the back of the building and increasing beeps merged to a steady whine. He switched off the tracker. There was nothing behind the building but a large garbage dumpster. Larry looked inside and saw the bones of St Petroc strewn amongst a nest of shredded office paper. He put the bones in his pocket because he figured Johnny would want his homing device back and crossed the street to the payphone. Ten minutes later Johnny made the call.

'I'm on Fifth,' he said. 'He parked up and went in a bank. He went in with the bag and came out empty handed.'

'Yeah. I found all the crap from the clock in a dumpster behind the vet's place. He must have brought the bones for identification. Vet saw right away they were dog bones so they chucked them out and kept the clock case. Means we don't have a homing device any more.'

'What do we do?'

'Stay on duty. I'll see you at noon.'

'DTS Zurich is a bank for high net worth individuals.' Johnny talking. It was noon. He and Larry were outside the bank. Johnny was bleary eyed. The excitement had Larry wired. 'Founded on Nazi war plunder. Art treasures and gold hidden in salt mines near Salzburg. The bank is favoured by gentry, pop stars and third-world dictators. It's one of the rites of passage for Prussian aristos. If you go to the right school you get a DTS account, automatic. Account holders don't have to visit the bank. Clerks travel to their client's ancestral home.'

'So what does that mean for us?'

'This branch happens to have the largest safety deposit facility in New York.'

'So what is happening with this clock case?'

'It's a neat way of handing over the merchandise. At a guess I would say they have a deposit box with two key holders who never meet. The guy drops the merchandise in the box and when he returns in a couple of days there is a bundle of cash. Our mystery buyer is obviously anxious to put buffers between himself and the street. This would be a good way of doing it.'

'How do we recognize the second key holder?'

'You can't. All we can do is stake out the bank and see if we recognize the package coming out. Fingers crossed he uses the same Bloomingdales bag.'

It was a difficult stake-out. It was one thing to skulk in the shadows across from an apartment building but another to stand outside a bank on Fifth in daylight, with cops funnelling traffic and doormen in top hats looking out for limousines. Larry had to retreat down the road and watch from a distance.

At four-thirty, just before the bank closed, a power-dressed woman came out of the building carrying a Bloomingdales bag. The bag was soft enough to adapt to the shape of the object inside, and the object was the exact dimensions of the clock case.

Larry made a leap of faith. He followed on foot to a megalith on Third, a couple of hundred yards down from the Chrysler Building. The revolving name plaque said Red Robin. He squinted through smoked glass into the atrium. The woman showed a laminated pass to the armed guards at the desk and got in an elevator. The floor indicator ascended to the top of its scale and stopped. Larry crossed the street and looked up at sixteen thousand bronze-tinted windows. The Tooth Fairy's lair, safe behind mirrored glass.

CROCODILE FINALLY SNAPS

A big crocodile that had for years been poked and jabbed by its keeper to make it snap and lash its tail for tourists finally turned on its tormentor and ripped him to shreds. Owners of the Kenyan Reptile Park now face prosecution for cruelty to animals.

Witnesses say that Pik Best climbed on to the crocodile and poked the sixty-year-old animal in the stomach. The creature lashed out, causing Mr Best to fall over, then the animal fell on him and dismembered him within a matter of seconds.

There are no plans to destroy the crocodile.

Chapter Twenty-five

~~~~~

T hey met at Levy's Café.
'We'll start with the assumption the rock is at the top of the Red Robin building,' said Virgil. 'Anyone know what Red Robin is, by the way?'

'It's a toy company,' said Johnny. 'A big one. Makes Candi dolls. The boss hasn't left his office for three years.'

'Weird.'

'Weird is normal. All the bosses want a Bill Gates-style personality cult going, so they get a bunch of affectations. Maybe write a book. Dreary pinstripes trying to kick-start a little charisma. Convince themselves pen-pushing for sixteen hours every day is exciting and dynamic and not a wasted life like they secretly think it might be. But apparently this guy is genuinely bat shit. His name is Vladimir Blacque. He got stalked a few years ago. He lives in absolute terror of attack. Thinks there are assassins out to get him. Won't leave his office. Won't meet anyone. Won't eat food that hasn't been tasted.'

'All right,' said Virgil. 'So let's say he's sitting in his office with the diamond and a bunch of other valuable stuff. We want to liberate it for the proletariat.'

'Yeah.'

'We need intelligence. We need to know how to get into the building. Ideas, Johnny?'

'Architect's plans. Schematics. City Engineer's Department will have them. We have to persuade a guy to make copies for us.'

'Would the Sanitation Department have access to these plans?'

'Yeah. They need them for chasing rats through the sewers and foundations.'

'I might know a guy who could help.'

'Those plans just give you the basic structure of the building. You also need to have detailed intelligence of the layout, security procedures, the regime the owners instigated when they set up shop.'

'How?'

'Do what every industrial-espionage guy would do if he wants to find out about a company. Get a list of people recently made redundant or dismissed. People with a grudge against the company. People who don't mind dishing the dirt. Pump them for information.'

'Do it,' said Virgil.

'I called in sick at the *Graphic*,' said Virgil, sipping coffee in Larry's apartment. 'I can't find it in me to take pictures.'

Larry was sitting on his bed smoking a cigarette. The lights were off. The tip glowed in the dark.

'For a while or for good?'

'No. It's over with. I can't explain it, but the photo phase is finished. Like your dope habit. It's time to stop.'

'Good. It was a rut.'

'What do I do now? It was my life.'

'Paint. Learn an instrument. Help the poor. There's a million things you can do.'

'It's more than just losing a hobby. I don't know who I am without a camera.'

'All the more reason to stop. It will be good for you, believe me.'

'Life matters, you know. You see someone die before your eyes you realize every cell of your body wants to live.'

'So, no more pictures.'

'Don't know what I'll do with the time. It was the same when I quit smoking. All those empty hours stretching ahead.'

'You'll find something.'

GYMSLIP WIFE – We want a man to spank me hard enough to make me come, then fuck my mouth until it's full of spunk!...212 26 73264

BENT OVER READY – My husband will bend me over the bed & hold me. You fuck me hard as I scream out loud as I cum!...212 26 73265

COCK-WEARING BITCH – Feel 6″ of throbbing latex cock up you as I wank you wearing rubber gloves!...212 26 73266

SLUT WIFE – Meet me at the bar. I'll wear a short skirt and no panties. Touch my wet cunt as I swallow your cum in the toilets! 212 26 73267

BRING THE WIFE – I'll lick her cunt out until she comes, then as you wank all over us, I'll fuck her with a strap-on vibro!...212 26 73268

All calls charged premium rate.

Chapter Twenty-six

V irgil met Johnny outside the Sanitation Department building and surveyed the queue of miserable people waiting
to book exterminators.

'How do we do this?' asked Johnny.

'Just walk in like you know what you're doing. When we
meet Reynard keep your mouth shut and let me do the talking.
Just crowd him. Keep him intimidated.'

The two insinuated their way through the crowd and past
the reception clerks. They adopted a purposeful stride and
walked past the guy handing out appointment tickets at the
foot of the stairs.

'Personal business,' explained Virgil without stopping. Up
spiral stairs and across dim landings, always following the
snaking queue. The dispirited applicants had bags and winter
coats and looked like Jews fleeing a pogrom. Corridors and
anterooms, dust and shadows, then the grand double doors that
led to Reynard's office.

Virgil threw the doors wide and strode in. Reynard had
finished with his latest applicant. She was getting off his desk
and pulling down her skirt. He was wiping his deflating dick with
Kleenex. People wanted their apartments fumigated real bad.

Virgil and Johnny let her pass then closed the door. Virgil
took a seat and Johnny lined up behind him like a knuckle-
cracking mafia goon.

'What do you want?'

'Structural plans of the Red Robin building. You can get the
blueprints from the City Engineers.' Virgil laid down money.

'Carrot and stick. This is the carrot,' he gestured to the money. 'And he is the stick,' he gestured to Johnny.

'I don't have time. You've seen the queue.'

'And so we dance. Threat and counter threat. Why don't we just get moving?'

Reynard led them through a labyrinth of low-ceilinged rooms and connecting passages. Clerks studied the minutiae of contracts and forms.

'Don't you have PCs?' asked Virgil.

Reynard booted a PC and a Garfield screen saver dissolved to the slogan 'All Words Are Lies, Everything Is Fiction' before fading to inert glass. Johnny snorted with amusement.

A big room was shelved floor to ceiling with scrolls of city blueprints, hung with dusty webs. Reynard ascended a teetering stepladder and threw down a map.

'All yours,' he said. 'No one will miss it. Now fuck off and never come back.'

They studied the blueprints in Levy's Café. Johnny knew how to translate the geometric mesh of pencil lines.

'A hundred and twenty elevators running up the core of the building. Shafts don't go down further than the ground floor, so they are no good. Don't want to walk past reception. That's a no-no. Separate elevator at the rear probably for executive use. Same problem. But the service elevator rides the same shaft down to the plant rooms.'

'It's just like the service elevator at Metro Plaza,' said Virgil. 'We got one that goes way down.'

'What's this space at the bottom?' said Johnny. 'Looks like a subway line, but no subway runs under Red Robin.'

'The Zed Line. It runs right up the Avenue from Metropolitan to Red Robin.'

'Zed Line?'

'The first subway line. Built and sealed up. Never used. The main station is under Metropolitan Plaza and the tunnel runs north.'

'We could use it to get into Red Robin?'

'It's creepy shit. Rats everywhere and a community of weirdos living in the tunnel. But it could be done.'

*　　*　　*

Early evening. The traffic had thinned and stars were out.

'One more guy to call,' said Johnny. 'And I do the talking. We wouldn't want to piss this guy off.'

The guy lived on the top floor of an uptown apartment house. He was a charismatic man in his forties. He was dressed in black Armani and had a sun-bed tan.

'This is Dexter,' explained Johnny. 'Dexter is an economic astro-futurist and a close personal friend of Jackie Stallone. I've known him for a couple of years.'

'Hi,' said Virgil.

The chairs had leather padding which farted and subsided like a whoopee cushion. The room was white, with the twenty-two major arcana of the tarot deck lining the walls. The Lovers, The Tower, The Hanging Man. Dexter mixed three Bacardis.

'You're a business astrologer?' asked Virgil.

'I offer investment advice based on the stars.'

'Does it work?'

'As much as anything. It's like psychoanalysis. Doesn't matter if you're a Freudian or a Jungian: they all have an equal success rate. Doesn't matter if you listen to me or a computer tracker service to regulate your portfolio. It's a gamble.'

'Do you believe in astrology?'

'Some aspects. Capricorns always make far fewer car insurance claims than any other sign. It's all about drawing out what people already know. Tarot decks and the i ching make cryptic shapes and people bring their own meaning. Helps them know their own mind.'

'I understand you used to work for Red Robin Toys,' said Johnny.

'Yeah. Did some predictive work, some of it pretty concrete. Red Robin owns the St Francis Veterinary Surgery downtown. New Yorkers spend more on their dogs than the annual foreign trade earnings of Guatemala, so fluctuations in the yearly spend are a good barometer of inflationary pressure. Every couple of months we had a man walk down Third and collect a hundred cigarette butts. The amount of white left above the filter is a good indicator of consumer confidence. Vladimir likes shit like that.'

'You've met him?'

'Nobody meets him. He phones if he feels like it.'

'You don't work there any more, is that right?'

'That's correct. I got on fine with Seth, the previous manager, but he got blown up. Vladimir was okay to begin with. We talked every week over the phone. Then his secretary took over his life and started vetting all his contacts. She terminated my services right off.'

'So you don't feel any great loyalty to the company?'

'Why?'

'I need information pertaining to security. Stuff you saw. Stuff you overheard.'

'Information is my business. But I charge by the hour.'

'Understand what I'm about to ask you is in confidence. This conversation never took place.'

'All right. What do you want to know?'

'The service elevator that rides up from the basement. Does it go right to the top of the building?'

'No. It stops a storey short. All the elevators do. The top storey belongs to Vladimir and his secretary. Nobody gets inside his office but her.'

'How does she get in?'

'A key lets the elevator travel up an extra floor. Inside is her office and a steel door to Vladimir's room. The door has a retinal scan and a code number. Only she can open it.'

'What if there's a fire? Vladimir would have to leave his office or at least let firemen inside.'

'No. In the event of a fire he sits tight until an armed response unit comes to fetch him. The door stays shut. If you want to reach Vladimir, and it seems like you do, you have to get the secretary to open the door. You have to accept there will be panic buttons, and she will hit one. You will have to get into Vladimir's office quick and when you are inside you will have only a couple of minutes before the cops arrive.'

'All right. That's all I wanted to hear. Thanks for your help. And remember: this conversation didn't happen.'

Dexter showed them to the door.

'I'll look forward to seeing you in the papers,' he said.

BURIED ALIVE

Song Xuechui, a fifteen-year-old boy from Peking, buried his fourteen-year-old brother and his eleven-year-old sister alive in a pit he dug in the garden. He believed that as an only child he would have a better chance of attending university. He initially told police the children had been kidnapped.

Chapter Twenty-seven

Virgil signed papers and a doctor got ready to switch off the machine. His mother had bronchial pneumonia and couldn't breathe without a respirator. A couple of squiggles with a biro and her legal protection was gone. Death was just a matter of reaching out and flicking a switch.

They asked him if he wanted to say any prayers. He didn't. They asked him if he wanted to hit the switch himself. He didn't want to do that either. So they turned off the machine on his behalf and the rubber diaphragm ceased its steady rise and fall.

Virgil sat in silence while his mother died. When the ECG flatlined the nurse unplugged it and wheeled it away. He leant over the bed, kissed his mother, whoever she was, and pulled the sheet over her head. Nothing to do, nothing to say. He left money at the desk along with instructions for her ashes to be sent to St Sophia's church. Arrangements had already been made with the priest to have her ashes scattered and a blessing spoken. He didn't need to be there when it was done. He had to admit the woman in the bed was nothing to him. She had been blank like a silver screen and he could ascribe to her whatever emotions he wished. Pretend she listened and cared when he came each week and told her his news; pretend she was glad when he entered the room. Visiting her was the mental equivalent of fucking a rubber doll.

Virgil made his way to 110th and looked at the crib in St John the Divine.

* * *

Marcy posed for a shoot at Turkel's place. Not a word about her night was Haas. Willie Turkel crouched and dived like a sniper working the ridges.

Virgil put Turkel at late forties, early fifties. The doors of his studio were open, so Virgil could see into the apartment beyond. New decor: penises. African phallic statuettes, paintings, drawings, vibrators, ivory strap-ons from China. Turkel liked to describe himself as 'an ageing voluptuary'.

'Take a look around,' he said.

The guy's shelves contained current hardcore books dedicated to all manner of peccadilloes. Pictures stacked in labelled compartments; the taxonomy of lust.

Horrifying images. A theatre of cruelty. Sex as Grand Guignol. Enemas, lactating breasts, amputees, wheelchair fellatio, tattoos, body piercing, auto-asphyxiation, chicks smearing themselves with faeces, necrophilia, guys getting their scrotums nailed to a table and loving it.

There was old stuff. A collection of manila Olympia Press books included a first edition *Naked Lunch*. There was a tattered but complete set of John Willie's *Bizarre*. There were photos by Jeanloup Sieff, Helmut Newton, Eric Kroll and Robert Mapplethorpe. There were leather-bound copies of De Sade and nineteenth-century erotic novellas from France with explicit watercolour illustrations and titles like *Journal Secret d'une Jeune Fille*. There were pictures of Betty Page. There were portfolios of arcane erotica tied with silk bows which contained Beardsley illustrations of *The Lysistrata of Aristophanes*, pictures from the fevered imagination of Marquis von Bayros, satirical Rowlandson cartoons of grotesque Regency gentlemen fucking their servants, Hokusai school pictures of delicate Chinese maidens taking it doggy-style.

Photos of a human pin-cushion, a hermaphrodite with a dog, a man tattooed head to toe, an albino sword-swallower. Pain and self-hate, and a vestige of humanity, airbrushed out. Torture equipment and mutilated flesh were reduced to aesthetics.

When Marcy was done she wrapped herself in a bathrobe.

Virgil showed Turkel the box of pictures he had brought with him. Prints of bodies crushed, bloated, half eaten and burned.

Turkel licked his lips like a gourmand about to sample some appetizing dish and held the pictures to the light one by one.

'Quite superb,' he said. 'An almost total lack of grain. What film do you use?'

'A slow Ilford. Sometimes a superfast Kodak.'

'You must have very steady hands.'

'These are the last pictures I'm going to sell. I'm moving on.'

'I don't think so. You can't deny your art.'

'Cash.'

Turkel handed over the money and Virgil was glad Marcy was there to see the deal go down. He wanted to show her he was a seriously solvent individual.

Virgil got an envelope of money. Turkel got the contact sheets.

'These really are the most exquisite morsels,' said Turkel doing his vampire act.

'You want fear?' said Virgil. 'Here's fear.'

He pulled out his .45 auto and emptied the magazine into the apartment walls. Mirrors smashed, shelves fell, holes in the plaster as big as grapefruit. Marcy covered her ears. Turkel was still cowering under a table.

'Feel that?' Virgil was pressing the gun to Turkel's head. 'Hot fucking metal. This is real. This metal. It's not a game, not a posture. It is one hundred per cent hardcore reality.' He left the guy sobbing.

Virgil and Marcy returned to the Mayflower. Marcy cooked and Virgil packed all he owned into a Samsonite suitcase. Letters, diaries, a few clothes. He would leave it at Penn Station tomorrow morning. They made love in their special way. They enjoyed the dark and Virgil told her the plan.

'If all goes well tomorrow we should be done by ten in the evening. Johnny is our ticket out of New York. He will meet us outside the Guggenheim at midnight in his limo. If we are not there he waits five minutes then leaves for good. You got to pack everything you need and be here waiting when I come back. If things go wrong we could have to split in a hurry.'

Marcy didn't say anything. She lay next to Virgil with her head upon his shoulder. Virgil listened to her breath.

'What are you thinking?' he asked.

'That you're a nice guy. I haven't met many good people. I just want you to know that I appreciate all you've done for me, giving me a place to stay, not judging me.'

'That's all right.'

'And I want to apologize for Willie Turkel. You don't know him and you don't understand him. I can see why he pisses you off, but he's a kind man in his own way. Whatever happens, you mustn't blame him.'

'You should have seen Lette Lipton when we found her. Cut up, face smashed in. That's Turkel's world. You can bet he knows what happened to her. One of his sick friends had a party and things went too far.'

'Like I say: there are some things you just won't understand. But I want you to know I love you.'

They held hands in the dark.

In the midst of decadence his talent flowered

an almost mystical vision of future shock
through the couplings of human and metal

TV images of wounded

'All crimes of addictive murder have a sexual element'

**What horrors have soaked into those
stones and might leak out again?**

Angel in a gospel of hate

appalling theologies

VISION OF THE FINAL DAYS

Baby catapulted from car

fireball

His service was closely integrated with a vast
apparatus of repression.

an influential icon of the American dreamscape.

screened for explosives

A NIGHT OF ARSON AND REPRISALS

The science and ethics of human extinction

new consumer desires

Bigger bang: tritium allows a much larger yield
from a smaller nuclear bomb.

High profile assassination is favoured over
attacks involving passers-by or non-partisan
casualties.

trained suicide squads

The war photographer TIM PAGE examines
the potency of the single, shocking frame.

white-out then darkness

**SOMETHING PERFECT, SOMETHING EXOTIC,
SOMETHING BEYOND REACH**

indicate the continuance of the idea that in
brutal extremity we can find truth.

I feed the appetite for pornography and death.

Chapter Twenty-eight

❦

T hey met at the Majestic. This was Virgil's idea. He was running the raid and this was his starting point. He had levered the plywood away from one of the back fire exits to give them access to the basement. Hurricane lamps gave them light.

Johnny showed up with Larry and led him to the basement room Virgil was using to store all they would need for the raid.

'My movie-nut friend has sculpted a face for each of us,' said Johnny. 'A lot less obtrusive than wearing ski-masks. Put the masks on, dress in your overalls and gloves. Don't take your gloves off for the duration. If you have a shit you wipe your ass with the gloves on, understand?'

'Yeah,' said Virgil.

'Virgil. You first.'

The pink foam latex mask peeled off a fibre-glass mould and looked convincing in the half-light once it was glued down at the eyes, lips and neck. The mask had crow's feet and foam padding in the cheeks to make Virgil look older and heavier. The blond wig with a ponytail made him unrecognizable.

Larry got black hair and smooth skin to make him look younger, and acrylic teeth to cover the nicotined stumps protruding from his gums.

Johnny applied swarthy skin and jowls that made him look like Nixon.

They each wore overalls with NY Exterminators, Inc. printed on the back, steel toe-capped boots and skin-tone surgeon's gloves.

They left the basement and Virgil worked on being a machine.

The three of them climbed into a rental and headed for Metropolitan Plaza.

As they drove Larry leant forward from the back seat and handed Virgil an unmarked carton a little larger than a shoe box. Inside was a big glass bulb held in an intricate brace of metal rods, Velcro straps and polystyrene blocks.

'What is this? A homemade atom bomb?' asked Virgil over his shoulder.

'It's a six-thousand-watt Xenon projector bulb,' said Larry. 'It's very delicate, so don't drop it. The inside is at ten times atmospheric pressure, so sudden shocks will make a bang like you've never heard. If we have to scare anyone then just throw one of these. Think of it as a stun grenade.'

'How many do we have?'

'One each. I've put them in our knapsacks.'

They parked a block away from the Metro Plaza and walked to the back entrance. People stared at Virgil as he walked down the street. He couldn't decide if it was because they thought his latex mask looked strange or because he was staring back at them.

Down the ramp to the underground car park and the service elevator. They made a human shield while Virgil levered the control panel and spliced the wires. The elevator took them down through the various sub-levels of the building to Zed Station.

'Here we are,' said Virgil, as they stood in the little airlock. 'Are we ready to go?'

The three shouldered their knapsacks and switched on police-issue flashlights. Virgil hit the switch and a heavy door rose upwards like a portcullis. Beyond was darkness and the rustling sound of night creatures. Virgil fired a couple of bursts from a flamethrower improvised from an aerosol of furniture polish and a Clipper. Rat noises decreased to a distance. He stepped into the darkness. Larry and Johnny followed.

Flashlight beams lit a vaulted ceiling and a station platform tiled in white marble. The magnificence of the structure was obscured by dust and garbage. It reminded Virgil of sea-bed pictures of the *Titanic*. Intimations of past grandeur.

They were standing where the track would have been laid had construction of the subway been completed. A passage mouth was up ahead, and Virgil expected to see dazzling light at any moment, to feel the fetid tunnel exhalation and have a train come screaming towards them. He recalled Marvin Copeland crushed under metal and fought the instinct to jump for the platform. But there was nothing but the sound of dripping water and furtive scurrying from the shadows. They headed into the dark.

Virgil worried about the structural integrity of the unmaintained tunnel as they walked but couldn't see if there were cracks and signs of imminent collapse above. Like his friends he kept his flashlight trained on the ground immediately ahead of him. The oval of light lit rocky debris, yellowed newspaper accounts of the Tet offensive and cigarette butts scattered like pine needles on a forest floor.

'Look out for broken glass,' said Virgil. 'There's a lot of it about.' Every few yards he scorched the ground with a jet of burning polish and rats squealed in fright. The embers of burnt garbage glowed in his wake.

With no landmarks to orient himself Virgil couldn't judge the distance they had travelled. He knew they were still underneath Third Avenue by the shudder of heavy traffic passing overhead. He was beginning to sweat beneath his mask.

They reached a gentle bend in the tunnel and saw fires up ahead.

'What's this?' asked Johnny.

'Mole people,' said Virgil.

'I heard bad things. CHUDS. They're cannibals. Cannibalistic Humanoid Underground Dwellers.'

'They're cool. They just want to leave their past lives above ground. Start again down here. This is their village. This is where the old tunnel runs parallel with the new, and that's how they get here. We have to show them we ain't transit cops. Let me go first.'

They walked slow to reassure the mole people they didn't

mean harm. The tunnel dwellers settled back in their lawn chairs and re-lit their joints. The spicy tang of fine Danish skunk reached Virgil's nostrils.

They were close enough for him to get a good look at the set up and he was surprised at the sophistication of the tunnel bivouac. What, at a distance, he had taken to be garbage fires were in fact bar heaters. Somehow an ingenious mole had spliced in to the street grid and was leeching power for heaters, kettles, TVs and even a VCR. There were about twenty tunnel dwellers, mostly black, and an even mix of male and female. They weren't vagrants. The cleanliness of their clothes and the order of their camp spoke of energy and self-respect way beyond the average junkie.

'I heard they were changing,' said Larry. 'Spending all their time down here in the catacombs and evolving. I read they can see in the dark.'

'They got a culture,' said Virgil. 'A runner collects welfare payments topside and buys stuff they need. That way they can stay down here living off rats. They call them tunnel rabbits. They cook them on a spit. And they are afraid of the Dark Angel they say haunts the lower levels. The devil himself. That's their theology. Sometimes Metro Outreach brings food. Unsold Kentucky wings and meatball soup. Won't be long before these guys are on the tourist map. Japs will come here between visiting the planetarium and watching *Stomp*. Better living down here than up there where sick fucks set fire to hobos while they sleep. Better than getting sodomized in a city shelter.'

They left the camp behind them and continued their journey. Virgil's legs were beginning to ache.

They became aware of the sound of running water. There was a crossroads. A trench filled with fast-flowing river water cut across the tunnel floor. The trench was fifteen-feet wide and couldn't be jumped. Even if the water was shallow enough to wade through it was flowing so fast they would be swept away.

'What now?' asked Johnny.

'There must be a way of crossing this,' said Virgil. He cleared his throat and called: 'Hello?' He called three times, and an old black man appeared on the opposite bank. He had a big mastiff following at his heel.

'Get those damn lights out of my face,' said the old man, and they lowered their flashlights.

'Can you get us across?'

'Show me your green,' said the old man. Virgil took dollars from his pocket. A bundle of ones made it look more money than it was.

There was a nylon rope slung across the trench at head height, secured at steel pegs on either side. The old man dragged a boat out of the dark. It was a yellow pedal boat, sixty-six, stolen from the lake in Central Park. The guy pedalled the boat across hanging on to the rope so the boat wasn't swept sideways into the dark aqueduct mouth. When he reached the bank he pulled the fibre-glass vessel on to dry land.

'Pleased to meet you,' he said, and folded a stick of gum into his mouth. 'Don't get a whole lot of tourists down here. Specially not wearing Hallowe'en masks. The dog won't bother you. Come on. Pay the ferryman.'

Virgil handed over the money and was the first to go across. The guy pedalled and Virgil pulled hand over hand. Larry was next, then Johnny.

'Will you be around later?' asked Virgil. 'We may come back this way.'

'I'll see you if I see you.'

They kept walking. Virgil's skin was itching beneath his mask and he wanted to tear it off.

After a while they found themselves travelling parallel to two great water pipes, each a couple of feet in width. The pipes took a right turn into a new tunnel, and Virgil said: 'If the maps are right what we have here is the pump tunnel. It draws water from the Hudson to the Red Robin air-cooling plant and pumps it out again. Tunnel extends about fifty yards then goes vertical. We got to watch our ass up there. These skyscrapers are little city states.'

The pipes took up much of the tunnel and they had to squeeze down the passage single file. Johnny went first because he had the building blueprints memorized. Larry went last because he was feeling claustrophobic. He was trying not to let on how much the journey had tired him, but his laboured breathing and the rattle in his chest filled the tunnel as they walked.

The pipes turned upwards and the passage ended in a wall and an iron ladder. Johnny climbed up and shone his torch over the heavy hatch above. He climbed down again.

'Lock and chain,' he said. 'A good lock. Let's hope it isn't bolted the other side.'

Virgil took a hacksaw from his knapsack, looped his legs through the rungs at the top of the ladder and set to work on the chain. His legs cramped and his arm ached from holding the chain taut to saw upon. It seemed to take an age, but a scratch turned to a groove and then a deep cut, and the lock and chain tumbled into the dark, just missing Johnny's head.

'This is going to take two,' said Virgil, so Johnny climbed up and helped him lift the heavy lid and throw it back.

Light, fresh air and the hum of machinery. The main plant room. Virgil checked left and right to make sure no grease monkey was around, and the three of them climbed out of the tunnel. They closed the lid and brushed the dirt off their overalls as best they could. Johnny and Larry looked sinister in their latex masks, and Virgil felt more alone than he did when they started their expedition.

They were lost in a maze of plant machinery. Chillers big as a ship's boiler. An electricity sub-station. Hoist motors for the elevators. Water- and air-handling systems. Johnny checked each corner looking for engineers and security cameras. He got his bearings and led them to the freight elevator. Partitions and glass made an office space, and there was a guy inside reading *Esquire*. His feet were up and he didn't look like he was moving for a while, so they jumped him and tied him to a swivel chair with kettle flex, and filled his mouth with kitchen roll. They summoned the freight elevator and got inside.

'How are we doing?' asked Johnny.

'Good time,' said Virgil. They watched the indicator numerals ascend past Ground and upwards to 99 then stop.

'Here we are. One level short.'

Virgil stood on Johnny's shoulders to reach the inspection

doors above.

Johnny joined Virgil and Larry on the roof of th
clung to the greased cable, frightened of the y
beneath. He coughed a mouthful of puke over t
elevator and the spinning gobbet fell away down
darkness.

'We have to climb,' said Virgil. 'Get up the la
those slide doors. Vladimir's secretary will hit the
After that we are on the clock, gentlemen. An
minute response time from the cops.'

Larry was wheezing through the plastic lips (

'How you doing, Larry?' asked Virgil. 'Try to r
to collect your stone.'

Virgil climbed the ladder to the foot of the sh

'Jemmy,' he called. Johnny passed up a ty
wedged it in the crack and got ready to lever t
He pulled the .45 auto, chambered a round an
weapon in his pocket.

'You promised no guns,' hissed Larry.

'Shut up. Get ready.'

Virgil levered the doors apart a couple of incl
the tyre-iron away. It clattered down the shaft.
doors wider and wriggled and squirmed throu
Johnny next, then Larry.

Virgil dashed a Xenon bulb on the floor and
made his ears ring. Vladimir's secretary was at
Warhol car crash behind it. A tall redhead, big
She was paralysed by shock, puce like coronary
pressed the .45 to her temple.

'What's your name?' asked Virgil.

'Holly.'

'Be cool, Holly.'

Johnny checked under the desk. A panic butto
LED to indicate the silent alarm was active.

There was a video camera over the steel door leading to Vladimir's office and Virgil shot it out. He also put a bullet in the junction box for Vladimir's office communications.

Virgil dragged Holly to the steel door.

'Code and retina scan,' he said. 'Or it's your head.'

She complied but still the door wouldn't open.

'The code and eye thing is just to identify myself,' she explained. 'Vladimir opens the door from the other side.'

There was an intercom on the door frame and Virgil used it.

'Open up, fucker. I've got your girl.'

A frightened voice crackled from the speaker.

'I've called the cops. They're coming with guns. Leave her alone.'

'Let me in or I'll poke her eyes out with this screwdriver.' No response. 'Right. First eyeball.' Virgil covered Holly's mouth with his hand and made a high-pitched, girly scream. 'Hear that?' shouted Virgil. 'That's her right eye put out. If you don't open the door in the next ten seconds she's blind for life.'

No response.

'Three . . . two . . . one . . .' The sound of heavy bolts sliding back and the door swung open.

'Thirty seconds gone,' advised Johnny.

The room smelt like shit and there were food wrappers strewn over the furniture and floor. A sleeping bag in one corner. A fridge and microwave in another. Antiques of incalculable value lined the walls.

A man was battering the office window with a chair so he could call down to the street for help. The chair made no impression on the vacuum-sealed triple glazing.

'Put the chair down, fucker,' said Virgil.

Vladimir was fat and dishevelled. He hadn't shaved for a while and his skin was so white it was almost blue. He knelt in front of Virgil.

'Kill me,' he said, holding his arms out in a Christ pose. 'Just leave her alone.'

'If I was an assassin you would already be dead.'

'What do you want?'

'Both of you lie down, face down. Hands behind your heads, legs crossed. Larry. Fill the bag.'

'Thirty seconds,' said Johnny.

Larry swept jewels, sculpture and artefacts into his bag.

'The stone,' he cried, tossing the diamond in the air and catching it. 'The Dog Star. Say hello to Daddy.' He kissed the rock and dropped it in the bag.

Johnny looked out of the window. Cop cars were collecting in the street.

'Shit,' said Johnny. 'Dexter was right about a panic button. The cops are here. Hundreds of them.'

'Larry,' said Virgil. 'Time to go.'

Larry zipped the bag shut and hefted it over his shoulder. Virgil lifted Vladimir to his feet and kept the .45 pressed to the small of his back.

'You too, sister.' Virgil marched Holly out of the office.

'Bring up the elevator,' he commanded.

'How?' said Holly.

'With the key around your fucking neck,' said Virgil, and ground the muzzle of the .45 into her temple.

Once in the car Virgil bound their hands with nylon cord.

'Why are you taking us?' asked Vladimir.

'If it all works out you'll be free in a couple of minutes.'

Virgil stopped the elevator at floor 29 and Johnny kept his thumb on Door Hold. Virgil sprayed lighter fluid over the carpet and up the walls. He lit a book of matches and tossed it. Blue flame washed the corridor. Sprinklers hissed to life and a psychotically calm computer voice said: 'Ladies and Gentlemen, we are experiencing an emergency situation. Would you please exit the building in an orderly fashion using the nearest stairwell.'

Despite Johnny's finger on Door Hold the elevator doors began to close and Virgil had to jump to get inside.

'Bad move,' said Holly with a smile. 'The elevators return to Ground and stay there in the event of a fire. Nothing you can do.'

Virgil punched her in the gut. She doubled up coughing.

'You are going to walk us through the shit down there and get us to the basement. After that you can go.'

Larry croaked and slid down the wall. Johnny peeled off his latex mask and Larry's face was pale, almost blue.

'Shit,' said Johnny. 'Heart attack?' Larry rolled his eyes. 'Christ. Some sort of collapse. He needs a doctor quick. How about we leave him? Cops would put him in an ambulance.'

'We take him to the Majestic and don't make a call until you and I are long gone.'

'He's sick,' protested Johnny.

'211 plus kidnap and arson. That's twenty years.' Virgil gripped the lapels of Johnny's overalls and pulled him close. 'Whatever it takes. If he dies on the way, that's how it is.'

Virgil triggered a flick knife and cut Holly and Vladimir's bonds. The gun pressed into her eye socket.

'Needless to say I'm not anticipating any surprises.'

The ground floor was in chaos and the group were desperately exposed as they crossed the foyer floor to a side door. Firemen with oxygen equipment and thermal-imaging gear were making for the stairs; paramedics hefting burns kits close behind. An old guy was receiving CPR in front of the reception desk. Security guards were leaving the building with stolen office equipment under their arms.

Outside, fire trucks with turntable ladders and hydraulic snorkel platforms had arrived and blocked the road. Fire control HQ vans. Paramedics. Firemen bolted delivery hoses to hydrants.

Holly let them through a small door with her keys and they ran down concrete steps.

'Good girl,' soothed Virgil.

A vault room filled with dolls in vacuum-sealed display cases. The head of each doll was partially collapsed and their eyes wept thick, brown tears. Bad rubber. Contaminants undoing the cellulose acetate polymerization process. They were kept in stasis like an Alcor subscriber waiting to be resurrected in the next millennium.

'I'd forgotten this place existed,' said Vladimir, and caressed the glass.

'What is it?'

'Samples for the sales force.'

The next room was space for life-sized replicas of Candi doll parts; store-front mannequins and prosthetic limbs destined for Cambodian landmine victims. A petrified crowd of Dorians, Heidis and Mary-Janes; blurred nakedness through sheaths of bubblewrap; airbrushed faces and lacquered hair.

Holly led them to the basement plant room. They lowered Larry down the hatch and Johnny followed to look after him. Larry was half conscious, wheezing with congested lungs.

Virgil was set to cut the hostages loose but he heard voices, footsteps and a dog bark from the direction of the service elevator. Breach to barrel pumps. Cops.

'Down the hole,' he told Holly and Vladimir.

'You said you would let us go,' she protested.

'Change of plan. Down the hole.'

Virgil dropped the hatch behind him finding reserves of strength to move an object it had taken two to lift. He and Johnny hurried the hostages down the passage double time to the subway tunnel and then south towards the sound of running water. But when they reached the point where river water cut across the subway line the ferryman was nowhere to be seen.

'I bet all the sound carried down into the drains,' said Johnny. 'He's long gone, and his dog with him.'

'That rope tied to the pegs. Reckon we could shimmy across?'

'Larry couldn't. Our two guests wouldn't. Best bet is to find another way out.'

'Have to go back the way we came.'

They travelled as fast as they could, with Larry stumbling along and the two reluctant companions in tow. They hurried back the way they came, north past the pump tunnel entrance and into unknown territory. They reached a three-forked road and took the middle path.

Two hundred yards on they hit a wall. The tunnel abruptly terminated in breeze blocks. There was a metal door, like a ship's bulkhead hatch, secured by a wheel, but the wheel wouldn't shift.

'What do you think?' asked Johnny.

'Obviously there's something behind this wall,' said Virgil. 'But this door won't be forced. Shit. We can't go back. Nothing back there but water and cops.'

'Think they'll follow?'

'They'll be coming with dogs and shotguns. What's that up there?' His torch beam lit a rusted cube of metal with a grill.

'Some sort of air-conditioning unit.'

'Looks pretty corroded. See if you can pull it down.'

Johnny jumped up and grabbed the unit. For a moment his legs swung in thin air then he braced his feet against the wall and pulled at the unit. It creaked. Flakes of metal and brick powder drifted from the bolts. The intake began to give way and Johnny jumped down. The metal box slowly drooped then fell away from the wall and hit the tunnel floor with a crash. The box was so rusted it broke apart as if it were porcelain.

There was a hole where the unit used to be. Virgil used the wreckage as a step and shone his torch inside.

'Some sort of room,' he said. 'I'll climb in and see if I can reach the door from the other side.'

His head and shoulders disappeared in to the hole then his legs and feet. A couple of moments' silence then the wheel on the steel door began to turn. Virgil let them in. He picked an iron bar from the air-unit wreckage then closed the door behind them using the bar to jam the lock mechanism shut.

'That should slow the cops up a little,' said Virgil. He took the Xenon bulb from his rucksack and placed it on the sill where the air unit used to be. 'The cops will have to come in through the hole. They'll knock the bulb off as they do and that'll shake them up a little. Make them cautious.'

They shone torch beams around the room in which they found themselves. A brick incinerator with a dusty radiation sticker and the instruction Place Clothes Here and another sign pointing to the showers.

'Shit,' said Virgil. 'You know what we have here? A fucking nuclear bunker. This must be some sort of decontamination area. A place to wash away radioactive dust.'

'A government place?' asked Larry. He was making an effort to get with the programme.

'Not neglected like this. Must be for company executives. Maybe a big company that went bust, like Pan Am. I wonder what building we are under.'

There was a rifle rack on the wall and Virgil tried to picture the bunker inhabitants defending their refuge with M16s.

They walked through corridors and rooms taking many turns and meeting several dead ends. There were stairs and they followed them up and up. Virgil felt it was like playing Dungeons and Dragons for real. It was hard to keep his bearings and he wished he had a ball of twine so they could retrace their steps through the labyrinth if they had to.

The necropolis was still partially equipped and the cobwebbed teleprinters and food cans dated the place late fifties. There was a telephone exchange, all Bakelite and plaited cable, an operating table in the sick bay and collapsible cardboard coffins in the morgue. One room contained a rotting Steinway piano and an old Harley under a tarpaulin.

'Jesus, this is creepy,' said Larry. He was walking unaided. 'It's like an Egyptian tomb. Pharaohs taking their gear to the afterworld.'

'Imagine what it would have been like down here if the bomb dropped,' said Johnny. He imagined the Empire State toppling like a felled tree. Half the people of Manhattan evaporated. The other half irradiated and flash blind. 200 mph winds. Then centuries of winter and nothing alive above ground except rats and roaches. 'Think of being in here with desperate people banging on the door to get inside. Or maybe the tunnel would collapse and you would be trapped for ever.'

'Designers would have thought of that,' said Virgil. 'That's why there must be another entrance. A main entrance. The door we just used doesn't lead to the surface. You would have to walk a couple of miles down the tunnel to get to street level. No good if you have to take shelter in a hurry, so I would say it was the back door. There must be a main entrance up ahead that gets you to ground level fast and discreetly. When that three-minute warning was broadcast the executive fucks would want a bolt hole they could use quickly without drawing attention to it.'

A distant bang echoed down the corridors.

'Either that bulb rolled off the ledge on its own or the cops are on our ass,' said Virgil. 'We had better get out of here double quick, folks.' He gave Vladimir and Holly a shove in the back to propel them forward.

Twisting and turning through bathrooms, kitchens and dormitories, they arrived at another decontamination area and tank-metal door. They quickly stepped through and shut the door behind them. They were in another tunnel but one laid with track. They were no longer in the old Zed Line.

The tunnel was filled with the roar of an approaching train, and they hugged the walls in expectation of fighting the vacuum ready to suck them under the train wheels. But no train passed and the noise died away.

'Must be parallel tunnels,' said Virgil. 'Any idea where the subway runs side by side?'

'I haven't got a fucking clue where we are,' said Johnny.

'Keep moving. And watch the third rail everyone. One false move and you get six hundred volts DC up your ass. Current would blow off extremities. Hands, feet, head.'

'We get the picture.'

Virgil was worried about the points system. If the rails shifted by hydraulics a foot in the wrong place would be scissored clean off.

'Make this fast, people,' he said. 'I don't like being in here. Let's find our exit and use it.'

They travelled a little further and extinguished their torches when they saw light up ahead.

'That isn't a subway station,' said Johnny, squinting to see pillars and roof girders.

'Shit. You know where we are, don't you? Grand Central. And fucking rush hour as well. What do you think?'

'You mean step on to the platform in front of all the commuters?'

'We don't have a choice,' said Virgil. 'Besides, we still have our masks. All we have to do is keep these two under control.'

'All right. On to the platform and keep going. Just a couple of streets to the Majestic. Should make it. As long as these two don't fuck around.'

Virgil grabbed Holly and Vladimir by their collars.

'You heard me. This is the deal. We walk through the station and the street. Be cool and this time tomorrow everything is back the way it was. *Capiche?*'

They nodded.

'Here goes nothing.'

They strode into the light where commuters, blue-collar and suits, craned to see what the hell was going on.

'Excuse me, please,' shouted Virgil in as confident a voice as he could manage. 'Clear a space. Coming through.'

The commuters backed off making room for the five to climb on to the platform.

'Thanks very much.'

They strode up the steps and through the bustle of the main hall avoiding cops and using gaggles of rucksack-laden tourists as cover. The two hostages were hemmed in. Virgil and Johnny either side, Larry behind.

Out into the street. Christmas shoppers. They needed to go west to Times Square, but 42nd Street was too crowded. They crossed the road and travelled down 41st, which was empty but for delivery trucks. They passed the back of the public library and were into Times Square. They were among tourists queuing for movies and rush-hour bustle. There were traffic cops in the road and Virgil pressed the .45 into Holly's side to keep her in line. She was the one most likely to make a move, not her boss. Vladimir was utterly pliable. He was looking around at the people and up at the sky like he was seeing it all for the first time.

They crossed the road and reached the alleyway leading to the back of the Majestic. Once they were inside they whooped with relief and Larry lit hurricane lamps.

Vladimir and Holly were tied to chairs and had duct tape pressed over their eyes. They were left in the room that used to be Virgil's darkroom. Then Virgil, Larry and Johnny went into the room next door where their everyday clothes were hung and peeled away their latex masks to release the sweat that had built up behind the rubber.

'Holy Christ, what a relief to get that shit off,' said Virgil. They climbed out of their overalls and put on normal clothes.

Larry succumbed to exhaustion, lay down on the floor and slid into a light sleep.

'Is he all right?' asked Johnny.

'For a little while. See his hands?' Larry's hands seemed independent of his snoring body. They crept over his chest like spiders and worried at his throat. 'Death crawl. Happens with terminal patients near the end. The mind knows it is being dragged down by a diseased body. The hands start clawing for a way out.'

'Hospital?'

'See how he is in a minute. I'd rather leave it to him.'

'Okay,' said Johnny. 'Let's take a look at the treasure.'

Virgil spread his raincoat on the concrete floor and upturned the sports bag. Gold and silver and jewels spilled out. More wealth than Virgil had ever seen. They divided it into three piles, having no better measure of value than weight. Johnny packed his share in his knapsack and got up off the floor to leave. He shook Virgil's hand.

'Great play, Virgil. Midnight at the Guggenheim. For Christ's sake don't be late.' He ran up the steps to the alleyway and was gone. Virgil packed his share and shook Larry awake.

'How you feeling, Larry?'

'All right. Just had a funny turn. Where's the stone?'

Virgil put it in his hand and Larry caressed the jewel.

'What are you going to do now, Larry? What's your route from here?'

'Just away. Why don't you see how our guests are doing?'

When Virgil returned from checking on Holly and Vladimir he found Larry in a chair and said, 'They're all right. I got to go. I'm heading West, and I won't be back again.'

'It's been a pleasure, Virgil,' said Larry. 'Even if you are a sick fuck. Enjoy life. Seize the day. All that bullshit.'

'Consider it seized.' Virgil shouldered his load. 'Take care of yourself, Larry.'

'*Vaya con Dios.*'

Larry watched his friend walk down the corridor and up the steps to the outside. He never saw Virgil again.

BLACK HOLE AT THE CENTRE OF THE GALAXY

Astronomers believe they have discovered a massive black hole at the centre of the galaxy. The mass of the singularity is millions of times greater than the Sun and increases as it sucks in planets and stars. The void at the centre of the Milky Way was revealed by Andreas Eckart and Reinhard Genzel at the Max Planck Institute for Extraterrestrial Physics, near Munich. The astronomers watched the movement of stars for five years and found the speed of stellar movement is reduced the greater the distance the object is from the middle of the galaxy, just as they predicted if stars were influenced by a decreasing gravitational pull. The mass of the object around which the stars are turning is estimated to be 2.4 million times greater than the Sun. Since no star of that magnitude can be seen at the centre of the Milky Way astronomers conclude there must be a vast black hole.

Chapter Twenty-nine

L arry waited till midnight, when he was sure Johnny and Virgil were out of the city and long gone, before untying the two captives. He showed Holly and Vladimir to the alley behind the cinema.

'That's it,' he said. 'You're free to go.' He leant over Vladimir and spoke in his ear. 'Life is too fucking short to shut yourself away. Remember that.'

Holly and Vladimir backed away like they thought Larry was going to shoot them in the back. Halfway down the alley they turned and sprinted for the street, tripping over garbage sacks in their haste to get away.

Larry could have gone on the run. Bought a ticket for the Keys or New Orleans. But the Majestic was his home.

He stopped on his way to the roof to catch his breath in the deserted auditorium. Adrenalin kept him moving through the job, but it had all but broken his aged and diseased body. He was panting and phlegm rattled in his throat. His chest burned. He had the diamond in his hand and felt a sense of completion.

After a couple of minutes' rest he climbed the remaining steps to the roof.

It was snowing again. Big flakes cascading from the night sky. From his vantage point he could see the traffic on 42nd Street and, to his left, the monumental neon of Times Square. Joe Camel lifted a cigarette to his lips and lowered it again with the regularity of a metronome. Emaciated models for Calvin Klein underwear. A seamless skein of hot images; advertisers trying to press his buttons, fuck with his self-image, pushing sex and anxiety.

Larry sat down to rest his tired bones and examined the scintillating facets of the diamond cupped in his hands. Eternal perfection held in arthritic, liver-spotted fingers. Metamorphosed carbon. Super-compressed shit: the stuff dreams are made of. He leant back and let feathery flakes caress his skin and melt to dew.

Sirens approached down Broadway. Holly and Vladimir must have found a cop and told their story. A crash from the street below as a tactical point man kicked through the plywood boards to enter the Majestic foyer. Larry was glad to hear them. Their barked commands and crackling radios were company.

He put a handful of snow in his mouth and let it melt to water. Virgil's silver pill box was in his shirt pocket. He had stolen it while Virgil's clothes were lying over the back of a chair. He swallowed the cyanide pill and hoped it wouldn't hurt. The last thing Larry saw was a big Toshiba sign and letters red like an ocean sunset.

Virgil stashed his share of the loot in his luggage locker at Penn Station and hurried back to the Mayflower. He ducked around each corner and stairway like he was dodging bullets. He was scared the cops would be waiting and was ready to run at the first hint of an ambush.

There was no one lying in wait for him.

He opened the door to the apartment, said, 'Time to go, Marcy,' and hit the lights.

Blood.

Great slashes of arterial spray across the far wall. Coagulated blood hanging off a house-rules notice in petrified drips. Blood soaked into the rug turning it crimson. Blood on the TV screen; the TV turned on, cathode backlight projecting red against the far wall like a sixties lava lamp. Happy sounds from a low-calorie muffin mix ad. Blood on the table next to the window mixed with bone shards and gobbets of flesh. Bloody streaks across the floor, like a heavy object had been dragged across the apartment to the door. The streaks terminated at Virgil's feet.

Flashback to Lette Lipton: dismembered, bisected, beheaded, face caved in.

Scenario #1: Knock on door. Marcy opens door. Psycho pushes inside, overpowers her, cuts her to pieces.

Why did no one hear screams?

Scenario #2: Knock on door. Marcy opens door. Marcy smiles because she knows the psycho, expects his company. She willingly submits to the blade and bone saw and Willie Turkel is there taking pictures. He soothes her, strokes her hair as life pisses away through a punctured jugular, tells her it's all right; it's art.

Virgil took the main stairs to the atrium. He vomited twice on the way down.

People, traffic noise, the city streets. Virgil just walked. It was like a session of ECT; absolute horror crackling from temple to temple, scrambling all thought and feeling.

He found himself sitting at the counter of Levy's with a cup of coffee. A banal still life in front of him: ketchup, napkins, ashtray, sugar bowl. He was so spaced the objects seemed alien artefacts.

On the street again. Virgil got his sack of valuables from the locker at Penn Station and waited on the steps of the Guggenheim for Johnny to show.

Midnight. Christmas Eve.

The white limo pulled to the kerb. Johnny got out and opened a door to the passenger compartment. Virgil threw the treasure inside and said, 'Keep it. It's yours.'

'What the fuck are you doing?' asked Johnny, but Virgil turned his back and walked away.

Virgil pressed the bell. The door opened a crack.

'Who is it?'

'Virgil Strauss. Don't you remember me, Mathias? We were at college together.'

'UCLA?'

'That's right. Days in the sun. I was in town and I'd thought I'd drop in on my old pal Mathias.'

Haas opened the door and let Virgil inside.

'Take a seat,' said Haas. Virgil sat on the sofa. The radio news was on. Carols in the background.

'Wife not at home?'

'She's visiting her parents. I'm sorry, but I can't quite place your face.'

'Yeah. Time. Changes us all.'

'Well, quite. Can I get you anything to drink?'

'Bourbon would be nice.'

Haas turned his back and busied himself at the drinks cabinet.

'So what have you been up to, Virgil?' he asked.

'Photography. I work for the *New York Graphic*. It's a fun way to make a living. I took a break from it recently, but you can't deny your vocation. I can't wait to start again.'

Virgil took his .45 from his pocket. He folded a sofa cushion over the muzzle.

'You seem to have done okay for yourself,' said Virgil.

'Yeah,' said Haas, turning around with drinks in his hands. 'You got to do some dog-eat-dog type of stuff to make it these days. But I suppose you know that, working at a newspaper.' His brow furrowed in puzzlement as he saw Virgil with the cushion. Virgil smiled.

'This is from Marcy.'

The cushion baffled the muzzle flash and the gunshot was a puff of feathers and muted whipcrack anyone next door might think was a blown fuse. Haas grunted like he took a heavy punch to the gut. He dropped the glasses. The midriff of his sweatshirt turned from grey to red. The man toppled backwards over a coffee table and lay in a mess of flowers and fragments of vase.

Virgil sat still and listened to the news. Schedules disrupted after the starboard engine of a McDonald Douglas 88 fell off and crushed a tenement building by the East River. Newsflash drama from anchormen improvising on air. Bubbling gasps from Haas as his lungs flooded and he drowned in his own body fluid. Blood frothing out of his nose. The last vocal sound the man made was a sneeze.

The engine originated from Flight 299 out of Pensacola,

Florida. The Douglas 88 was in a parking orbit around JFK waiting for a landing window. As the plane passed over the city an engine underwent rotor burst and spat titanium turbine blades. The disintegrating nacelle detached from the fuselage, as it was designed to do, and fell four thousand feet to earth. Live reports of bodies pulled from burning wreckage. Death toll 121 and climbing.

Haas' left leg twitched.

Virgil loaded his Leica with film and took pictures. A moustache of viscid blood under the dead man's nose.

He crossed the room, slid back the window and stepped out on to the balcony. The gun in his hand, the camera strapped around his neck.

The falling jet engine had cracked the mantle of the city: ruptured gas lines, gushing water mains, severed telecom conduits. A tenth of the city was without power. Looting had begun. The skirling cry of sirens all over town converging on a mile-high smoke plume. The airways would be fizzing with emergency traffic now. The hive mind responding to attack.

Wraiths prowled the street below the balcony. Teeming traffic from this world to the next. All the dead captured by Virgil's lens, languid phantasms as insubstantial as breath, drifting from the shadows of doorways and fire escapes to promenade beneath the street lights, sporting their bullet holes like carnations.

Virgil in a rattling cage elevator going down, down. He had killed and was now banished from daylight and company and love. Forever exiled to the penumbra, the lip of night.

Nine shots left in the camera.

Seven shots left in the gun.

Virgil loved New York.

Printed in the United States
by Baker & Taylor Publisher Services